EVENING STAR

SAM KEATON : *Legends of Laramie*

Books by
Sigmund Brouwer

SAM KEATON: LEGENDS OF LARAMIE

Evening Star

Silver Moon

OTHER FICTION

Blood Ties

Double Helix

The Weeping Chamber

Wings of Dawn

NONFICTION

Can the Real Jesus Still Be Found?

The Carpenter's Cloth

Into His Arms

EVENING STAR

Sigmund Brouwer

BETHANYHOUSE

MINNEAPOLIS, MINNESOTA

Evening Star
Copyright © 1994, 2000
Sigmund Brouwer

Evening Star is a revision of *Morning Star*, published in 1994 by Victor
Books/SP Publications.

Cover design by Ann Gjeldum
Cover illustrion by Chris Cocozza

Published by Bethany House Publishers
A Ministry of Bethany Fellowship International
11400 Hampshire Avenue South
Minneapolis, Minnesota 55438
www.bethanyhouse.com

Printed in the United States of America by
Bethany Press International, Minneapolis, Minnesota 55438

Library of Congress Cataloging-in-Publication Data

Brouwer, Sigmund, 1959–
    Evening star / by Sigmund Brouwer.
      p.   cm. — (Sam Keaton legends of Laramie)
     ISBN 0–7642–2366–6
     1. Laramie (Wyo.)—Fiction. I. Title.
PS3552.R6825 E94   2000
813'.54—dc21   00–009923

SIGMUND BROUWER is the award-winning author of numerous books including *The Carpenter's Cloth*. In addition, his coolreading.com Web site reaches out to instill good reading and writing habits in the next generation. Sigmund and his wife, recording artist Cindy Morgan, divide their time between Tennessee and Alberta, Canada.

To L.M.

I've always loved the glories of the old Wild West, and I would like to express my gratitude to the historians whose dedication has preserved that era, allowing the rest of us to cherish its spirit of freedom.

To them, and to you who may be reading this as more than a mystery, I would like to apologize for any of my research mistakes which I may have passed on during my attempts to make the fiction as historically accurate as possible.

CHAPTER *1*

WHILE ALL OF THIS BEGAN because of my attempt to rescue an irksome Indian, it wasn't until much later that I realized it was me who needed rescuing. God, I believe, is a persistent cowboy himself, going deep and wide into the mesquite for stray souls like mine, and when He fashioned the lariat to pull me close, He threw it by putting that Indian directly in the middle of my path.

To make sense of this, I have no choice but to confess that my life until that exact moment in Laramie had been a gradual retreat from anything of meaning. I was like a stubborn longhorn, preferring deep snake-filled canyons over green grass and clean water. Cowboying is a good life for that kind of escape, as it allows a man to keep his own business with a surliness that invites no intruders.

For that reason, I suppose, God knew it would take no less than that Indian to get my attention.

I had just stabled my horse and was intent on getting rid of six weeks of range dust with cool beer down at one of the saloons on Laramie's main street. My mistake was in taking the short route from the stable to the saloon, an alley between the hotels and train station.

I was walking with no particular thoughts in mind when I heard some strange thumps. Thumps mixed with grunts and a couple of gasps. Thumps like someone whacking a pole against an ornery pack mule. Thumps from behind a small crooked shed just beyond the shadows of the saloon.

I shrugged and turned toward the saloon.

Then another thump—and the gasp became a strangled yelp.

I wandered to the shed and stepped around the corner.

What I saw was a big shaggy man standing over a runt of an Indian curled on the ground. I watched two kicks, both a good sign the Indian's ribs didn't much pain the big man's toes.

"Afternoon, partner," I said halfway through the giant man's next kick.

"Tend your own business," he said as casual as if he might be ordering a beer. He paused to mop the sweat from his brow. "This horse-thievin' Injun's getting what he's due."

Some white folks hold that the only good Indian is a dead one. This cowboy seemed intent to prove the saying. He delivered another kick that resulted in another thump. The Indian gasped again. He was slight, with greasy braids flopped below a big hat and ragged clothes covered with dust.

That cowboy stood maybe four inches taller than me, which made him plenty big. I'm pushing six feet myself and got all the muscle a man needs to outwrestle the most mulish steer. But this man in front of me was so tall, I had to push the brim of my hat back to get a good look at his face.

What I saw didn't cheer me. Small, angry red eyes set

deep gave his face a look halfway between a pig and a grizzly. A dark matted beard helped that same impression. And, even accustomed as I am to the smells a man can cultivate after weeks in the saddle, I flinched at this one's ripeness.

"Get along, boy," he said. "This is my show."

I wanted to. Range dust caked my throat and beer was waiting.

The man raised his foot to give another whack. Behind him, the horse tied to a rail stamped nervously.

"Stop," I said without thinking. It wasn't that I took insult at being called boy. No, sir. Long ago my pa and ma had died over useless pride.

"Huh? Stop? Why?" He was so dumbfounded anybody might order him to do anything that he remained on one foot, the other reared and ready to kick.

"Well . . ." I said.

I couldn't think of a good reason for him to stop. This wasn't my business. And it was only an Indian. But I guess it was an Indian too stubborn to cry or beg, and that kind of perseverance always gets a person's attention.

"Boy, horse thieving's a mortal sin." The man mopped his brow again and then delivered the next kick.

I winced at the crack of boot against ribs. The Indian rolled slightly.

"The sheriff'd be happy to hang him," I mentioned. "Might save you all this work."

"Huh?" He didn't glance up. "You still here?"

I pictured the cool shadows of the saloon. Some cowboys at a card table. An open spot waiting for me.

I sighed. "I'm still here."

The man stared at me, genuinely puzzled. "I thought I explained. This here's a horse thief. An Injun, as you can plainly see. And I don't ever explain nothin' to nobody but once."

"Got money," the Indian managed to croak. "Got money."

"Shut up," the big man said to the Indian and absently added a half kick to encourage the silence.

Why hadn't I just walked along Main Street, stopping to look in the windows at fancy merchandise brought in from the East by train? Instead, I was half into something I didn't understand and had no idea how to leave alone.

"That's your horse he tried to steal?" I said, pointing behind the giant man for a change of subject. "You must be a smart one, catching an Injun in the act."

"Didn't," the man grunted. At least he'd stopped kicking.

"I thought you said—"

"Injun tried to buy my horse with this here gold piece." The man opened a giant paw and showed glinting yellow. "And any fool knows Injuns don't have that kind of money."

"But—"

"Boy, you test a man dearly. To buy my horse with stole money is jest like to steal the horse itself. And I take insult real easy."

He shook his head, a grizzly shaking off angry bees. His focus moved from the Injun to me. "In fact, you done pushed too far."

He took a step sideways of the Indian on the ground.

I made the mistake of touching the handle of my gun to reassure me it was still there. Not that I intended to use it. Gunfights are mainly something you find in Ned Buntline dime novels, stuff eastern folks believe happens every day out here. Only bounty hunters and desperate men are willing to risk a shoot-out, and it had been years since I'd been acquainted with either.

I never thought a man so big could move so quick.

Gunfights—real gunfights—usually take longer or shorter than this one did. The short ones happen with the few outlaws—like Jim Hickok—who learned to survive by any dirty trick: rigged holsters, sleeve derringers, and a shot in the back, front, or sideways when least expected. They ain't fools, and they don't leave survivors.

On the other hand, you can expect the longer gunfights from fools who carry a notion of honor with their guns. These generally start with insults and half-drunk cowboys. One cowboy says something like, "We'd best be slapping leather unless you is yeller," and the bartender moves everyone outside to keep stray bullets from shattering mirror. Then both cowboys walk toward each other on the street until someone finally breaks nerve and reaches for his gun, and then the slowest gun loses unless the fastest gun can't aim. It ends with mostly one or the other getting sent to a doctor for patching up, 'cause hardly anyone is steady enough to plug someone in the heart when they're so shaky and nervous about being plugged back. In other words, a fair gunfight builds real slow and don't cause much damage.

Not this one.

I'd barely touched the butt of my gun when the man flapped back his vest with one hand and reached across his stomach to draw with the other.

A cross draw's the deadliest if a man does it right, and it took only a wink for me to figure he was doing it as right as it can be done. In the same moment I realized that a part of my brain still remembered enough to instruct my hand to make a move of its own.

I had the advantage 'cause my hand was already on the butt of my gun. Without that lucky accident, I'd be dead. The Colt was out of my holster and jumping with the first shot before I really knew it was live or die.

I was able to fan the gun's hammer maybe twice more before something burned through my left arm and spun me around.

As I fought to stay on my feet, the next second was deadly quiet. Only the smell of cordite told me there'd actually been a gunfight and that I was still alive.

I weaved back to face the giant man again. Except I had to look down through the drifting gunsmoke to see him sprawled flat backward with his hat still wobbling tracks in the dust.

He wheezed bubbles of blood that snapped and popped at the side of his mouth. His eyes stared straight up at the high sun.

My stomach bumped. Then lurched. I managed to reach the side of the shed before I threw up. And threw up some more. It had been a long time since I'd seen violent death caused by my own hand.

When a bullet hits, it don't really hurt at first. Maybe as much as the sting of a bee. But given time, the nerves and vessels start to realize something's wrong. Awareness of pain reached me about the same time as distant shouts.

I stood, still unable to believe this had happened. Blood soaked through my sleeve. Approaching shouts grew louder.

Who was there to witness this had been a fair fight and not a murder?

The Indian. Maybe I could take a chance someone might take the word of an Indian as witness.

Except the Indian was gone. And so was the horse.

Depending on who I'd shot—whether he was local or not and how much anyone liked him—chances were fifty-fifty I'd hang. I didn't have much time to decide. I figured better safe than sorry. I'd ride out. Quick. The territories had plenty of range and not many people.

I stumbled in the opposite direction of the saloon to find my horses at the stable, wanting to build a lead before anyone knew it was I that had done the shooting.

I cursed each step of the way. My first gunfight since I'd assumed the name of Samuel L. Keaton. The first man I'd killed under that name. And now, no doubt, my first posse. With me on the wrong end of the chase.

CHAPTER 2

THE HALF-WIT IN THE SHADOWS of the stable nodded a friendly smile at the drops of blood that plinked onto the toe of my boot.

"Gotcha in the arm, huh?" he asked as he threw my saddle on Charlie. The half-wit's mouth remained half open. He was chubby and bald, with the unlined middle-aged face of a child in a man's body, and his head nodded and danced to whatever music always played in his poor mind.

"Gotcha in the arm," he repeated in his determination to prove he was capable of conversation.

He had watched me struggle to tie a wide strip of cloth tight between my elbow and the bullet hole in my lower arm only thirty seconds earlier.

"My friend, your powers of observation truly inspire amazement."

He beamed at the compliment.

"Knife or bullet?" he asked, happy to be in

a conversation he understood. "Most times around here it's bullet."

"Mosquito," I snapped as another wave of pain rocked me. "They grow mighty big here. Cinch that saddle good, will ya. I'll be riding far and fast."

"Ain't that something," he said. His large, shiny head bobbed as he whistled appreciation and got my saddlebags in place.

"Yup," I said. I closed my eyes to fight the pain and search for a story to send any posse in the opposite direction I intended. "Heading south to Colorado. Got a brother to meet in Denver."

"Now ain't that something the ride." He snorted at my stupidity. "Lots of folks go south. I mean ain't that something about a mosquiter big 'nuff to tear a hole in a feller's arm."

I took in the sweet smell of hay and horse and felt sadness that I couldn't just stay and lose myself in this peace of still air and dust dancing in the sunbeams. I wanted the moment so bad, I stayed where I was, leaning against Charlie for strength. He's a big horse, sleek and almost red, with powerful curves of muscle flexing each step. I paid double for Charlie compared to what most cowpunchers pay for a horse, but when a horse might be the difference on the range between living or dying, I always figure it foolish not to get the best you can, no matter how much sacrifice it takes.

"Did ya see it coming?"

I realized he'd repeated another question. Somewhere in the last few seconds I'd blanked. My reins were already in place, slack across Charlie's neck. My other two horses were tethered behind and ready to follow.

"Did I see what coming?" I felt a terrible thirst, too.

"That mosquiter. Be a real shame if a feller had no warning with critters like that around."

I dug in my pocket for a coin.

"Help me up, partner." I placed the coin in his manure-stained hand. "And give this to your boss man. This ought to cover the price."

He was gentle as he steadied me onto Charlie, but I should have expected that from someone not smart enough to learn how to be mean. I hated to take advantage of such innocence, but I had to think about a posse that would surely be gathering by now. Once they discovered no one near the body I'd left behind, the first place they'd check was the stable. It'd be nice if the poor half-wit wasn't to be found easy.

"Friend," I said. "To tell the truth, I believe that mosquito followed me in here. Once they get the taste of a man's blood, they don't quit easy."

The half-wit's eyes flared white, and he half ducked in fear as he looked around quick.

"Yup," I said. "Here's some advice for free. Run home and rest there a spell. Don't come out till tomorrow."

I felt bad for the story, until the first jog of Charlie's walk reminded me of the bullet hole in my lower arm. Then I felt nothing but a red-hot poker shoved into my flesh, pulled out, and shoved in again and again with each step.

Irksome Indian.

CHAPTER 3

IT DIDN'T TAKE LONG for that Indian to haunt me again.

I'd barely reached the outskirts of Laramie—with Charlie at a stately walk because the last thing I wanted was to attract attention among the buggies and wagons and horses and strolling people—when a black horse charged out from between the hotel and railroad depot. A familiar black horse.

The rider, naturally, was that slight figure with greasy braids, loose and ragged clothing, and a face already ugly with swelled bruises.

"Giddyup," I mumbled to Charlie. I squeezed my thighs slightly, and he responded.

Charlie moved from a trot into a smooth canter, and my other two horses kept pace behind. My arm told me it wasn't pleased with more bouncing. Despite my sacrifice of added pain that threatened to put me into a faint, the distance between me and that Indian shortened.

Me and Charlie passed the last house on the edge of town.

"Fly loose, bronco." I leaned forward and tensed for the explosion of hooves that would come as Charlie reacted to more pressure from the inside of my thighs. He bucked forward and we pounded dirt. For a moment I forgot my problems in the joy of raw speed on a great horse.

Then, still in the rhythm of gallop, I looked back—hat now fallen between my shoulder blades and tugging in the wind against my neck strap—and saw the Indian struggling with his black horse.

Behind the Indian, the edges of the buildings of Laramie dropped back. No sign of gathered horses. Good. All I needed was a twenty-minute lead and to not pass out from weakness. That'd be enough to hide my trail—I'd learned one or two tricks from my brother—and by changing horses every few miles, I'd be able to keep a pace no posse could hope to match.

The Indian kept following.

Hiding trail would be impossible if this didn't change.

I went so far as to spur Charlie, and he found that last extra juice. But at this pace, I'd kill him if we went longer than ten minutes.

Next time I looked back, that Indian was slipping from the side of his horse.

I looked back again, this time to see the Indian tumbling into the brush at the side of the trail.

Another quick glance showed how well the dead man had trained his horse. It had stopped to wait for its fallen rider. When I looked back the next time, that Indian was climbing back on.

Another hundred yards. My next glance showed that Indian in full pursuit again. Worse, the Indian was small on the dead man's big horse, and Charlie, with the burden of my one hundred ninety pounds, was hard pressed to keep our lead.

Something had to be done.

Charlie and I rounded a bend, screened by brush and the wall of a small gulch. I reined him to a stop and hopped down. I didn't waste time tying him to a bush. The other two horses puffed and blew on the end of their tethers.

Cowpunchers like to tell stories—'specially about outlaws and such stuff. In a good story, a fella like me would climb one of the nearby trees real quick—even with a busted-up arm and ready to puke from pain—wait for the following horse to get into range, and dive into the rider as he passed below.

I guess I'd never make a hero. My arm hurt bad. My head spun and was spinning worse each minute. The tree was too tall, and I had no hankering to dive into a horse moving at full gallop. Hit or miss, either way, the punishment would be the same. And I'd be the one suffering.

So I braced my feet where I stood, sucked in some deep breaths to keep the blackness from closing in on me, drew my Colt, and held it as steady as I could with both arms.

Charlie stood to the side, breathing hard but not heaving for air.

I waited.

Before my arms could get tired, that Indian rounded the bend. He saw me standing there and yanked hard on the reins.

The big black horse braced its feet and almost skidded, it stopped so quick. It pitched the Indian straight over its head, and I had to step aside to miss getting hit as he thumped to the ground at my feet.

Made me feel real good about choosing not to dive from a tree.

"You," I said with a toe prod into the moaning Indian. "Whatever reasons you got, I don't want company this ride. Understand?"

His groan sounded close to agreement.

"Good," I continued, "I'd hate to get in the habit of plugging people."

Right then I heard three distant shots from the direction of Laramie. The signal told me the marshal was gathering all the men who could ride and letting them know where to find him.

I weaved my way back to Charlie and placed a hand on my saddle.

There was only one thing wrong. Besides the fact that I'd shot a man. Besides the fact I'd been shot. Besides the fact a posse was only a few miles away.

I couldn't climb Charlie.

It was something I could always do anytime, even in the middle of my sleep. Just grab the horn of my saddle, swing a foot into the stirrups, push up, and swing a leg over and on.

But try as I did now, my body wouldn't listen.

Then I realized I was sitting on the ground. It puzzled me deeply to be staring at the dust. It puzzled me more when my nose started pushing its way into the dust with the rest of my body fallen forward to encourage it.

I wasn't able to puzzle about it for long. A black blanket of surrender drifted over me and I was gone.

CHAPTER 4

"JEST SHOT MY THIRD ONE of the week," the marshal announced as he pushed open the door. Long low rays of dawn's first sunlight fell over his shoulders across the width of his small office and into my jail cell. I closed my eyes until I heard the door shut behind him.

"Third stray dog," he continued. "Nope, ain't much glory in marshaling when folks expect you to shoot stray dogs."

I said nothing.

The fact that he'd spoken as he walked in meant he'd known I was awake. Which meant he'd taken the effort to wait outside at the edge of one of the front windows and watch for some time to be certain I was awake, as I hadn't the stomach to move much on the miserable cot. It also meant he wasn't the regular fool most towns are forced to hire to carry a tin badge.

"Coffee or water?" he asked in conversational tones. "Got plenty of both."

I'd woken to the aroma from the blue-enameled jug that bubbled on his potbellied stove. July or not, it was still early in the day, and its radiated heat felt good. But not being able to reach that coffee had become the first indication of how bar cells might limit a man.

"Coffee'd be appreciated," I said. I rose to a sitting position. My left arm, in a sling, fell none too gently against my side.

The marshal nodded, slapped his hat free of dust, and hung it on a nail on the back side of his door. Aside from the improvised coatrack, the office held little furniture. A desk, cane chair. Locked gun rack. And the potbellied stove in the center.

I guessed the marshal to be in his midforties. He was my height, slope shouldered with an easy, confident way of moving. His dark mustache, trimmed, barely covered his upper lip. Sunlight gleamed from a large bald spot that left matching dark hair only around his ears. Put the Stetson back on that head, and he'd look ten years younger.

His jeans weren't too dusty, and his shirt was long-sleeved with cuffs hanging loose. The vest over that shirt was pale, finely worked leather.

I saw no badge but did catch a gleam of a steel pin on the front of his vest. So he wore the badge facing in, where he could show it if he had to merely by opening his vest. This was a man who didn't feel the need to impress strangers, unless he had a marshal's duty to get better acquainted.

"Probably wondering why I'd leave an important prisoner like you unattended," he said as he moved around the office. "Fact is, town council's filled with men who couldn't find their backsides with a chair seat. I'm down to one deputy now, and rumor has it they'll likely stop paying his wages, too."

He worked his holster loose and set it on the nearby desk.

I noticed the marshal was careful to lay it so that the butt of the pistol faced the front of the desk. A Colt .31 fire-shot percussion. Not a fancy gun compared to the revolving action of the new .44–40, but reliable, and a .31 caliber hole is persuasive enough. It'd be within a half step and easy to pull loose no matter where he moved within this cramped office.

I also noticed he banged my cup upside down to clear it of bugs or spiders before he filled it with coffee. He stuck the full mug between the bars of the cell and waited for me to take it. He held his palm around the mug part, leaving the handle free for me. The coffee must have been near the boiling point. I wondered how much effort it took him to keep his face steady like the cup wasn't hot at all.

I got to my feet. It hurt some. I walked slower and groggier than I needed to. It wasn't much of an ace to carry, but it was all I had.

The marshal waited, giving me plenty of time to grab his arm.

I declined. I'd seen enough already to make judgment.

"Thanks for the coffee," I said.

I took the handle.

He didn't release the cup. Still giving me time to grab his arm.

I looked into his eyes and smiled a smile that I meant. This man had plenty sand.

"Don't expect a play from me," I said. "Not with a busted wing and your right hand free. Loose cuffs like that, I'm figuring you for a pocket cannon rigged to pop loose anytime you stretch."

He let go of the coffee and smiled back.

I barely saw his right arm move. By the time I blinked, I was staring into the twin black holes of a derringer so close to my skull I could barely focus my eyes on the gun barrels.

"One fool gave me a run once," the marshal admitted

without wavering those two barrels. "Pulled me into the bars so bad I nearly broke a cheekbone. Burying him, though, was cheaper than a trial. But you—"

He glanced down at the puddle of coffee I was pouring at our feet.

The cup dropped from my fingers to give me an open hand that I slapped into his right wrist. I used my momentum to slam his wrist and hand and derringer into the iron cell bars.

He grunted but didn't drop the derringer.

I wrapped my fingers around his wrist. Stiff-armed, I could lean that wrist into the bars to pin him there and keep my distance from his flailing left arm. My leverage gave me an advantage, and I was able to twist his hand so that the derringer had enough angle to blow away his jaw. I managed to curl one finger around the trigger.

We stared at each other. He refused to say a word.

I let go his wrist.

"Wouldn't mind more coffee," I said. "That is, if we're through circling each other like roosters in a pit."

He flexed and unflexed his right hand. "Sure," he said. "Maybe you want sugar in your coffee." He scratched his chin. "I noticed the first cup didn't agree with you."

"Sugar's fine." I reached down and picked up the cup. A snake for a man would have caught me under the chin with a boot right then, and I knew it. But I figured him for a good risk, and if not, split lips or loosened teeth were a small price to know what I'd be dealing with over the next while.

I discovered he was the kind of man who kept his word. He was generous with the sugar.

He poured his own coffee, sat back in the cane chair at the side of his desk, and slowly sipped as he watched me over the edge of his cup.

I sat back down on the bed and returned his gaze.

I guess the rooster circling wasn't finished yet, because I found myself smiling inside to remember some of Clara's advice. Much of my memories of her were filled with the pain of regret—losing a one and only love will do that to a man—but every so often I remember something that gave me pleasure. She'd told me time and again that the first one to speak loses, and I doubt anyone ever outnegotiated that woman or, for that matter, had had more varied situations among men to practice her own advice.

I sipped my own coffee and waited.

"Tarnation," he finally said, "it ain't natural. Most men fresh to jail ask more questions than a jealous woman."

"All right," I said, content that he'd spoken first, "where are my horses?"

He waited. So did I.

"That's it? All you want to know is about your horses?"

"Yup," I said. "Not too hard to figure where I am. Knowing where I am makes it easy to figure how I got here. And my bandaged arm tells the rest."

He took another sip. "What about what'll happen to you? Ain't interested in that?"

"I die from gangrene if the arm don't heal. Or I hang. Or I get let go. Not much else possible, and since you ain't doctor or judge, your best answer's a guess, just like mine."

He drained his cup, set it on his desk, and brought his feet down so that he could lean forward.

"Then what about the man you shot? No questions there?"

"I won't deny it was me what done the shooting. The man was kicking an Injun to death, and I happened by. It was a fair fight. A man draws a gun, he takes his chances. Just 'cause he picked the wrong time to take a chance don't mean I need to know his name."

"Fair fight?" His tone remained conversational. "You ran."

I finished my own coffee. "No witnesses to back me up," I said. "I took my own chance. It didn't go the way I expected. And I'm here in this cell to pay for taking that chance."

"A judge might look poorly on that. He'd ask why a man travels with his own remuda of the finest horseflesh I seen in a while, like maybe that man is in the habit of outrunning posses and needs a couple of fresh horses right handy."

"Same man might just prefer being ready for whatever's always waiting around the next corner. This is Injun country, and no disrespect intended, it ain't exactly free of outlaws."

"No disrespect taken." The marshal stood and began to pace. He didn't look my way as he spoke without inflection.

"Done checked you out already," he said. "'Course, I had two days to find out from what ranch you hailed. That's how long you were laid out, weak and cold from losing so much blood. Two days. Surprised? 'Course not. And if you were, that poker face wouldn't show it."

His pacing continued. "What I learned wasn't much. Sam Keaton they call you. Strange in itself. Most times cowboys look for a handle to hang on people. Itchy Jake, maybe. Six-gun Boy. Curley. Slim. Tex. Spider. None had much to say about you, like they couldn't get a handle at all. Just said you mainly kept to yourself and knew horses, was the best with a remuda they'd seen, the best at breaking broncs."

He stopped. "Now this."

I raised an eyebrow as he continued.

"The fact you figured me for a pocket cannon shows you ain't a typical cowpuncher. Plus the fact you beat me plain and simple with gunplay. And the fact you didn't blow my fool head off when you had the chance."

"Why didn't I kill you?" I remembered heaving my guts

at the side of the shed. "It appears I've developed a bad reaction to the sight of blood," I explained. "Besides . . ."

He studied my face as I worked up the energy to grin.

"Besides," I said, "you left the keys on the desk by your holster. So you dead and me behind bars wouldn't have got me out anyway."

"Lucky for me," he said with irony. "Though I noticed you just danced around the whyfors of you being so good with a gun."

He moved to his desk, hitched his pants, and with a small movement, hopped backward to land sitting.

"Lucky for me," he repeated softly as he lost himself in his own thoughts.

I didn't let him drift long. "About my horses. They shouldn't be paying for my mistake."

"Stabled," the marshal said. "One-arm Wilson's got them. No proof they were stolen, and I found enough money on you to pay their keep."

"Obliged," I said. I could see my own holster and pocketknife on the far corner of his desk. I pressed my back pocket and felt the bulge of my wallet. "Won't surprise me to find out you only took what was needed out of my billfold."

He ran his fingers over his bald head and sighed. "You do have a roll of notes there. I hope you can spend the rest."

My blood ran cool. "Meaning you can make a pretty good prediction on whether I hang or walk free?"

" 'Fraid so."

He shook his head. "Town owes you a favor. You killed John Harrison. It's a certain fact you won't have to worry about a mob and old Judge Lynch."

"Our departed friend didn't appear to be a saint," I agreed, even though the name wasn't familiar. "He drawed first, and it didn't take much provocation for him to do so."

The marshal's eyes widened. "Harrison drawed first, and you still beat him?"

It didn't appear to be the proper time to mention I was still sore at myself for missing bad enough with my first shots to take one in the arm. I didn't feel better, either, to blame my poor shooting on the passage of years.

"That makes it more of a shame," the marshal said. "Shoot anyone else like that, and you'd be a local hero resting in a hotel. Trouble was, Harrison was a deputy here, half brother to and especially appointed by the crookedest and meanest snake of a sheriff to run a territory, a fellow by the name of Henry Reed, the same sheriff who's hung men for looking at him crossways. And that same sheriff ought to be in from Rawlins any day now, looking to take revenge on you."

CHAPTER 5

I'VE SEEN IT HAPPEN BEFORE. The blood excitement that spurs a certain kind of woman. This is the woman who pretends not to notice two men courting her at a dance but on the sly finds a way to egg them on to a fight, then stands back quietly to pant slightly with flushed cheeks as they bloody each other with fists or, better yet, with knives or guns.

Most folks, I guess, would be quick to associate this particular woman with the soiled doves who trade their company for a cow-poke's wages. I won't deny you'll find her among them. I did hear a story about Hickok shooting a man in Dodge, and the dance-hall girl that clapped her blood-covered hands in glee to be so close to a dying man.

On the other hand, I don't believe many of those women chose their lives for the chance to see the raw side of life. After all, few women get soiled unless somewhere along the way there is the first man who takes advantage of a bad situation, with plenty other men after to help her dance the same lonely sad dance again and again. Not only that, I got my own reasons for knowing that a lot of these women have scraped their souls so bare, they'd be the last ones to delight in the misfortunes of others or, for that matter, point at someone else's sins.

Nope, as rare a woman as she is, one with a bloodlust shining in her eyes is just as apt to appear much farther away from the railroad tracks and hotels—banker's wife to schoolmarm. And it doesn't take her long after the blood's been spilled.

This one pushed open the marshal's door before I'd finished my shave.

"Marshal Evrett?" She waited in the doorway. A bonnet covered most of her hair and small-featured face. Her long black dress was tightly collared. She carried an open basket in one hand, a small leather-bound book in the other.

"He just went for breakfast at the hotel," I called across the office from behind my bars. "No more than a half minute ago. I'm surprised you didn't see him on the street."

The woman lifted the hem of her dress and moved through the doorway. "He left you here alone?"

"He mentioned something about sending a town councilman down to stand watch."

She narrowed her focus on me where I stood with a basin of tepid water on a chair nearby, piece of mirror propped in the windowsill, and towel wrapped around my neck.

"That's a straightedge razor in your hand!"

"Helps a man remove lather."

"I shall keep my distance."

"If it sets your mind at ease, ma'am," I said. "Marshal Evrett offered me his derringer earlier this morning, but I declined."

She pursed her lips in silent disapproval and stared at me

while I finished shaving. I wiped the traces of lather off my face and set aside the towel and the basin and straight blade.

She stared. Hard.

"Any message you'd like me to pass along to the marshal?" I said to break the silence. "I suspect I'll be here when he returns."

She didn't smile at my attempted humor. "Do you believe Jesus Christ died on the cross to remove your sins?"

"Ma'am?"

"Do you believe and repent?"

"You do cut to the chase, ma'am. I ain't even scheduled for a trial, let alone the hangman."

"There is the blood," she shivered, "of another man on your hands. I have arrived here to do the Lord's work."

She moved a step closer to the jail cell. Her young face was darkly intense.

"Food for your body." She hefted the basket.

"Food for your soul." She hefted the leather-bound book. "It was Jesus himself who commanded His followers to visit those in prison. If only Marshal Evrett would receive the word along with his prisoners."

Now I understood why Marshal Evrett had left so quickly. He'd been standing at the window, gazing onto the street, when he'd cut the conversation short. He had seen her coming and made good his escape.

The woman unwrapped the cloth of the basket. I smelled fresh biscuits and sausage. My mouth moistened, and I realized with a start how hungry I was.

She pulled the marshal's chair closer to my cell, set the basket on the floor beside the chair, then sat and faced me, hands primly folded in her lap.

She caught my hungry glance at the basket.

"The soul is more important than the body," she said. "Prayer before food. Is there repentance in your heart?"

I dry swallowed. It had been two days since food, and I didn't know how long since fresh biscuits. Did she have butter in that basket? Maybe some jam preserves, cheese . . .

"Prayer first, then food," she said. "Is there repentance in your heart?"

She took my silence as agreement.

"My name is Miss Ackerman. Pull your chair close and sit."

I did, not even disgusted with myself for letting my stomach control my actions.

She put her hands through the bars and took my hands from my lap. Her eyes grew wide as she examined the blood-soaked bandages on my left arm.

"As brother and sister in prayer," she said, "we shall take your sins to the Lord."

She stared into my eyes in silence for so long that I didn't have to use my imagination much to sense her new tension. Her shoulders began to heave with each breath, and I wondered if she even knew she carried the bloodlust. As for me, my interest was in the basket of food.

"Tell it now," she whispered, "how it happened. Why you did it. How you outdrew Harrison, faced him down with the fear of death in your heart. How it felt to . . . to . . . kill a man by putting a bullet . . ."

Her palms were warm. She squeezed my hands. "What I mean is, pour it out to the Lord. He will listen and forgive."

Clove mint breath, hot and close. Small beads of sweat on her upper lip.

"Pour it out," she urged, "how you took a man's life with the single flash of a gun. A killer facing a killer on a road to hell, each with the skills of a lifetime of dealing death. . . ."

She lightly bit the tip of her tongue, then leaned so close now that for her eyes to search mine, they had to dart back and forth.

She finally closed her eyes and pulled my hands closer. Ignoring my grunt of pain to have the left arm wrenched, she squeezed my hands harder with hers and groaned, "Oh, Lord, we beseech thee to—"

The opening of the door interrupted her.

She dropped my hands and stood quickly and straightened her dress. "We . . . we pray for a thirsty soul! We . . ."

Then her voice trailed as she turned, and we both saw the new visitor.

An Indian. At least an Indian to her. To me, it was *the* Indian. Short and scrawny. Face and braids even greasier with dirt than before. The edges of his felt hat hung over his ears and forehead. His bulky black coat was belted by a sash of red cloth. The deerskin medicine bundle strapped over his shoulder showed what I thought to be Sioux beadwork.

He stared at both of us, no expression.

"Haven't you heathen learned to knock?" the woman said to the Indian. "Now get."

To me, here was a good example of someone not doing the Lord's work. Miss Ackerman had been talking pretty enough when it was convenient to use the Lord as a calling card. But the tone of her voice now to the Indian had anything but the love of Jesus in it. A Christian like her wasn't going to bring me closer to God.

"Get, you filthy animal," she said loudly, using her hands to make shooing movements.

The answer from that irksome Indian was that impassive stare and forward movement.

Miss Ackerman backed a half step in deference, even though the Indian was no taller than her.

The Indian took another step in my direction. Still said nothing.

I didn't know how I felt about this Indian haunting me again. If he were a white man, I'd be begging him not to leave. All I needed was a witness to swear the gunfight had been a fair play, that I'd shot in self-defense. But few'd take an Indian's word in a white man's court.

Was I curious at his appearance again?

Not really. There'd been more than a few times on cattle drives from Texas that families of Indians had come begging for lamies as we crossed their land. Trouble was, give them one calf that was going to be left behind anyway, and they'd follow us days for more cattle, either pitifully screeching or shaking war spears, and generally making a nuisance until melting away whenever we got within ten miles of a soldiers' outpost.

I'd already saved this Indian once. Maybe he figured I was soft enough to contribute more.

I quickly signed to the Indian that I had nothing.

More impassive staring.

While I could understand why the Indian hadn't responded to Miss Ackerman—English doesn't make sense to most Indians—I wondered why this one didn't sign back. With nearly a dozen tribes and a dozen tongues just on the Great Plains alone, sign language was the only way Indians ever managed to communicate when they met during wars or palavers or trading sessions. According to mountain men, it had been done that way for centuries, and every Indian child learned to sign even as they learned to speak.

I tried signing again. I held my hands chest high, using mainly my right hand as I had been taught by those mountain men. After jabbing my forefinger at the Indian so he knew I meant him, I gave him the sign action for desire, holding my right hand closed very near my chin and forming an incomplete circle with my thumb and index finger at mouth level. With a slight wrist movement, I brought my hand to my lips, making the motion of drinking.

What is it you want?

I repeated the actions. *What is it you want?*

Only that unreadable stare from black eyes answered. Then I remembered that the Indian could talk—he'd croaked something about having money just before the shoot-out—and realized I was wasting my efforts. If he didn't want to communicate, he wouldn't.

The Indian pulled a bowie knife from the depths of his coat.

Miss Ackerman drew in a scandalized breath. "Grab your razor!" she told me. "I'm a helpless woman."

I wasn't worried. If the Indian meant real harm, he wouldn't be choosing the marshal's office.

"Try praying," I suggested to her. "I'm behind iron and God ain't."

The Indian slashed down with his knife and speared one of the sausages in the basket.

That hurt.

The Indian stared at Miss Ackerman while he stuffed the sausage into his mouth. He didn't wipe away the juices that dripped down his chin.

"Oh my," she said, fascination and a tremor of bloodlust back in her voice. "I've never seen one this close. He does smell, doesn't he?"

"He probably prefers fire smoke to perfume," I said. "Injuns don't smell bad to other Injuns."

The Indian speared two more sausages and left them on his knife.

He took the final step to the jail cell and with his other hand threw a folded piece of paper onto the floor.

Then, knife still held high with its trophies of sausage, he turned and left as quietly as he had arrived.

Miss Ackerman turned to me, the high points of her cheeks now reddened circles.

"Shouldn't we get Marshal Evrett?" she said, staring

down at the note she handed me.

I didn't answer. I was too busy with the note.

For that matter, I didn't even hear her leave. Not with immaculate handwriting in clear ink on a piece of paper that started with the words, *These are the instructions for your escape.* . . .

CHAPTER *6*

MISS ACKERMAN WAS THE FIRST that day to want to get a look at the man who outgunned John Harrison, but she wasn't the last. I can't say the others carried the shiny-eyed bloodlust that I doubt she even knew she had, but in Miss Ackerman's favor, none of the others carried a basket of food along with their curiosity.

A banker named Crawford stopped by, fat and sweating in a dark vested suit, to discuss with Marshal Evrett the details of a town ordinance that might forbid tobacco chewing in banks and churches, since Laramie was no longer a frontier town and some of the ladies now objected to the poor marksmanship of those too lazy to step closer to the spittoons. To which Marshal Evrett replied that he had enough difficulty stopping the rougher element from wearing guns in similar establishments, and had Crawford ever considered purchasing more or wider spittoons. It was wasted advice, because the banker was too busy gawking past the marshal's shoulders at me to pay any attention to the conversation.

Two elderly ladies arrived shortly after the banker's departure and inquired of Marshal Evrett's health. He dryly informed them it hadn't changed much from the previous year, when they'd been kind enough to stop by and ask while he was guarding a captured stagecoach thief who'd shot the driver's two lead horses to stop the stage, a crime equally serious to that of robbing the passengers. Then the sheriff surprised those elderly ladies by offering them the chance to wake me from the nap I was so desperately trying to pretend. He later informed me that subjecting me to their twittering questions was the only punishment he could think of to repay me for letting Miss Ackerman spread it about town that he'd offered me his derringer.

The monotony of the heat of the day continued, interrupted by at least a dozen other visitors, all of whom spoke to Marshal Evrett while staring at me. I can't say as I blamed them. A town like this had precious little entertainment, and I'd given all the respectable folk something to talk about besides the lack of rain and who had missed church the previous Sunday.

Not one of these visitors, however, remotely resembled who I imagined Rebecca Montcalm to be, she being the one who had signed the note delivered to me by the Indian.

I had the words memorized now.

These are the instructions for your escape. My Indian messenger will reappear at dawn two days from now, armed with a pistol and with rope. He will enter the jail and at gunpoint force the marshal to open your cell. It is imperative that you then tie the marshal securely to enable you the necessary time to establish an escape route that will not be traced. The Indian will accompany you and, when

appropriate, will deliver further messages to you from me.
Do not abandon the Indian. He is the key to great wealth.
Rebecca Montcalm.

Naturally, I had my share of questions. How was this Indian involved yet again? What wealth? And who was Rebecca Montcalm?

From where I lay on my side on the cot behind bars, each time the door opened, I'd crack my eyelids open enough to decide whether the new visitor fit the picture in my mind that I had of Rebecca Montcalm. And each time I was disappointed, I felt a vague uneasiness that I ignored as best as possible.

It wasn't until nightfall, when I could pace my cell without worry of having to answer to curious strangers, that I understood that uneasiness.

It was the fact that I had such a preconceived notion of who Rebecca Montcalm should be. Somehow, I imagined her to be young—beautiful, of course—with creamy white skin and red lips delicately pursed as she wrote the note in the shade of a parasol.

When I realized that, I shook my head in disgust at myself.

When it comes to women, men are the biggest fools to wander the earth. No matter who we are, we're willing to believe that there is something special enough about us that any woman secretly desires us and would act on that desire if only the situation and lack of opportunity wouldn't prevent her from expressing that desire. That was something I'd learned from Clara in Denver, and she'd played enough men for fools to know.

Clara had explained it to me one rainy late fall afternoon after I'd wondered aloud about the screeching outside that came from a scrawny redheaded cowboy who mooned after one of her dancing girls, an equally scrawny blonde with a pocked face who was trying to sleep in the room across from the kitchen where we sat.

I worked at the dance hall, a reasonably respectable place, for when the cowboys paid to dance, that was all they got. That led to much of my work, which was escorting drunken and disappointed cowboys off the premises.

It was a slow day, and we had brought out a deck of cards. At the renewed screeching outside the window, Clara had laughed, a laugh that now, nearly two decades later, could still make me smile whenever I allowed myself to remember those times.

"That crazed cowpuncher is soaked wet and singing for the same reason you're at this table and about to lose a week's wages in five-card stud."

I blinked. Sure, we had nine dollars in the pot—half mine—but my four hearts showed against her fives and sevens, and I was about to up the ante again because my hole card was the jack of hearts. I had a flush, and because one of my hearts showing was a five, it cut lower the already considerable odds against her holding the full house that would beat my hand.

"Clara," I said, smiling as I carefully counted out my coins and pushed them into the pile between us, "you're wrong. Twice. This five-dollar raise makes it two weeks' wages, and I ain't gonna lose."

"That's my point," she said, matching my bet. "You *think* you're a good poker player."

I shrugged. Cool I was. I'd probably sprouted a few chin whiskers by then, and as all boys that age in a man's body, I was fully convinced I would live forever plus another two years.

"Put your mind to it," she said.

I looked closer at her then, the tone of her voice was that sharp, almost bitter. Clara was maybe two years older than I, but her eyes were all grown-up. They were green, flecked with gold, and watched the world from a face not quite chubby and also pouty enough that I knew, young as I was, how it could draw a man in. Her hair, blond and fine, was cut in straight bangs that emphasized the smoothness of her jawline. She was wrapped in a thick robe that afternoon, a steaming cup of tea at her elbow, as if she were an old woman trying to warm her bones.

"You've been at the dance hall almost since you were a boy," she snapped. "In that time any of these cowboys ever tell you they can't ride a horse as well as the next?"

I thumbed my hole card, flicking the edge against the table.

"And any of them ever tell you how lousy he is at cards?"

I flicked the edge again.

"And any of them ever finish a dance, hitch his belt, and tell you how sadly he just disappointed a woman's expectations?" Her eyes were wide with heat now. "No, no, and no," she said. "Men are such fools that each and every one figures nobody can outride him, outpoker him, or outlove him with women."

Thinking about it in those terms, I had no choice but to agree. So I nodded.

"But the world proves every day that some men do get outrode," she said. "Every poker game has its share of losers, and women do say no to men."

As if to prove her point, the redheaded cowboy's screeching stopped dead, like maybe the blonde had emptied a chamber pot on him from out the window, as indeed I discovered later she had.

"What you got to ask yourself is this," she continued. "If all those other men are fooling themselves into thinking they're God's gift to the world when it's so obvious they're not, how do *you* know you're not fooling yourself, too? Anytime you start thinking the sun sets on you is the time you're ready to take a fall. That's the time you got to ask yourself why you're any different than all the others who think they're special but get outrode, lose money, and sing in the rain for nothing."

With that, she flipped over her hole card. A seven of spades. "Full house," she said. "And two weeks' wages is a small price if you understand half of what I'm trying to explain."

I winced.

"Dealt from the bottom, my full house *and* your flush," she told me. "Next time, watch the cards. If you think it was an accident special for you that my robe fell open slightly as I leaned forward to deal, you're as big a fool as the next."

Years later, one night while I'd been riding herd in the north of Texas, I had also been given cause to think of that afternoon with Clara. A she-coyote had called from just outside the firelight, and before anyone could move, one of the dogs had bolted into the darkness beyond. Barely a minute had passed before a hideous snarling and howling tore the softness of the night. The she-coyote had been in heat and used that to draw the dog away from safety to a pack of he-coyotes that had been waiting in ambush. I'd shaken my head, remembering Clara's words, and knowing the dog had fallen for an open robe and the certainty that only he deserved the gifts offered by that she-coyote.

––––––––

Here, in one of the few jail cells in Wyoming Territory, I knew with sudden certainty where my uneasiness came from. All day, again and again, I'd asked myself how the Indian was involved and who was Rebecca Montcalm.

In my relief at the thought of escape from the meanest sheriff to run a territory, I hadn't asked myself the most obvious question, the question I'd ignored by choosing to believe something as inherent to the conceit of being a man as that some beautiful woman was out there hoping to help me because her heart fluttered at the very sight of me.

What I should have asked first was why some woman would want to risk her own arrest by helping just another drifting cowboy escape. The only answer could be that she wanted something from me. And whatever it was, it had to be worth a lot.

Then I thought of the female coyote circling camp just outside of the range of the firelight and asked myself the toughest question of all.

What price would I have to pay for my escape?

CHAPTER 7

THE NEXT MORNING, I was disinclined against any immediate affection for Marshal Evrett's returned deputy. Where Marshal Evrett had offered coffee to start conversation, Deputy Smickles chose to fling a dipperful of water at my face to take my attention away from what little early morning town activities I could watch through the window bars opposite his desk.

"Don't look much tough without your gun," he said. "And there's plenty more water iffen you decide to keep ignoring my questions."

I unhurriedly wiped my face with the towel near my shaving basin. I waited until my face was completely dry before I turned to study him.

He stood with his hands on his hips, a half laugh of swaggering confidence across his face. He was big and, in the menacing manner of a bull, seemed to take more space than he actually did. He was also young, with a blocky wide face that would sag into impressive jowls as he let himself go to seed. And go to seed he would. From what little he had already said, I guessed he wasn't smart enough to learn from observation some of the lessons that age brings as it slowly grinds a man down. There would come a day when—in the same way that there inevitably comes the day for a woman who has always relied on her beauty alone as a calling card—his physical presence would not be enough to get him his way. If he was lucky, it would be a while until he ran into someone both unafraid and capable of beating him, because when it happened, he would face fear for the first time, and then the decline would begin.

While I was unafraid—simply because there are many things worse to happen to a man than mere physical pain—I did not know if I was capable. I did not want to find out. A smart person with a mean streak is to be treated with caution, but intelligence tempers the meanness. Mean and stupid, though, is a dangerous combination; there is nothing to rein back the urge to hurt. With Smickles, you could add to that frightening combination the strength of a bull, youth's lack of discipline, and that petty need to show power so common to government people and bank tellers.

To show weakness, I decided as I stared him down, was to excite the bully in him.

"Not tough at all, are you?" he repeated.

"Probably don't look tough with my gun, either," I finally said. "Otherwise Harrison wouldn't a drawed on me."

The half smile drooped for a second, to be replaced by a sneer. "Yeah, I heard that story. That he drew first. But I don't place much stock in it. Not with you the only person to do the accounting of it."

I shrugged. "He wasn't backshot. You don't need witnesses to know that, only a good look at the body."

"Two in his leg, Doc Harper said." A frown punctured the deputy's smugness. "Front side, so you didn't backshoot. I'll allow you that."

Leg? Two shots in the leg from less than twenty feet. Had I lost that much over the years?

"Doc says the one that killed him hit him in the side, just under the arm. Like maybe he was falling back and twisting sideways from the ones that took him in the leg. I figure you stepped out from behind a corner with your gun already drawn. That's the only way you could've gunned down Harrison."

"You sound dead certain."

"Durn straight, I'm certain. It's what I'll say in the trial too, iffen I get called to witness. There weren't much better with a gun than Harrison. It'd take a real name to outshoot him. Wild Bill Hickok, maybe. Wyatt Earp. Maybe even Harrison's own half brother, Henry Reed. This is a small territory. If I ain't heard of you, you ain't good enough to gun him down."

Once maybe, those names might have held my interest. Not now.

"You mind if I go back to looking out the window?" I didn't wait for permission.

"Henry Reed might want to kill you himself," Deputy Smickles said to my back. "He'll call you out, then gun you down slicker than skinning a jackrabbit. Then we'll see quick how it was you ambushed his half brother."

From what I'd heard about Henry Reed, calling me out would be the last thing on his mind, especially with any hint at all that I might be good with a gun. No, he'd rig it so that I wasn't carrying, then shoot me in the back of the head and make it look like I'd been trying to escape. Not that I'd blame him for cutting the odds. Prudence becomes more and more of a virtue for the few gunfighters who grow older.

Deputy Smickles mistook my silence for fear.

"I guess you don't want to lay eyes on ol' Henry Reed," he crowed. "Not with some of the things they say about him."

I gazed down the street. My angle from the window showed nothing of interest. Nothing, that is, to a man walking free as feathers in the wind. But to someone behind bars, it's a glorious thing to be able to bow and sweep a hat at a pretty woman as you stand on a street corner. I'd be happy even for the anger that hits when you accidentally step on a fresh horse apple as you cross the street.

And beyond that, even though I couldn't see, I knew was the valley that stretched northwest, widening to miles of open range between the mountains on both sides of Laramie. Already I'd spent hours in my mind feeling the sun and wind across my face as my horse stepped among the sagebrush and tumbleweed.

Smickles would not rest in his efforts to get a reaction from me.

"One story I heard was that Henry Reed once caught a horse thief and knocked him cold," Smickles said. "Then he took two o' them stolen horses and reined them to a tree. When the horse thief woke, each ankle was tied by a long rope to the saddle of a different horse, but both these two were now loose and just grazing. Reed himself stood close by with a pistol pointing in the air. He waited until the thief woke up clear enough to understand the situation, then smiled and pulled the trigger. Them horses tore in opposite directions, and that horse thief screamed murder as the rope drew tight. 'Cept nothing happened. Instead of getting ripped in two, his boots slid off. Henry Reed had greased the inside of those boots while the horse thief was out cold."

Smickles paused, then spit tobacco juice. "So now Henry Reed says to this thief that there's two horses left, and if he don't tell him where the rest of his rustling friends is hid, he'll tie the rope directly to the man's ankles instead of some greased-up boots."

Smickles laughed. "You can bet your ranch this varmint told Henry Reed exactly what he needed."

The deputy's boots thumped across the floor as he moved close enough to lean against the cell bars. He spit through the bars at my feet and grinned evil delight. He leered through the bars at me.

"I think Henry Reed will kill you slow and make you beg."

He spit again. A glob of brown splashed onto my shoulder.

It wasn't just that he spit on me, although few things are a worse insult. I think it was his leering grin. And the frustration of two days of sitting here like a chicken in a coop. I broke one of my steadfast rules. I let emotion control my actions.

I started to wheeze, as if I were trying to yell something in anger.

I stumbled closer to the cell bars, hand on my throat as if I were choking.

I struggled with words, gulped a few times, and struggled more, until Deputy Smickles and that fat, ugly, hateful grin had leaned close enough to the gap of the bars.

I bent at the waist, clutched my stomach with my good right arm, then started my sucker punch with that right arm from as low as possible and drove upward with my legs, shoulder, arm, and fist.

Had I hit one of the iron bars, I would have broken every knuckle on my hand. For a second, from a burst of pain across my hand, I thought I had miscalculated that badly.

A geyser of blood told me different—blood from the split

skin on my middle knuckles and blood from his upper teeth and nose.

It *was* stupid.

I'd rocked him all right, with a punch as solid as I could throw. He fell away three steps and landed sitting. But not out cold. I knew then, as I think I did before the punch, that I'd pay high for losing discipline.

It's probably vanity to think I'd be able to outlast Smickles in a fight somewhere open when I had two good arms. Now I was down to one arm, cramped in an eight-by-twelve-foot jail cell. And him with the key on his belt.

He bellowed.

He was so insane with fury that for several seconds his coordination failed him. His arms and legs flailed as he tried to scramble to his feet, his bellow rising with his frustration. Then, on his feet, he charged the cell and tried to yank the door loose from its hinges.

He bellowed more. Even after slowing down enough to realize he should reach for the key he carried, his bellow continued.

Above the blood and gore of his mouth and nose, his face was purple now, veins massive on his neck. He bellowed and shook with total loss of control as he fumbled with the key, then cried with rage because his shaking hands could not insert it into the lock.

So I did something even more stupid than that first sucker punch. But Smickles couldn't get any angrier, and I figured I might as well get my licks in while I could.

As he leaned forward and concentrated on the key, I threw another punch through the bars and into his face.

CHAPTER 8

SMICKLES HAD THE SHOTGUN leveled at me, and his knuckles were whitening on the trigger when Marshal Evrett walked through the door.

"Pull the trigger, Smickles," Evrett said, "and you'll hang in his place."

Smickles wiped blood away from his mouth. "He's trying to escape, can't you see."

A man walked in behind Evrett. Evrett spoke to the man without taking his eyes off Smickles. "With your keen journalistic eye, do you see a cell door open?"

"Am I supposed to?" the man asked.

"Nope."

"It appears secure to me."

It wasn't, of course. The iron bars were swung wide, but Smickles filled most of the narrow opening into my cell, even half turned as he was to answer to Evrett.

"See," Evrett said to Smickles, "the prisoner isn't trying to escape."

Smickles wiped with his other sleeve. "I'll kill him yet."

"Fool." Evrett snarled. "I warned you good to keep clear. Keaton's faster than a snake. Didn't I tell you that?"

I did not feel faster than a snake. In the previous five minutes, Smickles had done a good job of working me over in the jail cell. Good enough that for the second time in a week, I'd passed out. My shirt was still wet from the dipper of water Smickles had thrown into my face to wake me again. A few teeth were loose, but my tongue couldn't find any jagged edges, so I guessed by the numbness of my arms and ribs that most of his kicks had missed my head after I'd fallen and curled into a ball.

The groaning pain would arrive later, just like it did whenever I'd been thrown too often in a day of breaking horses. And I'd have to wait until I watered again to see if Smickles had done enough damage to my innards to make me pass blood.

None of that mattered. Not the tightness of my skin as the bruises started to swell. Not the urge to empty the contents of my stomach. Not the blood that dripped from my nose.

None of it mattered because I wasn't dead.

Sure, there had been more than a couple of times before when I'd nearly bought it, but all those times, it happened so fast that it wasn't until it was over before I'd realized how close it had been. Like turning a stampede at night. Or outrunning some troublesome Apaches during my trip in Texas.

This had been different. I'd been on the edge of my cot, staring into the black holes of that shotgun, helpless and waiting for the explosion that I wouldn't ever hear, filled with an eternity of sadness that my entire life had been reduced to an ending as common and meaningless as this, my insides splashed against a dirty brick wall and no one to mourn me.

And now I was alive. I clutched the edges of my cot to hide the shaking of my hands.

"Smickles, get out. Stay gone for a week," Evrett said. "Touch another prisoner without my permission and I'll work you over myself."

Smickles glared but left.

Evrett left the cell door open.

"Keaton, you need a doctor?"

By then, I was dipping a towel into the water of my shaving basin and sponging off my face.

"More water" was all I said. I squeezed the towel dry, and the water in the basin became pink.

"Making a note of that?" Evrett asked the journalist. "He's not only stupid enough to find a way to punch an armed deputy, but stubborn."

The journalist nodded with a half-polite smile, as if he didn't know if Evrett was serious.

Evrett stepped into the cell and poured water from a bucket into the basin. Despite the situation, I almost smiled. As little time as had passed from my request for water, Evrett had still made sure his holster was empty before moving into the cramped cell beside me.

"The man's got a few questions for you," Evrett said. "Until I walked in to find you and Smickles in a spat, I figured it'd be a way for you to pass time. You up to it now?"

"You know how I love to talk," I said, finding the energy to speak dryly. "And how I've got no interest in passing time with the books you haven't yet brung."

Evrett snorted as he stepped out of the cell and swung the door shut. "Books. Nobody believes me when I tell 'em I've got a cowboy who asks for books instead of better meals."

The journalist was scribbling on a pad of paper. "Interesting, literate," he mumbled to himself, "a refined killer."

His voice was nasal and pinched. It went with the rest of

him. Derby. Striped vest. Gray flannel pants. Narrow face and straggly mustache. Light hair—almost blond, almost gray— and pale skin that made it hard to place his age unless you were satisfied with a guess somewhere between twenty-five and forty-five.

He squinted through wire-frame glasses as he alternated between peering at me and at his paper while he wrote.

"I play piano, too," I said.

He scribbled again.

"And bite the heads off chickens."

He stopped scribbling. Only the part about the piano was true, but I'd wondered how far he could be pushed.

Evrett broke the new silence. "Samuel, the man's name is Will O'Neal. Hails from New York."

"I'm on a western swing for the *Times*," O'Neal explained quickly. "Collecting material for a series of articles. Cattle, Indian wars, that sort of thing."

I stared at him as I set the damp towel down. Although some of my cuts had begun to clot, my bruises were now calling attention to themselves, which didn't improve my mood. And I've never been able to understand why a grown man would want to make a living by meddling into the affairs of others.

"So, um," O'Neal coughed, "Marshal Evrett—that's two 't's,' right—informs me that you engaged John Harrison in mortal battle because he refused to stop extended physical abuse of an Indian."

"Chew that a little finer," I said.

"Eh?"

"He means speak plain English," Evrett explained.

Something was bothering me about all this. Evrett struck me as a sensible man. I couldn't understand why he took pains for an Easterner, one who was a journalist at that.

"Harrison drew a gun on you," O'Neal said after a moment's thought, "after you told him to stop kicking a red-skin."

Evrett grunted approval at the translation.

"If you want the story, ask the marshal," I said. "Marshal. That's one 'l.' "

O'Neal drew back. "No need for hostility."

"Go outside and lie down until a team of horses and a coach runs you over," I said. "Then you'll know what I feel like right now. If after that you want to spout big words and horn in on my business, we'll talk."

He put up his hand to protest. "This article could make you famous. Right up there with John Hardin and Wild Bill Hickok. I'm told only them and a handful of others were as adroit, uh, good with a gun as John Harrison."

I stared at him until he looked away.

"All right," he tried, head down as he concentrated on the pad of paper, "I can get the details from Marshal Evrett, but tell me at least, did you know the Indian?"

More silence.

"I mean," he faltered, "why would you risk your life over an Indian unless you knew him, and even then, why bother?"

I moved to my cot. It took every ounce of effort I could summon to lie down without groaning or showing pain, and even then I felt new sweat break cold on my forehead at the messages my body sent me.

"Mr. Keaton?"

He didn't even rate that I should turn my back to ignore him. I just lay there, face up, and closed my eyes.

"Mr. Keaton? Mr. Keaton?"

"I'll tell you what you need to know, Will."

For the next five minutes, Evrett gave him a background on Harrison, the posse chase, and the gunfight. In the brief silences, I could hear the scratching of pencil on paper.

The creaking of the marshal's chair told me Evrett had risen.

"Do you think Keaton knew the Indian?" O'Neal asked as footsteps told me they were walking to the door. "I'm looking for that angle for my story."

"Keaton hasn't said," Evrett admitted. "But if I find out, I'll let you know. Staying at the railroad hotel?"

"Next couple of days."

"Hope you enjoy Laramie, Will," Evrett continued in that warm confidential voice. "By the way, what paper you say you work for?"

"The *Times*."

"That's what I thought you'd said. Small world. I got a cousin lives in New York. Seems to me I remember him telling me that he met some fancy editor there said he works for the *Times*." Evrett snapped his fingers. "Editor's name was Jim McBlain, right? Big redheaded guy, likes the bottle."

O'Neal laughed. "Ol' Jim McBlain. Real slave driver, too. That's why I'm working so hard to keep my facts straight."

"I don't blame you," Evrett said. "Look, any time I can help, stop right by."

The door shut.

I opened my eyes.

Evrett walked to my cell and watched me, thumbs in his belt loops.

"Sure you don't want to walk along beside him with a parasol and shade his head from the sun, too?" I asked.

Evrett laughed. "Wondered if you'd get savvy onto it."

"I haven't heard you call anyone by his first name yet. And you sweet-talked him as if he were the only girl on a dance floor between here and Canada."

"I did at that."

"Have good reason?"

"Yup."

He grinned.

I waited.

He just grinned.

"So," I said, "what was the good reason?"

"Tell me more about yourself, Keaton. A man as good as you with a gun has to lay tracks, but yours are all swept clean."

I grinned back. It hurt, moving my face that much. "Should be an article in the *Times* that'll tell you all you need."

Evrett shook his head. "Keaton, I got information you should be trading for."

"Will it stop me from swinging?"

Evrett sighed. "You got any answers for me, Keaton?"

I closed my eyes.

"Thought as much," he said.

He turned and I heard a light slap as he put his Colt back into his holster. "You're a stubborn cuss, Keaton. Trouble is, I like you enough to ask if whiskey'll cure any of that pain you're bust determined not to show. Share a bottle?"

I grunted again and opened my eyes. "If you're headed to the hotel for it," I said, "we might as well spend my money on it."

Evrett chuckled, shook his head, and locked the front door behind him as he left.

In his absence, I had plenty to puzzle about. Like after I had passed out from Smickles' beating why I'd woken with my boots twisted on my feet, as if he'd pulled them off and halfheartedly shoved them on again. Like why my hat had been moved, and the mattress of my cot was spilled over the side of the frame. Like why, just before the sheriff had arrived, Smickles had leveled the shotgun and offered me my life if I'd tell him where the gold was hidden.

There was one other thing.

The piece of a telegram that must have fallen from Smickles' pocket as he'd leaned over me while I was passed out.

FIND LETTER STOP LEARN ALL YOU CAN STOP SHOOT ESCAPING PRISONER STOP

Letter? All I'd ever seen was a note, the one from Rebecca Montcalm that I'd taken care to memorize and rip into tiny pieces, long since scattered.

Who from a distance wanted me dead? And why?

And what gold?

I had a bad feeling it involved that irksome Indian.

CHAPTER 9

SLEEP THAT NIGHT was difficult. The cot was hard, with a lumpy straw mattress, and my aches stiffened and grew worse. Any turn, no matter how slight, woke me, and I was forced to stay on my back to nap at all.

Finally, I just shifted and found me a muscle I hadn't known existed. When I was finished cussing out the ceiling, Smickles, the Indian, and everything else I could add to the list, I heard a key turn in the door of the jail.

Smickles? Was he so stupid that he wouldn't realize he'd be the first person accused of murder should I be found dead in my cell?

I hoped not. Marshal Evrett had left me alone for the night. He knew, as I did, that the bars were securely set in the brick, and the cell lock and door locks were complicated enough that I couldn't escape without dynamite. And dynamite was a dumb bet—even if I had outside help to use it—because enough dynamite to bust me loose would probably kill me in the process. I relaxed almost immediately. Unless Smickles had taken to wearing strong, cheap perfume, he was not the dark figure who closed and relocked the door after stepping inside.

I watched without moving. My eyes were adjusted to the darkness, the moon threw dim ghostly light into the room, and I saw she did not appear to be carrying a weapon.

Was this Rebecca Montcalm? But how would she have gotten the key? And why not send the Indian as originally planned instead of risking herself?

The woman tiptoed across the floor. As she passed the potbellied stove, the red glow of dying embers threw a shadow across her face, but my straining eyes could not make out her features.

At the cell, she fumbled with another key, which made a slightly scratching sound before the lock tumbled open. The door creaked, and she pushed through.

I took deep long breaths as if asleep.

She moved beside my cot. The moon was at her back and threw her completely in shadow, a shadow that fell across my face. I closed my eyes.

She knelt beside the cot. I still did not know her intentions, and I listened carefully for a sudden movement of cloth, the only warning I'd have if she drew a knife to plunge it into my neck or belly.

"Darling," she crooned, "you awake?"

I struggled to sit on the cot. I couldn't contain a grunt of pain as I rose.

"Oooh," she said, "Smickles told me you might be hurt."

"Smickles?"

"Who do you think gave me the keys?"

I groaned confusion. It must have sounded like more pain.

"My name is Suzanne," she said, "I'm here to keep you company, if you want."

I shook my head, trying to clear that confusion. "I thought Smickles wanted me dead."

"He told me that, too," she said. "His nose is broke good. But he also told me that he don't dare do nothing to you now. Not even Smickles likes to cross Marshal Evrett."

"Why'd Smickles give you the keys?"

"Money," she said. "Money. He ain't mad enough to say no to business. Smickles takes half of what I get for keeping prisoners company. You ain't hurt real bad, is you?"

I snorted laughter, about all a person can do when life gets ridiculous. Which happens far too often. You find yourself in a strange situation that a week earlier you would deny could ever happen to anyone, let alone yourself. For me, I'd been scouting the high hills between Laramie and Cheyenne for wild horses, my biggest concern whether to shoot a grouse for supper or to fish a nearby stream for young trout. Now, I was a couple days away from the noose unless a woman I didn't know and her sidekick Indian managed to rope the marshal at dawn to allow my escape. Someone else wanted me dead for gold I'd never heard of. And I was in a jail cell about to say no to a warm and willing bundle of all woman when, with my hanging approaching, it probably didn't matter what happened to the money she wanted from my wallet. 'Course, if this were a logical world, it'd be men who rode sidesaddle.

"I miss something?" she asked at my brief laugh.

"No, ma'am." I thought of the keys she held. "What's to stop me from trying to escape?"

"Smickles and his shotgun. He's right outside."

Dumb question. They'd probably done this more than a few times before. Extra money on the side never hurt, and how many prisoners would ever complain about this sort of attention?

I took a deep breath and stood to pace with awkward,

pain-stiffened steps. "Suzanne, how about I pay you for conversation?"

She stood, too, and tried to put her arms around my neck as I paced back toward her.

I took both her wrists in my hands to stop her movement. We were sideways now to the moonlight, barely inches apart, and the soft light across the side of her face brought out all her prettiness and hid all that she had lost over the years. In that moment, as she looked up at me with questioning eyes, she was a young girl again.

"Conversation?" She must have felt as sad as I did to be suddenly aware that we were two lonely people.

"I'm looking for answers," I said, equally quiet. "Find out who sent Smickles a telegram."

I wanted to know more about the Indian, but didn't dare let anyone hear Rebecca Montcalm's name, otherwise I'd have asked about that, too.

"Telegram?" She stepped away from me. "But how—"

"Stop at the railroad office. Ask on the sly. It's a message that came in yesterday, maybe the day before. I'll pay whatever you make in a week."

If dawn brought me escape, then I didn't need the information. If the Indian didn't appear, the information might not help anyway. But I was tired of doing nothing, and this might be a start at unraveling whatever mystery was making my life, or imminent death, so complicated.

"That's it?" she said.

I nodded. "As long as you don't let anyone, including Smickles, know why you're asking."

She thought for several moments.

"Why not," Suzanne said, "but I'll need some money now. Smickles will expect some as soon as I step outside."

"How much?"

"Two dollars."

I gave her four.

"Samuel?"

"Yes?"

"You're a decent man." She bowed her head, suddenly shy. "I hope the hangman don't get you."

She let herself out without another word.

I could not fall asleep. In those terrible hours of silence, with just me and four brick walls and iron bars and moonlight creeping slowly across the floor of the jail, I found myself wondering why I'd not pursued the company she had been offering.

The best answer I could find was that those long, long moments in front of the shotgun had changed me. Each time I closed my eyes, the dark holes of the barrel appeared in my vision, and I felt again the same ache at the meaningless and common way I would have died.

Call it God's first attempt to get my attention. Because of that shotgun, I could not deny the nagging feeling that I was missing something, that life had to be bigger than finding ways to satisfy the varied demands of my body. I also could not escape the feeling that deep down, I'd always known life had to be bigger, but along the way, I had always chosen whatever distractions it took to keep me from wondering about God. Except now, try as I might, I couldn't ignore what some certainty told me was beyond. If I turned my back on whatever instinct now pulled me to seek the answers, if I chose distractions like Suzanne, I would have to fool myself real good not to find those distractions sour and hollow.

These were thoughts to which I was not accustomed. I worried at the thoughts and worried more at the fact that I even had those thoughts. I worried at them like poking my tongue again and again at a sore tooth, until the moonlight faded into the gray of early dawn.

Marshal Evrett arrived as the sunlight began to brighten.

And dawn came and went without any sign of the Indian, his gun, or his rope. Or his rescue attempt.

CHAPTER *10*

I WAS DESPERATELY TIRED of jail. It didn't help that I was still so sore it took great effort to lift my arms high enough to hold a shaving mirror in one hand and use the other to carefully scrape my razor through the lather on my face—an awkward move, even freshly out of a sling.

"Mighty particular man," Marshal Evrett observed from where he relaxed with his feet up on the desk. "I ain't never seen a prisoner so determined to keep his whiskers at bay."

A spasm of pain in my arm betrayed me, and I nicked the side of my chin.

" 'Course," Evrett continued, "I ain't never had a prisoner so hard to figure. From where do you hail, Keaton?"

I took one last swipe with the razor. "Most men take insult at questions like that," I said. "On the range, a man's taken for how he works."

"Yup," Evrett said. "But most men ain't a marshal."

I wiped my face with the towel that was almost brown now from yesterday's dried blood. I frowned at the fresh blood from the new cut.

"And most marshals," I said without taking my attention from removing the last of the lather from below my ears, "are drunks too stupid to worry about how they might die by pinning on a badge. Which leads me to ask—from where do you hail, Evrett?"

"More important, Keaton, is where I want to go."

Evrett swung away from his desk, stepped to the front door, and locked it. He put in the left window a sign that had in handwritten block letters "MARSHAL GONE" and pulled the blinds down. He also pulled the blinds of the window on the right side of the door.

By then I'd set aside my shaving basin and wiped clean my razor. Shaving, with the scar to avoid, usually took me less than fifteen minutes. Today I'd been able to drag it into half an hour. But now that I was finished, I had nothing left to pass the time.

"Wyoming's been a territory six years now," Evrett said. He was at the potbellied stove now, pouring a coffee. "I figure statehood's maybe ten years away."

He offered me the coffee. I accepted it with a nod of thanks.

With his back to me as he poured another coffee, Evrett spoke more. "There's money in cattle, but only if you have money first to buy a herd. Otherwise a cowpuncher's life is hellish, and it's got no future."

I had nothing to argue there.

"Gold is a fool's game. Coal? Well, all you have to do is look down the tracks to Rock Springs to know that coal's got a great future here. But it's dirty and kills if you're a miner, and again, it takes investment money if you're not."

He faced me and blew over his coffee before sipping. When he finished the first mouthful, he rambled more. "Soldiering? Civil War's long finished. No government money in soldiering, and when the Injuns are gone, even less. Uniform's a bad choice if you want a future."

"That leaves law," I said. "You're betting that Wyoming gets more people and gets more civilized. That soon it'll take more than stupidity to hold a badge and a wage."

Evrett smiled. "Yup."

"You're a man with foresight," I said. "Even if your coffee tastes like mud."

He smiled at that, too, then became serious. "Marshaling's fine for now," Evrett said. "But I aim to do it right enough that it becomes just the first step. A young state will provide plenty opportunity for the man in the right place at the right time."

"It will at that," I said. I pointed at the shaded window. "But I can't figure what all this has to do with closed blinds and a locked door."

"Everything." Evrett moved to his desk, pulled open a drawer, and took out a large piece of folded paper. "Keaton, what it means is that I can't afford not to be the best marshal Laramie has seen. And I don't rest when something in my jurisdiction has even one more question than there are answers."

The paper looked like a poster.

He set his coffee down, opened the paper, and showed it to me.

It *was* a poster. An old yellowed Wanted poster. With a reasonable likeness of my face, in full beard, across the front.

" 'Robert Adams,' " he read, although it wasn't necessary—for I knew the words far too well. " 'Wanted in the state of Colorado for bank robbery and murder.' "

Evrett looked up to see my reaction. I stared back.

"I had a stack of posters brought in by train from Denver," he said. "That way I knew I'd get the last twenty years' worth. Took me about five hours last night, going through real slow, again and again. It was the beard on the drawing that fooled me. 'Course, now I understand why you're so careful to shave."

I continued to stare. Evrett held my gaze. Neither of us flinched.

Then he let out a long breath, and his face lost some of its hardness.

"More coffee?" He brought the pot over without waiting for my answer. "Keaton, I'm glad you didn't deny that was you."

I raised an eyebrow.

"See, I bet myself how you'd react to the poster. I told myself you'd keep that poker face, no different than if I'd opened the door and told you the sun was shining. I told myself that you were man enough not to start saying it must be someone who looks like you, or that the artist got someone else's face wrong enough to look like you, or a whole lot of other things that I've heard from your side of the bars. And I'm purely tickled I won my bet."

"Makes my heart beat pitter-patter, too, Marshal."

That brought a grin. "It should. Because I told myself if I had you figured right, I'd listen to your side of the story behind that poster."

"Does it make a difference?"

"Might. I was forthright with you. Folks don't know how high I got my sights aimed. Now you do. Why don't you return the favor and tell me a bit about yourself."

It was my turn to let out a deep breath. "There's no one alive to back what I say."

"Which is why you decided to live on the run?"

"Something like that."

I didn't know where to begin. It'd been so long since my brother had died, so long since I'd managed to bury the memories. I swallowed several times to moisten my mouth until I felt I could speak without croaking my next words.

"Ever hunted men for bounty, Marshal Evrett?"

He shook his head.

"Don't start," I said. "It's a terrible game. Especially the last part of the chase, when they know you're on their trail. Some run harder, some double back and try to kill you."

"You know this?"

"I know this." I closed my eyes briefly. "I was younger then. Didn't understand fear. Mine or anyone else's."

I paused to think of a way to explain it. "It's like the innocence of a boy's cruelty," I finally said. "He'll catch frogs and blow air in them with a straw till the frog explodes. Or nail a cat's tail into a piece of board and let dogs loose on it. Senseless cruelty. But innocent because the boy's so thoughtless, he's never considered the pain it causes."

Evrett grunted. "It shames me to say I can remember doing things like that myself."

I smiled sadly. "Along the way you learned that shame. Good thing, too. Some don't. My brother . . ."

I looked past the marshal at the dusty blinds and tried to remove myself from my words. "My brother and I thought it would be great adventure to hunt down desperadoes. We brought some in alive. Others dead. Never once wondered how it might feel on their end, to be tired and afraid and hunted."

I tightened my lips briefly and shook my head. "You'd be surprised how many cried the last few miles into town. Or cried when they realized the bullet they'd just taken in the gut was going to kill them."

I stopped again.

"You learned shame, too," Evrett said softly.

"My brother died. To another bounty hunter's bullet. And I had to run. If a man don't learn it from that, he don't have a soul."

There it was, in my mind, the word *soul*, like God was tugging at mine.

I concentrated on finishing the last of my now lukewarm coffee. Slowly.

"The poster . . ." Evrett finally prodded.

"We found our man that day," I said. "Fellow by the name of Nick Caxton. Tracked him across the territory, town by town, and finally caught up with him as he was running hard back in our direction from a couple towns ahead. He'd just robbed a bank with two others. Then he'd shot both of them in the back to keep all the money for himself. We caught him shortly after. Put us in a pretty good mood, it did, knowing we'd collect bounty and whatever reward for returning the bags of money. So we decided to hole up where we was."

"What town?" Evrett asked sudden-like.

"Pueblo. Caxton had robbed the bank in La Junta."

Evrett nodded. It was a trick I'd have used myself, trying to trip a man on details without giving him time to prepare.

"My brother went to get our horses in the morning. He took the prisoner with him. Another bounty hunter ambushed them both outside the stable. One of the dangers of the trade, that bounty hunters are always trying to steal prisoners from other bounty hunters."

"Where were you when your brother was shot?"

"Does it matter? I wasn't there to back him up." I didn't notice until I caught Evrett looking at my hands that my fists were clenched. "By the time I got there, he'd been hit and a woman bystander shot dead. That other bounty hunter, he killed Nick Caxton, just walked up to him where he hid behind a horse with his hands tied and shot him in the heart. My brother died as the crowd started to appear. And the bounty hunter made it look as if my brother and I had been the two with Caxton to rob the bank, and that I'd killed the woman. The money was in our saddlebags, in cloth sacks clearly marked National Bank. It put me in jail. Later I had a chance to run and took it. I've been on the hoot-owl trail since."

It was not quite the truth and there was more, but I'd said all I wanted to.

Evrett studied my eyes. Something must have satisfied him, because he relaxed. "It'd be a fearsome thing," he said, "to hold the power of a man's life. Did you ever wonder if you should let one go? Ever wonder if a man you caught deserved to die?"

"Not then," I said.

Evrett swung around quickly at a single knock at the door. He glanced at his watch, then at me.

"I'd have liked another five minutes," he said. "You're the first one I've wondered about. I don't think you deserve to die. So I'm going to do something about it."

It didn't make sense to me, so I held my peace.

He walked to the door and pulled it open.

That Indian, hat brim low across his greasy face, gunnysack over his shoulders, walked in and pointed a gun at the marshal.

"Shut the door first, you fool," Evrett growled. "No need to give anyone out there a reason to panic."

The Indian lowered the gun. Evrett stepped around him and kicked the door shut.

The Indian raised the gun again and blinked those unreadable black eyes.

Evrett shook his head in mild disgust, walked over to my cell, pushed a key into the lock, and opened the door.

"The Injun's got rope in his sack," Evrett said. "But he

doesn't appear to have the sense to tie me good. I'd prefer if you did that."

I stared disbelief at Evrett.

"Do me a favor and tie me in my chair," he said as he backed away. "I don't need the extra discomfort of sitting on the floor, and who knows how long it'll be until someone decides to check up on me."

I still couldn't move.

"Well hurry, man." Evrett was now in his chair, his back turned to me. "When the train arrives, it don't stay long at the station."

CHAPTER *11*

"YOU'VE GOT SUZANNE to thank for part of this," Marshal Evrett said. "And make sure those knots are tight."

I grunted as I pulled on the rope, kneeling as I was on the floor and busy cinching Evrett's wrists to the back of the chair. This was so unexpected, I barely felt the pain in my left arm. The Indian just stared at me impassively.

"Suzanne?" I asked between grunts.

"She spent a cozy half hour in your jail cell last night around midnight."

I looked up as the Indian shot a sharp glance at Marshal Evrett, but it was so brief I decided it had been my imagination.

"Wondered if you knew her little working arrangement with Smickles," I said. "I don't believe I'm the first visitor she's entertained."

"Smickles is so dumb he believes he's smart, and I do my best not to change his mind. It's a lot easier for me to watch him if he thinks I've got a blindfold covering my eyes."

I straightened. There was at least twenty feet of rope left. "Ankles too?"

"Yup."

I began to bind his boots together. "Suzanne reports everything she learns to you?"

"Yup."

"You know about the telegram."

"Yup."

"This too tight?" I asked.

"Nope. But it'll look better if you take that last piece of rope and tie it around the leg of my desk."

"Done," I said as I shifted to loop the rope as instructed. When I finished, Marshal Evrett was trussed tight. All he could move was his mouth.

As if reading my mind, he said, "When you gag me, use a clean handkerchief. Top drawer."

"I don't think I'm ready to gag you. When's the train arrive?"

"Maybe ten minutes."

"Let's talk."

"Keaton, that's exactly why I'm taking this gamble."

The Indian was now staring at the floor.

"There's too much strange happening in this town," Evrett said. "So I'm offering a deal."

I chuckled. "You're in a good position to barter."

"Keaton, you could have blown my jaw off three days ago. I'm not worried about your end of this bargain."

I took my holster from his desk and began to buckle it around my waist. "What's strange?"

Instead of answering me, Evrett spoke to the Indian. "Step outside. He'll be just a minute."

The Indian began to move.

"Leave the gunnysack."

The Indian dropped it on the floor. There was no thud.

When the door had closed, Evrett spoke to me again.

"Plenty's strange. Start with the Injun. I found out Harrison had left Laramie and taken a train eastward, alone. When he returned to Laramie four days later, he had the Injun with him."

"My bad luck," I said.

"That's what I was figuring," Evrett said. "That you were telling the truth about your gunfight. That you were at the wrong place at the wrong time and had never laid eyes on the Injun before. When you sent Suzanne to ask about the telegram sent to Smickles—you not knowing she'd tell me about your request—it seemed like something an innocent man might do, one not involved with any of the strangeness."

A fly landed on the end of Evrett's nose. He twitched. I waved it away with my hat.

"You see," Evrett said without pause, "I want to know about the telegram, too. And the gold."

"Gold? By mentioning it, you appear to know more than I do."

"Nope. I heard Smickles ask you about gold when I walked in to find him entertaining you with that shotgun."

I pulled my Colt out, opened the chamber, and held it upside down to catch the shells that fell out. Three—the three I'd fired at Harrison—were empty. I reloaded as Evrett continued.

"Then there's that New York slicker, O'Neal," Evrett said. "I can't figure how he fits in, but my gut tells me he does."

"Oh?"

"I heard he was asking around town about you," Evrett said. "The kinds of questions I'd been asking. Made me suspicious, so I bought him a beer."

"You do like sneaking up on a person."

Evrett was accustomed to me by now. He just smiled and

plowed on with his story. "When O'Neal told me he was a journalist, I thought I'd let him loose, see more of him in action."

The lonesome distant hoot of the train reached us. Evrett continued in his steady voice as if he hadn't heard.

"Wasn't until O'Neal took notes that I knew something was up. You ain't the only gunman here that knows to read."

"I noticed you peering over his shoulder."

"He was just scribbling. That's when I decided to mention that my cousin knew the editor, Jim McBlain."

"And?"

"I ain't got no cousin. There ain't no Jim McBlain. Which means Will O'Neal ain't no journalist."

I began to search the top drawer for the handkerchief. Evrett might want to pretend he hadn't heard the train's whistle, but I didn't have that luxury. I needed to be on that train. After all, how much time before someone walked in to find Evrett roped to his chair? Not enough to make a good run on horseback. Second last thing I wanted was to ride northwest of Elk Mountain at the head of Medicine Bow range into the great basin without provisions and ample water. Last thing I wanted was to head into the mountain valleys the other way, moving too quickly to be careful in Sioux and Cheyenne country. Train was the best way of escape, and I needed time to get my horses onto the stable car.

"So I got to thinking," Evrett said. "Harrison and the Injun. Smickles and the gold and the telegram. And I couldn't believe that O'Neal showed up so soon by happenstance. It's all too strange. When I knew you was being set up for escape—"

"You couldn't know that," I said.

"Small town, Keaton. You'll recall it didn't take long for Miss Ackerman to spread the story about how I offered you my derringer."

I nodded.

"You think she didn't tell folks about that Injun? Or see that Injun drop the note? I didn't figure it was a love letter. So I sidled up beside the Injun yesterday and mentioned in passing how if I was trying to bust someone loose, I'd wait until the train was due to leave and probably disguise him in a dress."

I picked up the gunnysack. It was featherlight.

"Should be a wig in there, too," Evrett said. "And a bonnet to hide most of your ugly mug."

I checked the contents. Evrett was right. I'd be a flaming redhead in less than a minute.

"Can you tell me why the Injun wants you to escape?"

I shook my head. And again, didn't feel it very smart to mention Rebecca Montcalm's name.

"I feared that," Evrett said. " 'Cause somehow that Injun's tied to this, too. If you'd rung false about the Wanted poster, that Injun wouldn't have made it inside. Instead, you're going to tail that Injun and get to the bottom of all this mess—the Injun, Harrison, O'Neal, Smickles."

"Don't forget the gold," I said dryly. I'd never put a dress on before and I struggled with the zipper. Small consolation that the hem reached down to the floor and hid my boots completely.

"And the gold," he agreed. "I want the truth. And half the gold. Small price to pay for your life. Send me telegrams when you can to keep me posted of your progress."

"If I don't come back?" I said. Already the wig itched.

"You'll be back."

———

Five minutes later, I stood in the shadows of the train station as I watched the Indian lead my three horses up the ramp into the stable car. He already knew that he'd be traveling there with the horses. While some Indians did travel passenger coach on their way to Washington for treaty talks, it was rare, and the way this Indian looked, it would draw considerable attention to have him beside me.

I wasn't worried about the tickets. The conductor would take cash once we were on board and moving. I'd spoken briefly to the stablehand in the railcar explaining just that, with my head down and in as high and a squeaky voice as I could manage. I was grateful the conversation had lasted less than ten seconds, because I didn't figure I made the most acceptable woman in the world. For that matter, I intended to be out of this hot dress the minute the train wheels started rolling. I hadn't seen anyone I recognized get into the passenger car, and my shooting of John Harrison had happened recently, so unless a body was from Laramie and had seen me in jail, there would be nothing about my face to excite anyone into figuring me for a prisoner on the run.

Still, no sense in taking unneeded chances. I waited in the shadows and watched passengers board, expecting to enter the train myself at the last possible moment.

I did have another reason for watching. Rebecca Montcalm.

What had she written? *The Indian will accompany you and, when appropriate, will deliver further messages to you from me.*

On the short walk to the station, I'd tried to put myself in her shoes. First, the Indian would have relayed to her the marshal's conversation about choosing a different time than dawn for an escape attempt. Then she'd have had to decide if Evrett was on the level. She'd decide yes, because if Evrett wasn't on the level, he would have said nothing at all and been on his guard for the Indian to try busting me loose. So she changes her plans, has the Indian show up just before the train arrives, armed with the gun, rope, and a dress for me. And the only way she could stay close enough to me and the Indian to deliver messages would be to board the train. While that was easy enough to figure, it still drove me crazy to wonder why she'd want me to escape, or why she'd insist I stay with the Indian.

I looked for her now, even though I had no idea who I was looking for. Fat? Pretty? Young? Old?

And I'd look for her on the train, too. Somewhere on the way, she'd have to get to the stable car to talk to her Indian. With luck, I'd find her then and also find a way to shake some truth from her.

While I watched, a man stepped down from the train and pushed his way through the small group milling about. I froze, for that man's face had appeared in every nightmare I'd had since the day I'd watched my brother die.

CHAPTER *12*

THE MAN, OF COURSE, did not spare a second glance at me, by all appearances a large, plain woman standing awkwardly with her head half hidden in a bonnet. Had he seen me without my disguise, I doubted even then he would have remembered me, for when we'd last locked eyes, I had a full beard and my face was considerably younger.

But my own stare at this moment should have burned a hole right through him.

His eyes, first, marked him as unforgettable, no matter how the sun and wind might ever leather his face. They were cold and gray, eyes as empty of any emotion as the eyes of a dead man. His hair was gray also, although he was not an old man, and his face flat and wide, with a mouth that was merely a slash marked by thin, pressed lips.

He wore a buckskin jacket, open to show two revolvers tucked in his waistband, handles facing toward each other so that when he reached for his belly with his left hand, his palm would grip the gun on the right, and when he reached with his right hand, his palm would grip the gun on the left.

He was a small man but walked larger. He didn't swagger or bounce as many small men do but almost seemed to roll as on oiled wheels. People in front and to the sides made way for him, probably unaware that they were pressing back by instinct as they continued their conversations.

He was a killer, as I had learned, one of the few who could and would end a man's life with as little regret as if he'd ground a snake's head below the heel of his boot.

I found myself struggling to breathe, seeing him this close. Even though I'd never discovered his name, and thought of him as Gray Eyes, I'd known it would happen someday that our paths would cross. While the territories were vast, the numbers of whites were few, and they always gathered in the comfort of suffocatingly small and dirty clusters of towns. Those of us who roamed, no matter how much time we spent in the vastness, would always have to return to the towns, no matter how briefly. And there were too few towns to live a lifetime without meeting again.

Yet, knowing as I had that this moment would arrive, I was still not prepared. I'd dreamed of a gunfight. Or feared that I'd run. Now, neither, for this dress and a marshal roped to a chair meant I had no choice but to continue as if I had not seen him. I wondered if tonight the nightmares would begin again.

He had just stepped through the crowd when Smickles appeared from around the corner of the telegraph office.

It did not console me that Smickles' eyes and upper cheeks were purple-black with the bruises of a broken nose, or that Smickles was almost hangdog in his approach to the man with gray hair and gray eyes. What had happened with

Smickles was something I'd forget within days. But the man with gray eyes . . .

I was close enough to hear Smickles' first words to the man.

"Sheriff Reed," Smickles said, "I've got the room booked at the hotel, just like you asked."

————

Was it coincidence that Marshal Evrett had, in his mentioning to the Indian of the best time to escape, arranged for the Indian and me to board the eastbound train? I'd already shed the dress. The train had barely been clear of the station when I had found an empty sleeping compartment to give me the necessary privacy. Losing the discomfort and distraction of my disguise had cleared my head to let me think. I discovered, however, I would have preferred discomfort over my new thoughts.

The bounty hunter who had killed my brother was Henry Reed? I wasn't surprised that he was now a territorial sheriff. More than one man with a bad rep had played both sides of the law before. A fella named Henry Plummer done the same game in Montana in the early '60s, raising a ruckus during the gold-rush times, going as far as joining a vigilante committee and secretly arranging for the murder of fellow vigilantes. He once shot a man for laughing at his Connecticut accent and engaged in a number of other things that made him famous before he died at the end of a rope.

So Gray Eyes—I stopped and told myself to call him Wyoming Sheriff Henry Reed because that might take my mind off those eyes when I'd stared into them close—could use all his killing skills and earn himself that fierce reputation as a sheriff.

As to all of his past, well—I knew him as a bounty hunter, others might know him for something else, but in the West the past was something easy to hide. For me, it'd been so long since anyone had called me Robert Adams that I'd almost forgotten that name until Marshal Evrett had pulled out the poster.

Nor was I surprised that Reed and I had crossed paths. The frontier was large but the settlements few: places where men would drift together and drift apart. Many of us met and played cards in different towns, as if the geography separating us from previous meetings meant nothing.

What I didn't like was the fact that all of this had been brought to such a personal level.

He was my nightmare.

I did not want to think about the past.

To rid myself of those gray, dead eyes, I tried to concentrate on if and why the marshal had made sure I escaped on the eastbound train.

The train slowly picked up speed and began to meander through the few miles of dry plains, which remained until the tracks began to climb into the mountain hills south and east of Laramie.

Or was it not coincidence? Like it or not, I was now Evrett's bloodhound. And he'd mentioned that Harrison had done the same—traveled eastward alone and returned in four days with the Indian. The whyfors of Harrison's trip—why the trip, why the Indian, what about the gold—were questions I'd never be able to answer without help. I set them aside. What I could contemplate with less futility was the *where* of Harrison's destination. If he'd been gone only four days, the most he could go in one direction was two days, and that far if only there had been no complications in meeting— maybe kidnapping—the Indian upon arrival, wherever that arrival had been.

Someone tapped me on the shoulder. I removed my gaze from the tops of the cottonwood trees and the blue sky and faraway horizon and turned my head to the aisle of the train.

"Destination?" It was the conductor, a monkey of a man who compensated with a large mustache. In one hand, he held a paper punch that was attached to his belt by a shiny chain. In the other a sheaf of tickets.

"Funny you should ask," I said.

He found nothing funny about it and frowned slightly. I didn't blame him.

"Say I traveled for two days," I moved on quickly. "How far'd that take me?"

The conductor squinted and thought. He swayed slightly in the aisle as the *clack-clack* of iron wheels on iron track quickened in tempo to a *clickety-clack*.

"Lincoln," he announced. "Nebraska State."

"Lincoln? This train's doing at least twenty miles an hour."

He shrugged superiority. "Figure in stops every thirty miles or so for water and coal, layovers to let the western trains pass, then loading, unloading at each destination."

"Then Lincoln's fine," I said. It would cost extra if I didn't have to go that far, but now I had every possible stop covered. "I got three horses and a man with them."

"Payment in gold or bank notes?" he asked.

"Notes."

"Gold saves you a dollar on every ten."

"Notes."

"Fifteen dollars, then." His lips tightened in disapproval at someone willing to throw away money. For me, gold was too heavy to carry and too easily noticed. What the conductor didn't know was that over the years I'd had little urge to spend the money I did make, so saving money, especially now, was the least of my concerns.

He punched a ticket and handed it to me, then moved down the aisle.

I studied the ticket. In bold lettering in the center, the words UNION PACIFIC filled most of the boxed space. I didn't mind wasting some time thinking about the meaning of those two words.

How many years had it been since Union Pacific began to lay track west of Cheyenne as it raced through Wyoming on its way to complete the cross-country connection? Only seven, I decided, not because I had a bent for history, but because that's how many summers I could count since I'd earned wages by shooting buffalo to feed the Union Pacific work crews.

———

It had been a glorious year, not only for the wild and feverish competition to see which crew could lay track faster, or which camp could kill more buffalo—our camp had lost narrowly, as an army scout named Cody in the other had managed by himself to kill five thousand—but because even the crudest, ill-educated men understood the impact of the work of their hands. All of us sensed how the railroad would be a pivot point to change forever the land that absorbed our sweat and blood and buried the bodies of those around us who fell to dynamite, Indians, weather, or the brutal punishment of our labor.

How could we all know this with such certainty? Towns sprang up overnight at our arrival. Laramie went from a small wooden fort and a few tents to a town in less than two weeks. Cheyenne . . . by the time we'd gone the couple of hundred miles west to Rawlins, Cheyenne—barely a trading post when we'd left—had two daily papers, three hotels, two theaters, five churches, one school, twenty gambling saloons, and a firmly established reputation as uproarious hell on earth.

Each day, we saw trains follow behind us as far as we'd gone, bringing in lumber, glass, and store supplies in a fraction of the time and a fraction of the cost of the sacrifice it took for oxen-pulled wagons to do the same on the deeply rutted Oregon Trail. We all saw cattle go suddenly from worthless at two dollars a head to the basis of new fortunes at twenty-five dollars a head, because these same trains turned back eastward took cattle across the formerly impassable Great Plains to the markets of Chicago and New York.

The Indians also knew how the railroad would change their land forever, and they fought us every mile. They saw their buffalo go to our hunters, and the cattle move in where the buffalo had been, and an endless stream of white settlers follow the rails. But it seemed we were living for something larger than ourselves, and it didn't bother us greatly when Indians killed surveyors and burned the papers with markings that seemed so important to us whites. All of us were caught in the fever, and when we finished not much more than a year later, Wyoming had a string of real towns—Evanston, Green River, Rock Springs, Rawlins, Laramie, Cheyenne.

———

These were all the towns that were now marked in fine print around the outside borders of my ticket at which I stared.

The other towns, Nebraska towns, filled, in continuing easterly order, the rest of the outside edge of my ticket. Pine Bluffs, Sidney, Ogallala, North Platte, Kearney, Lincoln, Omaha—with Lincoln punched out in a neat circle, because that was as far as the ticket would go, and that was as far as Harrison might have gone.

Harrison. Yes, Harrison. I tried to think of Harrison and the questions he brought, but I couldn't.

The railroad was now in my head and, because of the railroad, the Oregon Trail it had replaced. Eighteen fifty-two, it'd been. Me thirteen, Jed fourteen, and my parents dizzy with excitement to be in on the wagons that pulled out of Omaha to follow the Oregon Trail.

If there'd only been a train then, I thought, *the prairies wouldn't have been this vast untamed and nearly uncharted wilderness. There wouldn't have been the graves that led to those lonely wild orphan years with Jed and the mountain men. Instead, him and I would probably be farming somewhere on the other side of the Rockies. If there'd only been a train then, we would not have found the life that led us to hunt men for bounty. . . .*

I bit my tongue. Hard. And tasted the salt of blood. I did not want the memories that Gray Eyes brought back.

Against my will, an image squeezed into my mind. *Of the shadow of a man raising a gun and . . .*

Suzanne! I told myself to think of Suzanne. If I'd have accepted her offer for company, I'd still be in jail waiting for the noose. Hadn't Evrett said it was my request for the telegram information that convinced him to give me the chance of an innocent man? And without her vouching for my intentions, I'd still be in jail, shocked as if dumped into ice water to see Sheriff Henry Reed walk to the front of the cell and glare through the bars at me with those gray eyes.

And after, as Jed's lifeblood spilled from the side of his mouth, those gray eyes had bored into mine as the man had pressed a pistol into the front of my nose and waited for me to beg for mercy. . . .

I bit my tongue again. No matter how I tried, all thoughts led me back.

Don't think. Do something. Anything.

I'd check on my horses. Ask the Indian tough questions.

I stood quickly. I ignored hard looks from people seated as I almost trotted down the aisle and moved from the passenger car to outside where a small walkway led over the couplings to the next car. I paused and drank in the coolness of wind against my face.

The train was just beginning to climb into the Laramie Mountains that separated us from Cheyenne. Scattered pines began to replace the cottonwoods, and the folds of the upper hills lost their soft edges to show the sharp lines of deep canyon shadows.

As always the land moved me, to remind me how it would be again to lose myself beneath sky and towering clouds, with the horizon always so far away that just breathing felt like I was filling myself with freedom.

Already some calmness began to take root.

Then I spotted the commotion in the next passenger car. I pushed across the coupling and through the door.

It was that Indian. Wrestling the conductor.

I figured it for an even match. They were about the same size and, it appeared, equally determined.

When I got closer, though, I discovered the Indian had a distinct advantage. Body odor. Here in the almost stifling warm enclosure of the passenger car, the greases and unwashed clothes of the Indian had maximum impact. The poor conductor was trying to push the Indian back while holding his breath.

It was a wordless struggle. Some passengers were watching with amusement. Most of those, however, were some distance away. The passengers immediately left and right of the two wrestlers were crinkling their noses in disgust.

I marched right through, grabbed the Indian by the scruff of his neck, and spun him around.

"Won't happen again," I told the conductor as I continued to push the Indian back. "I can't figure what got into his mind now."

The conductor brushed and flapped his uniform.

I took the Indian by the shoulders and kept pushing. He

was a scrawny one, all right, and I was surprised he'd done so well against the conductor.

But I was angry, more at myself than the Indian, and happy to find an outlet for that anger, so my own efforts simply overpowered him.

"Back to the horses," I said. "Before I wring your skinny neck."

He stumbled ahead of me. Through the remaining length of this passenger car. Through the next one. Then back to the stable car.

All of the horses were reined to heavy iron rings, and I took care not to stand behind any. A jittery horse is not something to tempt, not when one well-placed kick will cave in a man's skull.

"You *can* talk," I said. "And this would be a bloody good time to start."

The Indian reached into his heavy coat and pulled out another piece of paper. I guessed that's why he had begun to look for me in the passenger cars.

I sighed and took it.

Potter, it read in that same exquisite handwriting, *is where you shall disembark. Secure enough provisions for two weeks travel. You shall be repaid when you succeed. The Indian will give you further instructions upon your departure from Potter.*

One glance at the Indian's set face told me I would get nothing more from him.

I confess right then that it didn't bother me. It seemed now that the prospect of something so deeply puzzling was much better than worrying myself with thoughts of gray eyes.

CHAPTER 13

POTTER, NEBRASKA, WAS a railroad town, as new to the territories as the trains that stopped in it twice per week. There were two hotels down from the depot, wood siding on both already gray from unrelenting sun, mossy water barrels beneath the eaves troughing. Beside the second hotel stood a general store, complete with railing bereft of tethered horses, while the railing in front of the saloons farther down held nearly a dozen, their heads dipped in the murky water of the troughs at their feet.

This town was set in the middle of the Plains, its location chosen for no other reason than that the steam locomotives could go no farther from the previous town without stopping here for water. The streets lay north and south and east and west in orderly grids because that's how Union Pacific had decided to sell lots for maximum profit from its government-granted land.

I knew, because my mind was filled with

needless things to know. It was a habit I couldn't stop. I think I made a point to ask questions partly because I'd learned from the mountain men that survival might depend on knowing something trivial and unrelated to daily life, and partly because I marveled at how quickly the West was changing.

The mountain men had raised me only twenty years earlier, but already they were rare except in legend. Myself, I could remember how a town ten years earlier considered itself to be civilized if it held a bank and a doctor's office, and folks made do with what they could. Back then, in a town in Kansas, I'd once set out for a shave, and instead of finding a barbershop, I was directed to the livery stable, where for fifteen cents one of the hands set aside his hammer and moved away from the anvil to strop a razor blade across the top of his boot before scraping away my whiskers. Now even a place like Potter had a saddler, shoemaker, tailor, and cabinetmaker.

Ten years ago, I'd have to count out the grains of gunpowder and mold my own bullets before loading and crimping them into a brass cartridge that I'd carefully save for use again. That in itself was one good reason most men survived a gunfight. Miscount by a couple of grains—easily done—and a body'd never know where his bullet was going from one shot to the next. Now I could step into the store, like I'd done ten minutes earlier, and buy—as I was doing at the moment—a couple boxes of factory loads for my .44–40, the newfangled six-shooter with bullets to fit my rifle. Both repeating weapons were making life miserable for Indians now that we could fire more than one bullet for every twenty of their arrows.

One thing, though, was never going to change. Men. Halfway through my order of provisions, I heard shooting just outside the store, close to where I'd left the Indian with our horses.

I stepped out onto the wood sidewalk and squinted into

bright sunshine and the haze of heat and dust that pressed upon the streets of Potter. It took but a second to decipher the action.

For one who said nothing and did little, the Indian had an alarming habit of managing to irritate folks. He danced now as two cowboys took turns firing bullets into the ground at his feet. It was a timeworn trick used on greenhorns, and there was little humor in it.

Still, folks began to gather. Some frowned. Some laughed. But all other movement nearby, from passing wagons to conversations on the street, had stopped. Aside from the few other Indians who'd been lying around and now edged away with their dogs slinking behind, it seemed that the Indian and the two cowboys were on a dirt stage.

The Indian would hop and dance to each shot as one cowboy emptied two guns, during which spell the other cowboy loaded. It gave the Indian little time to rest.

Unfortunately, the Indian's problem was now my problem.

There were, however, a couple of tactical errors involved with challenging the two gunmen. For starts, they were two. And, judging by my last gunfight, I was rusty. Even if I did win a shoot-out, I'd be facing lawmen again. And, judging by my last encounter with the law, there were more enjoyable ways to engage myself over the next while.

I needed a more peaceable solution. One came to mind, so I stepped forward and started shooting at the Indian's feet, too.

This earned me a look of sheer hatred from the Indian.

It succeeded, however, in stopping both cowboys from further shooting. I stopped, too. I had three bullets left in my gun.

"Hey," one said.

"Hey what," I said back as I sighted down my pistol at the Indian's feet.

The cowboy who'd spoken was the shorter of the two. Sweat-stained dark circles under the arms of his checked shirt. I had his position memorized, too.

"Hey what?" he sputtered. "You c'ain't horn in on us."

"Looked like fun," I said. "Watch this."

I squeezed off a shot. Missed the inside of the Indian's boot by less than half an inch.

"I can get the next one closer," I said. I hunched forward and drew another bead.

"This is our Injun." It was the taller cowboy, slouched and with a potbelly. He spoke with as much hesitation and indignant surprise as was used by his companion. "Find your own."

I fired my next-to-last bullet. The Indian yelped. I'd nicked the edge of the sole of his boot. The Indian's next look went beyond hatred.

I ignored the heat of that look and glanced at the two cowboys and grinned. "Told you I'd get it closer."

Both were starting to frown at me now that the shock of my appearance had worn off. I smelled whiskey on their breaths. Good because it took an edge off a man. Bad because it made a man less predictable.

"But this is our Injun," the shorter cowboy echoed, except with more conviction, as if he were building an argument.

I needed to keep them off balance.

"Storekeep," I called past them, "empty me a box of shells, will you? I need the paper box."

Both of them turned their heads to see the storekeeper. They weren't bright. Standing so close together was another mistake. I could have dived and rolled and from a side angle plugged them both with my remaining bullet. But that would have landed me in jail.

They faced me again as I was pulling my wallet from my back pocket.

"You men look like shooters," I said. "Interested in a shooting bet?"

The tall one started to raise his top lip in disdain.

"Give you ten-to-one odds." I put my wallet back and cut in to stop him from speaking. "I miss, you get ten times what you bet."

The short one studied me. He finally conceded interest. "You'll shoot what?"

The storekeeper reappeared from the shadows of the doorway and handed an empty paper box to a man standing nearby, who in turn gave me a questioning look. I nodded, and he stepped forward to hand me the box. To do so, he passed between me and the two cowboys. Again, I could have drawn, because they made no effort to stop him from blocking their vision of me. As gunfighters, they were fools, destined to short careers.

"Obliged," I said to the storekeeper.

He stepped away again, leaving me and the Indian and the two cowboys in a large open circle of the street.

"What I propose is this," I said. "I'll set the box on top of my left hand." I held my hand out waist high and balanced the box as promised. "Then I'll draw with my right, fan my first shot with the left, and shoot the box at the same time."

The short one snickered. "Sure you will."

"Backing that disbelief with money?"

"Ten-to-one?"

"Yup."

"I'll bet ten bucks," he said. "That way you'll owe me . . . you'll owe me . . ."

"Hundred bucks" came a voice from the crowd. Murmurings greeted that.

"Bet thirty," I said. "Against three hundred."

"Me too?" the tall one asked, his eyes glazed with greed. Few cowboys made more than three hundred in a year.

"You too," I said.

"Done," the short one said. His partner nodded.

I motioned with my right hand for people to clear. They understood quickly and parted so that my shot would travel harmlessly down the street. To warm up, I drew my gun and slapped it back in the holster. Kept the paper box where it was on my left hand and drew with my right three times more. Then drew the gun and twirled it and slapped it back. Then drew and twirled and drew and . . .

"Quit dragging your feet," the tall one complained.

I shrugged.

It grew quiet.

Then I did it. Eased my left hand over to the right side of my body. Drew and spun my gun forward with my right hand while pulling my left hand into my hip so that in the same motion my left thumb fanned the trigger and fired the gun.

The box, in midair and still waist high, blew to shreds.

I would have been very surprised if it hadn't. Marshal Evrett's trick was the derringer rigged to an elastic on the inside of his sleeve. Mine was a revolver with a shortened gun barrel and no front sight to snag on my holster. And that holster had been sliced down the front, the leather of both sides then wetted and curled dry inward so that it would hold a gun but permit it to release easier.

And there was one other thing—besides practice and the knack of flipping the box upward and forward with the top of my left hand as I began to fan the trigger. I knew the gases of the exploding gunpowder funneled out the sides of a revolver. That bullet didn't need to hit the box, not with a blast of superheated air to do the work.

The box landed in pieces.

The cowboys gaped at me. The short one opened and closed his mouth, a toad gasping for air.

Each had just lost a month's wages. I wanted to forestall any nasty drunken outrage. My intent was to keep this from getting to the law.

"One more bet," I said. "A chance to win your money back before it even leaves your pocket."

The Indian—I caught myself almost thinking *my* Indian— had sidled closer to the crowd.

"We'll send the Injun halfway down the street, get him to toss two quarters," I said. "I'll use two guns and hit them both at the same time."

More murmurs.

"He cain't do it," the tall one whispered from the side of his mouth.

"I don't know," the short one argued. "You see'd what he done with that box."

"I miss," I said, "you keep your money, plus get another five bucks apiece."

They agreed so quickly they forgot to ask what they would owe if I hit the quarters.

I pointed at the Indian. "Get in front of that saloon," I commanded. "Stand aside, and when I give the word, toss both quarters as high as you can."

The Indian walked away, and the crowd gave me more room. I pointed my gun at the ground and pulled the trigger. As expected, it clicked dry. I holstered it again.

"Each of you give me a gun," I commanded the cowboys in a voice that was impatient as I stared in a distracted manner at the Indian. I also loosened the sling from my left arm and prayed moving it would not hurt too much. As they couldn't know I traveled with the Indian, the fools stepped up to me and did so. Which had been *my* gamble. By now, the Indian had reached the saloon.

"Toss," I shouted.

The Indian threw both quarters high. Each glinted briefly in the sunlight. I brought both my guns high to follow the quarters, then pivoted slowly and brought both guns low so that one faced each cowboy. The quarters plunked down. Neither cowboy spared the quarters a glance, not with their guns in my hands consuming their full attention.

"Now," I said, "if I shoot, I'll have clean missed those quarters. Care to win your bet?"

They shook their heads no.

A drop of sweat hung on the edge of the short one's mustache.

"Then unholster your other guns real slow," I said, "and kick them aside."

It didn't take them long.

"Good," I said. I raised my voice. "Show's over, folks." Then to the cowboys. "Back up some, will you. Sit on the edge of the sidewalk, but make sure you sit on your hands."

By the time they were seated, most of the folks had left.

"I'm curious," I said, squatted in front of them with their guns trained on their faces. "What'd the Injun do to upset you both?"

"N-nothing," the short one said. The drop of sweat on his mustache trembled, then fell. "We was paid."

Until then, I'd truly been only as mildly curious as my casual question might have conveyed. Cowboys drank and whooped 'er up, and by the time their heads cleared, they mostly regretted whatever foolish things they'd done. I'd aimed for this little conversation to cause them to sweat some fear, and afterward I planned to turn in their guns at the sheriff's office.

This changed it. I should have known any trouble involved with the Indian would not be coincidence.

"Paid?"

He clamped his mouth shut.

"Say I wanted this bullet to catch the corner of your ear," I said. "It might miss outside, which means your ear is fine. It might miss inside, which means you died with your boots on. It might snip just a piece. But whatever happens, this gun'll make enough noise you don't hear out of that side of your head again."

"Man just approached us in the saloon," Shorty said. "Gave us each five dollars iffen we'd play the hot-lead dance for a Injun. Then he took us to the street and pointed the Injun out for us."

"What'd he look like?"

"You just seen him," the tall one blurted, anxious to please now. "He was dancing for us. He tossed them quarters for you."

I sighed. "The feller who paid you. What'd *he* look like?"

"Skinny-like," Shorty said. "Walked funny."

"Yeah," the other added. "Like his clothes were itchin' him."

"What was he wearing?"

"Jeans. Fresh-ironed shirt." Shorty snapped his fingers. "Like they was new store-bought. I always itch myself till—"

I waved him quiet. Not that it took much motion with the gun to snap his mouth shut.

"Talked funny, too," the tall one said. "Fancy eastern talk. That's why I figured he paid us. Maybe hadn't seen gun-play before. Iffen that's why, he sure got his money's worth. I ain't ever seen no one fast enough to shoot a box—"

Another wave of the gun to silence him. "Where'd he go after he paid you?"

Shorty shrugged. "Didn't see."

I grunted. Then stood. "Git."

"Huh?"

"Git. Pick up your guns from the storekeep in the morning."

I backed up to give them room to stand. Old habits die hard. I'd seen more than one man die because he relaxed with his guns when it appeared everything was over.

Both cowboys left me in a shuffling half run, peeking backward to see if I would give chase.

I scanned the street. My—*the* Indian was standing beside my horses. A carriage behind a two-horse team headed toward me. A few ladies in calico dresses, others in hoopskirts, picked their way across the street, stepping widely around clumps of horse apples.

There was the saloon. Livery. Another general store. Newspaper office. Two hotels. If I wanted to watch the front of this store without being seen, where would I stand?

Many places, I decided. There were too many shadow-darkened doorways in this bright afternoon sun. Hotel rooms above the street. It'd be a waste of time trying to find the man who'd paid the cowboys to start the gunfight.

"We got provisions," I told the Indian. He stared at me.

"Provisions," I repeated, with exaggerated patience. "Victuals. Bullets. Nod your head if you understand."

The Indian nodded.

"That means we'll be leaving town. Plenty of daylight left."

More staring.

"So what I'm saying is we need some place to go."

More staring.

"Maybe your mystery woman has a destination in mind?"

The Indian reached inside his coat and pulled out a piece of paper.

The Black Hills.

That's all it said. But it was enough. Rumored to have

plenty of gold, north about hundred fifty miles in the Dako-
tas. Easy travel across the prairies. But death for a destination.
The Sioux held it to be sacred ground. I hadn't heard yet
about a white who had gone in alone and returned.

CHAPTER 14

"Won't be long," I told the Injun outside the telegraph office. "Think you'll manage to steer free of trouble?"

The Indian blinked, and his head moved up and down. Only slightly, and only once, but it was more than the usual impassive stare.

I was impressed. Had my earlier rescue of this stubborn mule of an Indian overwhelmed him with such gratitude that he was actually prepared to acknowledge my existence with such exuberance? Not for the first time did I wonder about his relationship with Rebecca Montcalm, or for that matter, where she was at this moment.

That question seemed less urgent as I walked up the steps. We were minutes away from leaving Potter. Because of that, it didn't even bother me that I'd been with the horses when the train stopped in Potter and was unable to check departing passengers for her. If she wanted to keep giving that Indian messages, she'd have to stay close, and once we got into the long and slowly rolling grasslands, I'd be able to backtrack easily enough to make a surprise introduction. And I might also find the truth behind all of this, not to mention permanently delay this suicide trip into the Black Hills.

The telegrapher had his back to me as I walked in, tapping the brass keys as he sent a message down the wire. Through the window beyond his bent shoulders, I saw the open prairie. The window was dusty, but not so much that I couldn't recognize the difference between dirt and the darkening sky as a towering thundercloud moved in from the horizon in response to the unrelenting heat that rose from the baked grasslands. Short violent rain would hit within the hour. It would barely settle the dust because the clouds had no place from which to draw moisture, but the swirling winds and sheet lightning that came with that brief rain would throw a good fright into my three horses and the two I'd bought for the Indian. It'd be helpful to get a few miles in before hunching down before the winds.

Even though it would save hardly any time, I couldn't resist the illogical urge to be doing something that would speed me along. I searched for something else to do, and as the clicks and clacks came in, I reached over the counter for a pad of paper and wrote a short note:

REACHED POTTER STOP NO NEWS YET STOP
DESTINATION BLACK HILLS STOP WILL HAVE
MORE NEWS IN TWO DAYS STOP

I put the pencil down, ripped the paper off the pad, set both back on the other side of the counter, then reread my message.

Two days? I guessed two hours. From what I'd been taught by the mountain men, if I hadn't managed to capture the mystery woman by tomorrow morning and return to Potter with the rest of the story for Evrett by tomorrow night, I was ready for a cane and rocking chair.

The clacking stopped. The clerk set aside the telegraph form that held his Morse code translation, then scurried to the counter.

"A message to the marshal in Laramie," I said.

He took the pencil from where I'd set it and licked the end while holding the pad in his other hand. His nails were chewed down to the quick and his movements fast and furtive, like a mouse.

"Yes?" he almost stammered.

I handed him the note.

His eyes widened. "You wrote this?"

" 'Course."

"But ain't you the gunfighter who just . . ."

That explained the stammer and the quick movements. It never failed to amaze me how quickly news traveled. Instead of telegraph poles across the country, they should just set up pickle barrels like in the general store where a few folks could gather round each one and gossip. It would disemploy this fellow in a hurry.

"Once a person knows to read and write," I said, "he can't figure out how to pull a trigger?"

"Yes, yes," he said. "Just don't hardly happen that way, is all."

He was right, of course. School learning in the territories was a rare prize. Most who had the luxury of education were brought up in a style of life that did not lead to punching cows or throwing lead. But not many gunfighters had had to endure Clara's constant nagging on the need to be civilized. When I'd pointed out that the dance hall she ran hardly appeared to be civilized, she'd tartly told me that the need was always greatest among savages. Unfortunately I'd never since seen anything to prove her wrong.

The telegrapher told me how much it would cost to send a message, and I added a dollar bill to the amount he requested and set it on the counter.

"You've overpaid," he said.

I noticed, however, that his nail-bitten hands remained on the money.

"The name Harrison ring a bell?" I asked.

He shook his head, but his fingers twitched. I folded and placed another dollar bill on top of his hand. In a quick movement, he covered it, too.

"Harrison was here in Potter maybe a week ago," I tried again. "Did you have or send any telegrams for him?"

"That would be confidential," he said. He lifted his hand to make sure he hadn't counted wrong. "Only the threat of violence could break my silence."

"Bang, bang," I said. "Is that enough of a threat?"

"Harrison?" he asked without hesitation. "Big guy? Stinks like a rotted buffalo?"

I nodded.

"If he ever heard back I'd told . . ."

"I shot him dead in Laramie."

"De . . . de . . . dead?"

"He irritated me," I explained.

The poor man didn't know whether to relax at that news or shake in fear to be facing the bearer of the news. I went back to my wallet again for two more dollars, which reassured him greatly.

The clerk pocketed the bills.

"I'll tell you what I know," he said. "Only Harrison never sent nothing."

"He picked up a message?"

"Nope." The clerk seemed to swell now that he had something I obviously wanted.

"Bang, bang," I reminded him.

"Harrison came in, told me his name, and asked if I had a telegram for him. Slammed his fist on this here counter when I said not. That's how I remember him." The clerk wrinkled his nose. "And the smell."

That information didn't help much, but it had been worth a try.

I got to the door before the clerk stopped me.

"You should know, however, his name was on another telegram," the clerk said.

I swung back.

The clerk held out his hand.

"Nope," I said. "It'll irritate me greatly to open my wallet again."

He pulled his hand back.

"What did the telegram say?" I asked.

The clerk closed his eyes to remember. " 'Harrison arrives tomorrow. Stop. Deliver goods. Stop. Then follow. Stop.' "

I waited, but the clerk opened his eyes.

"Where was the telegram from?" I asked. "Who picked it up?"

"It didn't say who it was from. But it came from the Denver office. And the fellow who picked it up, his name was O'Neal."

The Indian and I headed north on the trail to Scottsbluff. It was midafternoon now, and I kept my hat well forward so that the brim kept my eyes in shadow.

I rejoiced—and had no compunction about using a word that strong—to be under the skies again. My time in jail had made me ache to be unfettered, and while the train had shown me the passing countryside, it wasn't until I was on horse and become a tiny speck below the shifting clouds and blue sky that it felt as if I were free again.

The land here suited my spirit, for it was good for travel. Solid, not sandy, and free of rocks that might lame a horse. The climb was so gentle on these hills as to be barely notice-able—the only indication of rising land was the edge of the horizon as it dipped and rose in all directions.

The grass had begun to pale in the midsummer heat, but it had not yet thinned. If we stopped occasionally to let our horses graze and kept them at a walk, we could hold pace for hours without wearing them down.

To add to our ease, the storm on the western horizon that I'd seen from the telegraph office had blown itself out miles before reaching us, but the cool breeze it kicked up for half an hour was much appreciated. I was glad of the storm's re-prieve for another reason: I did not want to see the disposi-tions of the new horses tested just yet, for the Indian was as clumsy on horseback now as he'd been during the first ride while chasing me out of Laramie.

In fact, I was rapidly reaching the point of deciding that the Indian had some serious mental shortfalls, and that the wisest thing the Indian could ever do was to continue to keep his mouth shut—leaving me to guess at his lack of intelli-gence—because opening it would surely prove he was an idiot.

We had traveled only an hour—maybe as much as eight miles already—when I glanced back to see how the Indian fared.

My two horses were behind me, loaded light and haltered to the lead rope tied to my saddle. I fully expected to see the Indian and his horses directly behind. Instead, he had paused at a small depression of water just off the trail. The Indian had dismounted his horse and held the reins as he squatted, and he was about to cup his hand into the water to drink. His other horse stood beside them.

I groaned and pulled my rifle from the scabbard.

Did I worry that noise might bring wandering Indians in? No, not here, south of Scottsbluff in the more settled area of Nebraska so near the Pawnee reservations. And although we appeared to be alone on the trail, the wagon ruts showed it to be well traveled. The untamed Sioux wouldn't be a problem until much farther past the North Platte River.

So I aimed, fired, and saw the smack of water about three feet ahead of both horses' noses where they were about to dip into the water.

Both horses shied at the smack of bullet and the sound of the rifle. The Indian sawed so badly on the reins that his horse reared, then nearly slipped in the mud, while the other horse pulled back from the water, straining on the rope that held him to the Indian's saddle. The Indian staggered as he held the reins and then fell to his knees in the slime and mud.

I paused to load another shell to replace the one I'd shot. My new Winchester .44–40 held fifteen shots, and while some would have been content to continue travel with only fourteen remaining in the magazine, slim as the chances were, I'd have been plenty upset to meet a war party and regret not having that fifteenth bullet to fire.

After I replaced the rifle in the scabbard, I trotted my horses back to the Indian.

He was on his feet now. Again, that look of hatred shot my way.

"Alkaline," I said. "Didn't you notice the grass?"

The grass around the small depression was reddish yellow, a sure sign of bad water. Had he or the horses drunk, we'd have been held up a day, maybe two, waiting for the gas and pains to subside. And that's only if I'd have been able to pour grease into their stomachs, grease that would have meant a hard gallop back to Potter, since we traveled so light that I had none in the packs.

I didn't bother to watch and wait while the Indian

mounted his horse. Without further conversation, I turned and let my thoughts occupy me as my body eased into the rhythm of Charlie's walk.

Harrison arrives tomorrow. Stop. Deliver goods. Stop. Then follow. Stop.

My already considerable respect for Marshal Evrett increased, for the telegram message certainly proved correct his hunch that O'Neal had more involvement in this than a curious passerby who decided to pose as a journalist.

Harrison arrives tomorrow. I decided to assume the obvious, that Harrison did not send the telegram. He'd left Laramie, not Denver. Yet who in Denver would know so precisely his arrival and how? The logical answer was that the sender of the telegram had also sent Harrison.

Deliver goods. Could I conclude that the goods must be the Indian? After all, Harrison had left Laramie alone and returned with the Indian. Or was there something else that Harrison had carried back, something small enough not to be noticed upon his return to Laramie? If *the goods* was the Indian, why was he so valuable? And if *the goods* was the Indian, then Rebecca Montcalm was involved very deeply in this. If *the goods* meant something else, however, and the Indian, like me, was an innocent person caught in a complicated spider web, then Rebecca Montcalm may be as ignorant of the situation as I. But that still didn't explain why the Indian was so valuable to her. I fully intended to ask Montcalm those same questions when I caught her within the next day.

Then follow. The sender of the telegram had given an order to O'Neal, which I took to understand that the sender had full expectations for the order to be followed. In other words, O'Neal was an employee. But why give that order if Harrison was also employed by the sender? Did it mean that the sender of the telegram didn't trust Harrison? But if Harrison couldn't be trusted, why send him in the first place?

Another thought struck me. Was the sender of the telegram also the one who had given Smickles instructions to kill me? If yes, I knew with certainty that somehow all of this had to do with gold.

We were headed into the slight breeze that swept across the dancing grass and into my face. I scanned the dips and gullies around me for any sign of movement, a habit only a fool would forget—no matter how engrossing his thoughts might be.

Far away there was the hulking blackness of a bull buffalo followed by a half dozen cows. A few hawks circled. But other than that, I saw nothing to alarm me.

I gnawed again at all those thoughts.

I knew I could walk away from this. I was free now. And while Wyoming Territory would no longer be safe for me as Samuel Keaton, I could head to Texas again, maybe California, and drift in those regions with little fear of becoming reward money for some bounty hunter.

Yet I did not want to leave. Evrett had been right in his guess about me: I owed him my life and could not leave that debt, no matter that he'd dictated the terms of repayment. But there was more. I'd been raised just west in the mountains and had not returned to those dark tree-filled valleys and shadowed, high granite rocks because something about the open land and sky of the plains and valleys brought me peace. I felt comfortable in my wanderings here and was not sure if I would love the land anywhere else.

There was, too, the unalterable fact that I no longer felt all of that peace. Facing death through Smickles' shotgun had changed that. Although I did not want to leave the land, I had a feeling that aimless and enjoyable wandering might no longer be a good enough way to kill time until time returned the favor.

This mystery of the Indian and the gold—for that is what

I was facing—was something to preoccupy my mind and keep me from the emptiness I feared might await me out in the aloneness of the hills. I wanted to grip the mystery and shake it and hound it to the end.

Starting tonight, I'd be backtrailing to discover what I could about it and the gold from Rebecca Montcalm.

CHAPTER 15

SHORTLY AFTER DAWN, I stood beside the Indian. The red and black wool blanket I purchased in Potter covered him so completely that only the tip of his nose reached the crisp air. He slept soundly as I watched the robe rise and drop with each of his deep breaths.

We were camped in the fold of a hill on the edge of a bluff, with a dry stream bed far below us, making impossible any attack upward from that side. To reach this site, we'd gone a half mile past it at dusk the previous evening, then backtracked as night was wrapping black around us. It was an old trick, but enduring because it was effective. Should a Sioux or Pawnee war party happen across our tracks, they'd not find us near the main trail, and they'd have trouble following our path at night to our camp. With the vantage point from our summit, it would be difficult to surprise us, and as added precaution, I'd taken a long circling path to hobble two horses below us at the stream bed. If the worst ever happened, we could scramble down and escape on horseback, knowing any pursuers would spend half an hour getting their horses to the bottom of the bluff to begin chase. In short, this Indian had a good reason for sleeping so soundly.

Yet my muscles still ached from the beating by Smickles, and my own night had been sleepless largely due to the Indian and my deeply rankling failure to find Rebecca Montcalm anywhere in the last five miles of the trail. Thus the Indian's contented slumber irritated me, and I wasn't man enough to ignore my petty feelings.

I took my pistol and, from the hip, fired at a mound of dirt.

The horses up here stamped some, but the Indian yelped and thrashed as if shot himself.

"Daylight's wasting," I explained. "Hope you didn't wet yourself."

His eyes stared upward at me in rage.

"Be glad you heard that shot," I said. "The one you won't hear is that one that kills you because someone with more harmful intentions caught you sleeping."

I was holding a box of factory loads in my other hand. The Indian's eyes moved to it.

"Practice time," I said. I kicked at a stack of dried buffalo chips that I'd just collected. "Start the fire and get some coffee brewed. You'll find what you need in the packsack on the ground yonder."

I left as the Indian was struggling to rub sleep from his eyes.

I took Charlie, the roan horse, with me some hundred yards away from camp. A good cow horse doesn't flinch at gunfire—the last thing you want when firing from a saddle—and it would never hurt to keep him accustomed to the sounds and smells of exploding gunpowder.

I intended to shoot plenty—this morning and others—since I didn't know how long it would take for me to become confident with a gun again. There is—I've learned the hard way—no other way to reach competence in anything except through work, and gunfighting is no different, except that incompetence in that area rarely gives you the chance to fail again.

I began by sighting down my gun to fire steady two-handed shots at a small chest-high circle I'd scraped into the grass of a sidehill about twenty paces away. My left arm hardly hurt with the extra effort, and Charlie calmly grazed throughout all the shots. I made nine of twelve, with spurts of dirt to show where the bullets plugged in and outside the circle.

Next I practiced one-handed, still taking time to sight with my arm extended at shoulder height. A full chamber of six bullets with my left hand, then six bullets with my right, each shot slowly squeezed. Again, six and six. The results were much better with my right hand—my left arm was still weak and shaky from the bullet of Harrison's that had torn through the outside edges of muscle.

After that, I tried a series of shots from the hip. The trick there is to pretend you are pointing with your index finger. When you relax and trust that aim, you'd be surprised how accurate it is.

I did not stop until the box was empty. I could purchase more bullets in Scottsbluff, and I needed to reach the point again where the response of my body was simple and instinctive and unquestioning to the needs dictated by my mind. Without that, it is impossible to react properly under pressure. This is knowledge held by good generals who endlessly drill their troops during the long, slow days between campaigns.

I had also concentrated on loading the bullets as quickly

as possible. I'd pop open the chamber, flick the upside-down pistol downward to clear the hot brass shells, then take the fresh bullets from the cartridge holders of my holster in quick, short movements. Later, when we moved closer to hostile country, I'd take the other pistol from my saddlebag, and carry it, too, simply to give me extra bullets before needing to reload. While the covers of those eastern dime novels always show a cowboy with both guns blazing, that was, as far as I knew, a myth. In all my travels, I'd yet to meet or hear of a gunfighter who did that. For starts, it's much faster to fire by fanning the hammer with the heel or fingers of your opposite hand than it is to pull the trigger, so much so that a person can almost fire twelve bullets faster one gun after another than with both at the same time. And second, firing from two guns does little good when the bullets from either gun hit nothing—the only result you can expect with half your concentration on each gun, and something those fools in Potter should have known when I offered to hit those quarters with a two-fisted trick shot.

Why was I spending shells on shots with my left hand? Not only to strengthen it, but for the day that I might take a hit in my right arm during a long gunfight. Henry Plummer, the renegade sheriff of Montana, I'm told, once took a ball in the right wrist, so he practiced with his left hand until he was as terrifying in accuracy and speed as he ever had been. I'd also heard that after he was hung by vigilantes, some gruesome souvenir seeker had cut apart his right wrist and found the lead ball, shiny bright from rubbing, lodged among the tendons.

The sun was higher now, and bright, so that the tall slender stems of grass cast sharp shadows at my feet as they began to wave in the breeze that grew with the warming earth. I could feel my sweat rising and a few mosquitoes drawn to me by my heat. But I was not finished with the gun. I spent another half hour in quick draws—not firing—but merely snapping the gun out of my holster again and again. A Colt weighs a couple pounds, and my muscles had forgotten the toughness it takes to draw that split second quicker than someone with softer muscles. By the way my arm tired, I knew it would be several weeks until it became worth my while to actually fire shells and expect any accuracy from a quick draw.

I didn't need to hear anything to know the Indian was moving up behind me, not with Charlie nearby. His ears rotated toward a spot behind my back. Because he did little more than turn his head slightly and roll his eyes backward, I remained relaxed. Charlie would have stamped some at a stranger.

How fast could I still be, I wondered. I kept drawing and reholstering my Colt. The shadow of the Indian fell onto the grass just beyond my feet. He tapped my shoulder.

I spun, dove sideways, and came up with the Colt solid in my fist and centered on the Indian's chest, who was already stumbling backward, eyes widened white with fear.

I stood, twirled the Colt on my index finger, holstered it, and grinned. "Coffee ready?"

I was so accustomed to his silent glare that when it arrived, it almost felt like a greeting of friendship. I followed the Indian back to camp.

He'd found the small grill from the packsack, unfolded the metal legs, and placed it over a fire that was already dying. A blackened pot from the same packsack bubbled on top of the grill. I found my tin cup and poured.

One sip later, I gagged and spit out chunks of ground coffee. I pulled the lid free of the coffeepot to confirm my guess. I held it close to the Indian for his inspection.

"This here percolator holds the ground beans," I observed. "A lot of folks brew coffee by letting water rise and drip through it. Seems better than just pouring the coffee loose into boiling water."

My sarcasm had no effect, for the Indian, of course, just stared at me.

"Tell you what," I offered. "If you believe you're the ugliest, smelliest, most mulish Injun ever to devil a man's life, just keep your mouth shut and don't say a word."

I grinned at his silence. "Glad to see you so quick to agree."

I met his eyes and after a few seconds, he turned his head. I moved to the other horse to get more water, willing to wager that the Indian had been forced to turn his head not because I could outstare him, but because, unless I was entirely mistaken, I'd seen the start of a return smile.

———

We traveled until just before noon. Without urgency, there seemed little reason to push the horses through the punishing heat. We would resume in a couple of hours when the worst of the sun had passed.

I had another reason too for pausing here at the bottom of a hill: Rebecca Montcalm.

Somehow she'd outsmarted me earlier. I'd covered five miles of back trail in the gray of predawn and found no tracks leading away either. This meant not only did she know the ways of the prairie well enough to camp away from the main trail, but she'd also taken the time to brush away all sign of her movement.

I was bothered most by the mistaken assumption I had made earlier, an assumption triggered by the telegraph clerk's surprise that I could read and write. It was a justified surprise, too. He couldn't know that Clara had fought me long and hard to the point where it was easier to learn than to resist her nagging.

Neither, of course, could Rebecca know the same. Yet she had fed me a series of notes, fully expecting that I could read. Why, when to someone like the clerk, it was the opposite?

I'd decided that the answer was in the wording of her notes, all of which I'd memorized. *These are the instructions for your escape . . . it is imperative that you then tie the marshal securely . . . establish an escape route . . . the Indian will accompany you and when appropriate, will deliver further messages . . .*

Formalized phrases. I didn't know anyone who'd spent any time in the territories who used words so fancy that they showed up as big as a skinned horse on a dinner table. Nope, only an easterner would write that note, and only an easterner would assume I could read. So she was only an easterner then, yet one I'd been unable to find in country as familiar to me as city would be to her.

But I would not give up. What I'd try now was a simple waiting game. If she was bringing up the rear guard, sometime sooner or later she would round the far bend at the top of the hill. Her silhouette would be easy to see against the sky, while we were screened by the brush along another dry stream. That silhouette would be all the excuse I'd need to begin chase.

Except we waited long enough for the breeze to shift, and I was rewarded with nothing but a familiar stench. Dead buffalo.

I guessed it to be hundreds of buffalo. I hadn't seen any crows, which meant the meat had to be beyond the horizon ahead of us, and it took more than a couple dozen to rot so bad the smell carried from that far away. I wasn't looking forward to passing through the area.

I caught the Indian giving me a puzzled glance as he wrinkled his nose. It was my turn to shrug. Dead buffalo were common now that the rail could haul carloads of hide back to tanneries in Chicago and New York. Sometimes a man topped a hill to see the glare of sun off weather-whitened bones so far and wide that for a moment he believed the reflection came from a lake. Until he'd move close enough to see the handiwork of a couple of men armed with Sharps rifles who'd shoot for only the hide and tongue. I'd killed buffalo, too, for the railroad and when the meat had gone to good use, but now, with their numbers dwindling, I found it more difficult to comfort myself with any excuses for the slaughter.

The breeze didn't shift, and Rebecca Montcalm didn't appear. There was a benefit in the Indian's silence, however. I didn't have to endure the idle chatter that some men insist on as a way of warding off the vastness of the sky and land around them. I got to thinking, too, that a person could respect this mulish Indian for his tendency not to complain.

Finally I gave up waiting and led our tiny expedition northward into the breeze that carried the stench of dead buffalo.

An hour later, warned miles earlier by not only the stench, but by the hundreds of crows visible in wheeling circles, we reached the buffalo. I had some muscle liniment, which provided little relief to the bruises from my beating, but now helped greatly against the smell, for I rubbed it into my kerchief and then tied the kerchief around my nose, so that I looked like a bandit robbing a stagecoach. The Indian did the same, and we rode through at a trot. Close up to the buffalo, the biting peppermint smell of the liniment pressed tight against my nose barely held the stench at bay. It took five minutes of a good trot to pass by all the dead bodies, ground stained brown from the rivers of blood, bluebottle flies in clusters everywhere, and the obscenity of naked muscle and bone left to rot.

If that wasn't enough to spoil my mood, I didn't find Rebecca Montcalm that night, either.

In fact, we didn't meet anyone else until noon the next day, when we came upon a buffalo skinner who offered me whiskey in the bottles that I promptly shot from his hands.

CHAPTER *16*

IN A WAY, IT WAS pleasing to discover it had taken my body less practice than expected to remember the unthinking response necessary to be accurate in the heat of trouble. I'd sheared both bottles so quickly, it had sounded like one shot. Yet, in another way, it was less than pleasing, for bullets are designed to kill. I decided to remind this buffalo skinner of that fact before he might attempt something stupid.

"The next bullet kicks dust twice," I said. "Once as it hits your shirt, and once as it leaves."

I needn't have worried. The skinner, instantly sober, was too stunned to speak, let alone act. All he'd done was hold up the two bottles of whiskey—one in each hand—to invite me in a slurred voice to step down from my horse and join the fun. Now twin puddles of whiskey at his feet soaked into the grass as he stood unmoving, the necks of the shattered bottles still clutched in his hands.

He was short and pudgy, and he wore a battered felt hat with holes in the brim, holes that cast white circles in the shadow across his face. His goatee was ragged. Silver grizzle covered his chin and throat, grizzle crusty with the grease and caked dirt that also covered his filth-stiffened clothes.

Behind him, two old squaws rocked on their heels and watched me in silence from where they had been scraping a hide near the fire. Behind the squaws stood three tepees. By the markings on the buffalo-hide walls, Pawnee. Most Pawnee were on reservations, so these were renegades, or had been forced by hunger to chase buffalo. Either way, this group should have been reluctant to spend more than a couple days at one site, yet the grass between the tepees was well matted, bones and pieces of hide littered the paths between the tepees, and the fire pit overflowed with ashes.

There was, of course, only one reason for this, the reason that I'd taken savage satisfaction in swinging down from my horse to answer the skinner's invitation with .44-calibre holes. As the Indian and I had ridden near, I'd seen two Pawnee braves passed out at the edge of camp, their faces turned upward to the heat of the sun. Small children sat near them, accustomed already to the sight of their elders in that unnatural stillness.

What I had not seen were any younger squaws. But two mules and a horse hobbled near oxen, and two wagons loaded with buffalo hides, suggested why the squaws were not in sight. And why we'd heard screams from the tepee during our approach. I hoped I wasn't too late.

I looked past the skinner and concentrated on the flaps of the tepees, looking for any response from the other men who had ridden the mules and that horse beside those wagons. By the rifles—easily identified by length and heaviness as Sharps and still in the scabbards at their horses—I knew they were buffalo hunters, working with this skinner, most likely responsible for all the dead buffalo we'd passed earlier. Because they had left their rifles in the scabbards, and because my first two shots had not yet brought them out with guns in hand, I guessed them to be drunk, too, or that they'd spread so much whiskey in this camp that they feared neither theft nor trouble from the braves, a mistake I intended would cost them.

"Drop your pants," I ordered the skinner.

"Huh?"

I was angry enough that I wanted to shoot his left knee-cap. Instead I let my bullet hit the ground between his feet. Before the report had finished echoing, he was yanking at his belt.

"Good," I said when his pants, at his ankles, had effectively hobbled him. His trapdoor long johns were no cleaner than the rest of his clothing. "Now lie down."

He hesitated.

I cocked my pistol. He dropped to his knees and then lowered his chest to the ground.

"We ain't got money," he started to whine. "I don't understand—"

"I'd like to shoot you and your kind dead." It felt like I was biting each word. "Say anything more, and I will."

He must have recognized the rage in the softness of my strained words, for he buried his face in the grass.

I motioned to the old squaws and signed for them to move closer. They did, bloody knives still in their hands. I signed again, instructing them to sit on the skinner's back.

Toothless grins appeared. They were not gentle, these heavy women, as they dropped their hind ends squarely onto his body.

"These squaws ain't blind," I told the skinner. "They've seen what's been happening here. And I imagine they'll be happy to cut your throat if you try to get up."

His reply was a groan.

I holstered my revolver, grabbed the Winchester from my horse, and left the Indian behind me with our horses. Before I could reach the closest tepee, someone inside kicked the flaps open. Two of them walked out. A young squaw. And directly behind her a buffalo hunter. Her face was grim, resolute. His face was sun darkened, mean and leering. He held her braids in his right hand and a knife at her throat with his left.

"Stranger," he said. "Now that I got me a shield, we can have a civilized parley."

Instead of committing my aim at him, I kept the rifle waist high, easy to swing in any direction. I needed to be watchful and ready of the two other tepee entrances.

"I might shoot her dead."

He snorted. "You'd have done it by now. Besides, dead or alive, she'll keep stopping bullets."

One of the children ran up to the squaw and wrapped his arms around her legs. His head barely reached her knee. She reached down to tousle her boy's head. The buffalo hunter yanked her head back at the slight movement.

"So, stranger, what's your game? We ain't got money, just wagons of hide, and you won't travel fast with that."

What *was* my game? Again, I'd reacted with feelings. It was becoming a troublesome habit, one I'd thought long gone. Yet I'd shot a man for beating the Indian, hit Smickles for taunting me, and now let something as common—although vile—as trading whiskey for squaws goad me into this mess. Short of killing these white mongrels, there was little I could do. And I wasn't about to kill—nobody had appointed me judge, and I wouldn't have accepted the position anyway, not when I knew too well that my own sins made it impossible for me to throw the first stone at anyone.

"The game is simple," I finally said. "I want you and the others cleared out of this camp."

He snorted again. "That's no hardship. We'll just find another Pawnee camp."

Again, my anger felt so good it scared me. I raised my rifle and sighted on the half of his head that he allowed to appear from behind the squaw. "Drop the knife."

He smiled, a smile I didn't understand until the explosion of gunfire behind me.

I whirled.

Another man had reached the mules. He held a rifle in his hands, the rifle I expect he'd thought would kill me. Except my Indian had his arms wrapped around the man's waist and was struggling to throw him to the ground, an action that must have thrown off his aim with the first shot. The man raised his rifle butt to smash the Indian's skull, but as he brought the butt down, my bullet took him in the shoulder.

I spun again, slamming the lever action down and up. The buffalo hunter from the tepee had his head lowered in full charge. I didn't shoot. I can't say that in that instant of decision I had held off shooting for any concern about his life. I just knew it would feel better to hurt him with my own hands, and that I had the time to bring my knee up into his chin. I slammed my rifle butt down on the back of his head in the same motion, then stepped aside.

As quickly as that, the animal rage in me died. I had to run to get back of one of the tepees before I lost the contents of my stomach.

When I returned to the Indian, he was dusting himself as he stared down at the injured buffalo hunter, who moaned and clutched his shattered shoulder.

It wasn't difficult to decide what had happened. I'd let myself be lulled by talk while the other hunter had slipped out the back of the far tepee, then gotten to the rifle. I owed the Indian my life.

Before I could thank him, one of the old squaws rose from

the skinner's back and wailed with terror as she pointed at my Indian with a gnarled forefinger of one hand and covered her wailing mouth with the other.

I saw nothing to deserve such a reaction. The squaw was so old she couldn't be a stranger to death.

Yet her wail grew louder, and the other squaw pushed herself awkwardly from the skinner and also started to wail in chorus.

My Indian was as baffled as I. He stared back for several moments, then picked up his medicine bag where it had broken by its strap and began to gather the amulets and bones wrapped in dried feathers that had fallen from it.

I fired a shot into the air to stop the wailing. The only result was that the children behind me added to the wailing as they began to cry. A quick glance showed that three young squaws had gathered their children into them, making a protective circle.

"Where's your whiskey?" I shouted at the skinner.

"Whiskey?"

I knelt and placed the end of my rifle against his temple. "The rest of your whiskey."

I could hardly hear his reply above the noise, but I understood him to mean the saddlebags of the horse. I told him that I'd be taking their horses and guns, but that they could find them several miles ahead on the trail. Throughout that entire conversation, the wailing of the old squaws varied only in pitch.

The Indian and I broke every bottle before we left. It took until the next rise for the eerie sound of that wailing to lose itself in the wind that swept across the open prairie in front of us.

———

Nothing much happened between there and Scottsbluff,

except that we got caught in a thunderstorm that darkened the day into night, soaked the Indian and me into our first bath in days, and terrified our horses into a panic that only ended when we threw blankets over their heads to block the flashes of lightning.

After the days of heat, it felt so good to be drenched by the pelting sheets of cold rain that I stripped and ran naked in circles, yipping glee and shouting joy.

It was one of those crazy things that feels good just because of its craziness. It may have partly happened because of the relief of still being alive after facing down the buffalo hunters, still able to feel, hear, and smell the incredible show of something as common and awesome as a storm. It also may have partly happened because of the tightness, anger, and sorrow I'd been carrying inside about having shot another man. That he was still alive and that I'd fired to save my life and the Indian's did little to appease that tightness, and when the rain hit, I took it as an opportunity to forget everything except for the sensations of rain against skin.

Not even the Indian's sullen refusal to return with me to exuberant boyhood prevented me from dancing and slipping atop the grass until I could hardly raise another war whoop.

His attitude bothered me little, and when the sun returned shortly after, I had the satisfaction of watching him huddle and shiver in his sodden coat as he rode, while I basked in the returning heat, wearing only jeans that dried quickly in the saddle.

In Scottsbluff a day later, the Indian's coat almost got us in trouble. While most of it had dried, because he had worn it the entire time, the inside had not been able to dry, and it magnified his customary noticeable body odor.

We drew plenty of sour looks from people in the one eatery that served this stopping post for travelers on the Oregon Trail. This in itself spoke for the Indian's powers of attraction.

Many of the men casting those sour looks drove oxen and would not have been out of place sharing pens with hogs.

The only solution to this was to send the Indian outside, where he ate sitting in the dirt street. In the eatery I managed to find other conversation to divert the attention of people around me, and in so doing discovered that a lieutenant colonel named George Armstrong Custer was somewhere ahead of us in the Black Hills.

He'd been chosen to command an expeditionary force to disprove rumors of gold in the area, a move that the government hoped would divert prospectors from flooding the area at considerable danger to themselves.

The news of Custer's expedition did not fill my heart with gladness. By the reports, he was only a couple weeks ahead of us, and I could not imagine his presence would endear any new travelers to the Sioux.

Custer, of course, would have no worries—not with ten cavalry troops, two companies of infantry, and one hundred and ten wagons, along with three Gatling guns.

On the other hand, all I had was a couple of revolvers, a Winchester, and a mulish Indian with a smelly coat.

It wasn't until a half hour later, when I'd rejoined the Indian on the street, that I realized the significance of that smelly coat. For almost immediately, the Indian handed me another note from the depths of the coat. *Continue with dispatch.*

I read the note. And smiled.

The coat!

Whatever her game, Rebecca Montcalm would not stay ahead of me for long.

CHAPTER *17*

WE LEFT SCOTTSBLUFF at dawn—the Indian in his usual silence—and headed into a sky now clearing of the smudges of dark clouds that were the last of the storm.

I no longer worried about Rebecca Montcalm on our back trail, for I now understood why I had been unable to track her during the previous days. She wasn't following.

And why should she if she knew where we were going? I cussed myself for all the time I'd wasted in trying to catch someone behind me who was instead in front.

I believed that only two possibilities remained: one of them that she'd gone ahead to Scottsbluff and handed the Indian a note there and now was making her way separately north. This possibility I discounted. My earlier assumption that she was an easterner unfamiliar with the territories now held, except I had some admiration for how she had been a smart enough easterner to know the stupidity of trying to keep up as the Indian and I crossed the Plains. Given that, I figured she was too smart to have waited for us in Scottsbluff, not with the second and more certain possibility that she could simply travel ahead to our final destination and throw me off her trail by sending me on a different route with the Indian while she waited in comfort for us to eventually arrive.

I also think I could now make some reasonable guesses. At the bottom of whatever was happening, there was gold in the Black Hills—stolen money perhaps, or simply a miner's cache of nuggets—marked by a map. Whatever her relationship to this Indian—and it could be as simple as a hired scout—Rebecca Montcalm knew where the gold was. But with so little experience in the territories, she could not get it herself. Harrison, O'Neal, and whoever had ordered them by telegram from Denver also knew about the gold, but not its location. My innocent actions in saving the Indian from Harrison would have shown Montcalm that I was not party to the others who sought the gold. If there was anybody to be trusted, I was the one person—yet it was obvious she couldn't trust me with much more than allowing me to know the gold existed. Were I in her shoes, I would keep distantly safe, too, and string me along with notes for as long as possible.

In the end, it would still come down to the gold. If indeed she was using me to get the gold for herself, she would have to find a way to safeguard it so that once it was found, I didn't become another Harrison or O'Neal. Looking at it from her untrusting viewpoint, it seemed likely that her promise was merely a way to involve me until I was no longer needed, a time when I would become much safer to her if I were dead. I thought of the coyotes beyond the firelight, and how that he-dog had been lured to his death, and decided there was nothing Rebecca Montcalm could do to get me to trust her.

Until I met her, however, I could take some action in seeing how accurate my guesses were, even if the Indian refused to speak. For that, I was waiting until we reached water. Because I now knew how to find the final destination where Rebecca Montcalm waited for my arrival.

———

A few hours' ride after the midday rest break, we reached a creek. To cross it, we descended dried mudbanks torn deep during flood season. It took some coaxing to get our horses down, but the water, barely more than a trickle, would not be difficult to cross.

A stone's throw downstream, however, the water pooled as the creek bed almost doubled back on itself. There, tall cottonwoods provided dappled shade, and it was there that I directed our horses.

I dismounted and dropped my reins to allow my horse to drink at the grassy edge of the pool. The Indian did the same with his horse.

I fumbled with my saddlebag and found my soap, wrapped in grease paper.

"Strip," I ordered.

The Indian's usual sullenness disappeared in a look of questioning disbelief.

"You heard me," I said. "Strip."

He crossed his arms and shook his head no.

I intended to kill two birds with one stone. And one of the birds was the fact that the Indian stunk. Usually a man's bathing habits were his own business, and this Indian had smelled from the git-go, but over the last few days, he'd gotten to the point where he was unbearable unless the breeze blew away from him.

"It's not difficult," I said. "And won't provide you any pain. Take off all your clothing and set it aside. Then get into the water."

He shook his head again and started to back away from me.

"I'm not going to pull a gun," I said. "But if I have to run you down and strip you myself, I will."

And I would. This Indian had kept his heavy clothing on through heat and after rain, when I'd taken as much off as possible to let dry. There had to be a reason for it, and that was the second bird I was hitting with that stone.

My reasoning was that if Rebecca Montcalm was waiting somewhere ahead, she must have armed the Indian with a series of notes to give me along the way. So, while he was scrubbing himself with the soap, I intended to go through his coat and clothes and prove that guess correct by finding all those notes, notes that might also give me an inkling of what to expect in the near future.

The Indian backed away farther.

Without taking my eyes off him, I stepped to my horse and grabbed my lariat.

"If it comes down to it," I threatened, "I'll rope you like a steer."

The Indian came to his decision. He straightened and threw his shoulders back to gather his dignity. He first sat, then pulled off his boots and set his floppy hat beside them. Then he stood, turned away from me, and fumbled with the buttons of his coat.

The coat dropped to the ground. Followed by his pants, which left him in red long johns and a large checked shirt that in the breeze flapped around his butt.

He stopped.

"Go on," I said. "Soap ain't gonna give you blisters."

Moments later the shirt fell. He was now down to the long johns, which from shoulder to ankles sagged on his small frame.

Again, he stopped.

"Get on, will you. I ain't doing this for a thrill," I said. "And I won't even comment on your skinniness."

He crossed his arms in front of him. From where I stood behind, I saw his hands reach up to the top of the long johns, right hand on the left shoulder, left hand on his right shoulder. He didn't let the long johns drop. Instead, with great reluctance he began to peel them down from his shoulders. He had a slender neck—made more slender in appearance by a wide necklace of beads and animal claws—and rounded shoulders with skin so smooth that it startled me into a staggering revelation.

This was not a man.

"Stop," I said.

I'd seen all I needed. This irksome Indian was a woman.

CHAPTER 18

I REMEMBERED HOW I had smugly told myself that if anyone had the skills to backtrack someone on these prairies, it was me. Now I figured I'd have to drown to realize I'd fallen into deep water, for I'd been too stupid to figure this out earlier. This Indian had fallen from the horse during my first ride out of Laramie. This Indian had stopped for water at a poisonous alkaline pond. This Indian had made such a poor pot of coffee, and this Indian had steadfastly refused to speak. All of these were the actions not of an Indian, but of a woman from the East.

"Rebecca Montcalm," I said, for it could be none other than her, "you have plenty sand."

"Sand?" She spoke while still facing away from me, pulling up her long johns again.

"It's a term we use here for courage, ma'am. Courage and plenty nerve."

Save for the quick motion of pulling her

long johns up to her neck again, she had not begun to dress.

"I had little choice," she finally said. "There is little virtue in necessity." Another pause. "May I impose upon you to grant me the privacy of the bath you so recently threatened to force upon me?"

Her words carried an accent of preciseness I'd heard only once before, from a man depending on remittance money from parents who had long resigned themselves to his disgraceful ways and simply paid that money to keep his disgraceful habits an ocean away from where their friends might notice. This man had carried himself almost woodenly and, even when losing that remittance money in great quantities to the poker players who hung around Clara's dance hall, always spoke to me of the need to keep a stiff upper lip.

"Privacy? Of course." I suddenly realized how uncomfortable the filth of her disguise might have been to a woman with an upbringing in England. "I'll remove myself and return when you call."

"Thank you," she answered. "You don't know the envy I felt to listen to you singing as you soaped yourself at those other rivers."

My face flushed. It hadn't occurred to me how much I'd been sharing with this Indian. And I remembered my now understandably solo rain dance during the thunderstorm.

"Rebecca Montcalm," I said, "when I return, you have a lot to account for."

———

When I returned, she was in her long johns, the red material now wet, with her upper body covered by her shirt, also wet. Draped over a nearby branch were her pants, dripping dry. It explained why it had taken so long for her to call me. She'd washed her clothes, too.

She was standing in bare feet at the side of the creek,

leaned sideways to squeeze dry her unbraided hair. She smiled at my approach, leaned the other direction, and repeated the squeezing with her hands. Rivulets of water streamed down her wrists and dropped from her elbows.

"Would it be a great inconvenience if we waited here for the breeze to—" She broke off.

I hadn't returned her smile. The time she'd taken to wash was time that had let me grow angry.

"You, ma'am, have been a great inconvenience," I said. "Furthermore, you've played me for a fool."

"Have I?" She studied me. The muscles around her eyes tightened and her voice lost its light happiness. "I'm under the impression you left Laramie with an Indian because he saved you from the gallows. And because you expected great wealth. Both selfish reasons, it seems to me. Why should it matter I was that Indian?"

"Because . . ." I snapped my mouth shut. Put like that, I had no answer. On the other hand, how long had she led me along like a blind idiot?

I opened my mouth again.

"And my understanding of fools," she interrupted, "is that generally they only have themselves to blame for their foolishness."

I snapped my mouth shut again. She certainly had a way of getting a man's attention. I found myself looking closely at her, which became, in truth, my first occasion to truly *see* Rebecca Montcalm.

Before, as the Indian, her braids had been sloppy pieces of rope; here, her loose hair fell over her shoulders in thick, if damp, luxury. Before, the flashes of her face had shown greasy smudged dirt; here, her skin was a light dusk stretched smooth. Before, hidden by the bulky coat, she had walked bowed and head cast downward as if in shame; here, she stood tall and proud, and her shirt, weighted with water, no longer concealed the womanhood I had not suspected.

She returned my gaze with a calm dignity that defied the essential absurdity of a barefooted woman in saggy wet red long johns. In that moment, as my cloud of anger dropped to be replaced by an awareness of Rebecca Montcalm as the woman she was, it felt like my breathing had developed a hitch.

For she was beautiful. Definitely Indian, but beautiful.

Strands of her black hair danced against her forehead and high curved cheekbones. Her face showed a haunting untamable wildness, yet to me her half smile promised joy and long shared nights. Her features were unblemished and perfect, yet the duskiness of her skin stayed any porcelain fragility.

I've seen beauty before, the outward moldings of flesh that cause men to pant and follow, and seen enough of that hollow beauty not to trust it. But I thought of her long, uncomplaining hours in the saddle. How she'd shared the chores I'd thrown upon her. Danced the hot-lead dance without crying in fear. Fought the train conductor. Come up—regardless of the fact that in the end it had had Evrett's blessing—with a plan to bust me loose from jail. And finally, I remembered her grittiness as Harrison kicked her almost to death. Whatever magnificence Rebecca Montcalm showed on the outside— and it matched anything I'd ever seen, including Clara's—she had double on the inside, as hinted by the softness of her smile and happiness of her voice when I'd first returned to this pool to confront her with my anger. And as more than hinted by the steel of her own answering coolness and sharp reply to my rudeness.

Unaccountably, at least to me, for I felt like a tongue-tied boy, she averted her eyes to look downward.

I took my hat from my head, held it humbly against my chest, and searched for any words to break our awkward silence.

"Ma'am, what say I go back to my horses, turn around, come up here just like before. Except this time when you smile and ask about inconveniences, I won't say anything that gives you the opportunity to rightfully accuse me of being selfish or foolish."

She looked at me again and smiled. A nice reward for my efforts.

"Please save yourself the walk," she said. She extended her hand. "I should have done this much earlier. My name is Rebecca Montcalm."

"Samuel Keaton," I said. Her fingers were smooth and cool to my touch. "The pleasure is mine."

It probably struck her, too, the silliness of formalities given our situation, because she grinned with me.

"I can't imagine what the sisters might say about this," she said, gesturing at her undergarments. "For that matter, I can scarcely believe this myself. What on earth possessed you to demand me to strip?"

I explained. She nodded several times. When I finished, she was silent.

"So . . ." I said.

"So?"

We were low enough that the walls of the gully blocked any view of the horizon. A part of me prickled, only slightly, to be spending so much time in what was essentially a trap in the earth. But the breeze was pleasant here, and I wanted answers.

"So where are you going to start with your story?" I ticked off my questions, finger by finger. "Who are you? What are we chasing? How is—" I grimaced. "How *was* Harrison involved? And why me?"

She walked past me and up onto a rise of the bank, where she found a fallen tree to use as a seat. I was forced to follow.

I didn't like that, her subtle way of taking control of our conversation.

She ran her fingers through her hair, eyes closed with her face upturned to the sun. I swung my leg over the log and sat as if in a saddle, arm's length down from her. When she opened her eyes, I held four fingers out, to remind her of the questions I ticked, one by one.

"I'd like to know who I am," she said. "That's why I'm here."

She reached out and folded down my index finger. "I'm not certain what it is that we seek." She folded down my second finger. "John Harrison's appearance was a vaster surprise to me than it could have been to you." Now the third finger. "And I had no one to trust until I saw you risk your life for a total stranger."

With the final finger folded down, I was left with a fist, one that I pounded against my forehead in theatrical anguish. "You don't know who you are? Rebecca Montcalm is not your name?"

"It's the name the sisters gave me, on the insistence of a patron."

"You mentioned them earlier. Sisters."

She nodded. "I was raised in a convent on the outskirts of London."

I tried to keep a straight face. "Sisters. Convent. London."

She nodded again, with a frown of concentration.

Now I smiled. "Yes, ma'am. If you'll excuse me, I want to hold my hat under my horse's tail. I expect since the day's arrived that I'm sitting in the middle of the prairies with a nun in red underwear, that horse oughta be ready to drop gold clumps instead of—"

"I'm not a nun," she said. "The sisters raised me. I came

of age last December and left with what little inheritance remained. Left for here."

I lifted my hat and scratched my head. And grinned. "Ever since you were a bitty girl, you dreamed about being a cowboy, just like in them dime novels."

She stood. "Every night since I was a"—she spat the words—" 'bitty girl', I cried myself to sleep. I wanted golden hair and cream skin, just like the other orphans. Every morning, I looked into the mirror and saw cheekbones that resembled the ones of engravings of savages." Her voice dropped but didn't lose anger. "That's what they called me, the others, when the sisters weren't nearby. Savage girl. The older ones called me circus girl, something I didn't understand until I found out who my mother was. Then I vowed to find her land, to see what had been taken from her."

Rebecca's face became a mask of icy rage. I put up a hand to stop her outburst.

"No," she said. "You sit and listen."

Charlie snorted and stamped. That's what I should have listened to.

"It took a month in the belly of a ship to get to New York. Another month to reach Saint Louis, a month where every day men tried to rob me and worse. Since then, I've been kidnapped, beaten, and dragged across the wilderness by horse. I've stunk, been bitten by fleas, and had someone force me to strip. I'm alone and have never felt so alone in my entire life. And now you expect me to look at that smugly grinning face of yours and smile pretty in return."

She started walking away. "Go back to your horse," she said. "Fill your hat. I promise you it won't be gold."

She took several more steps without looking back.

Charlie snorted and stomped again. This time, however, I saw why.

Rebecca screamed anger when I picked her up by the waist.

By then, I was running full speed.

She hit me once across the face, but I didn't slow.

I didn't set her down until we reached the horses.

"Stand between the horses," I said. "Hold the reins and keep them around you."

I didn't wait for her reply. I was already sprinting to reach my Winchester.

She didn't argue. For now she saw what I saw, what Charlie had heard much earlier.

Warrior braves. Maybe a dozen. In full color. Outlined against the sky on top of the north wall of the gully.

I swept my eyes to check the creek bed for any others. And a dozen more rode slowly to the edge of the south wall of the gully to stare down in silence upon us.

CHAPTER 19

SILENCE AROUND US became unbearably loud, the swish of a horse's tail magnified, and it seemed I could hear each individual blade of grass as it whispered in the wind.

That's what fight fear will do to you once the panic disappears. Everything is keener—colors brighter, edges sharper. It was clear to see, at a hundred yards, the serrated tips of the eagle feathers that fluttered from a warrior's spear.

Ready for battle as I was, I did not fire the Winchester.

That would have been suicide.

Once, in Texas, on the Santa Fe trace, I'd been followed for several days by a large party of Comanches. Every time they moved in close, I dismounted, squatted on one knee to make myself a smaller target, and pointed my rifle at the foremost brave—a move that each time turned them back, until finally they'd quit. Had I fired and killed one, it would have forced them to take the fight to me, and ants would have picked my bones clean.

Today, we were probably dead anyway, but I wasn't prepared to give up on an outside chance. They hadn't attacked. Maybe they were just curious, passing through, and weren't willing to risk the death of one of their party.

"Rebecca," I said in a low voice, "we're going to walk our horses through the cottonwoods until we reach the overhang of the bank on the other side."

It was the best I could do. Our backs would be protected, for the overhang was deep and curved inward to match the bend of the stream, and the Indians would have to ride down into the gully to attack us. If necessary, we'd kill the horses to use them as a fortress wall in front. And we'd have water close by to reach during the night. If we lived that long.

"Move together," I said.

She stayed with me. Her face was grim, but panic had not frozen her. I'd seen men with more experience less calm and seen plenty others in this kind of danger lose their nerve enough to wet themselves.

I held my breath as we took the first steps. Our direction of movement would instantly tell the warriors our plan. If they wanted us dead, they'd either attack in the next few seconds or outwait us.

We reached the cottonwoods. Rebecca had not yelped once as her bare feet covered the rough ground. I took a chance and stepped away from our horses to get her boots and hat from where she'd undressed. No shots were fired at us.

A few steps later, I breathed some. Now the trees gave us protection. Another ten seconds brought us to the overhang. From there, I could only see the south edge of the gully. The warriors there had not moved.

"All right," I said. "We keep the horses in front and stay here."

"For how long?" she asked.

"I don't know. They might want us. They might want our horses. They might want to move on and have a good laugh at how they scared us."

She took her boots and pulled them on.

"Tuck your hair into your shirt," I said. "If they haven't yet guessed you're a woman, we don't want it to get their attention later . . ."

Far down the creek bed, the warriors from the north bank descended.

". . . or sooner," I finished.

"You're bleeding," Rebecca told me.

I became aware of the taste of blood and remembered. "You hit me."

"I thought . . ." She stopped. "You grabbed me. I thought . . ."

"In a convent, you learned what men wanted?"

"The sisters warned us . . ."

"Had it been my intention, it would have happened earlier."

"Yes," she said after a moment's thought. "You let me bathe in peace. You discovered I was not a man and didn't try what . . . what others had suggested when I was traveling as a woman."

In her place, I probably would have disguised myself the same. Hid that I was a woman to spare myself the grief. It must be some powerful thing to keep spurring her on, a woman alone on the unfamiliar prairies, when the very sight of her would lead some men to simply take what they wanted.

The warriors from the south bank joined the first group in the gully. I counted twenty.

"It's them," I said, pointing, "who you need to fear."

Bunched in rifle range as they were, I might have been able to hit four or five before they scattered. That encouraged me. When warriors were serious about killing, you either didn't see them, or they were riding at you full tilt.

"They mean to kill?" she asked.

"If they don't move on, and we can't win, that's what you would pray for," I said.

Out of the corner of my eyes, I sensed her remove her gaze from them to focus again on me.

"If they attack," I said in answer, "this is what we do." Without taking my attention from the warriors, I set the butt of the Winchester down and leaned the barrel against my leg, fumbled with the buckles of my saddlebag, and grabbed my other Colt.

"Watch my hands," I said. I did not look down but trusted she would. I opened the chamber of the gun. Closed it. Opened it. Handed it to her. Got the Winchester back into my hands.

"Open and close the chamber," I said.

I heard the click of oiled metal. Then again. My eyes were still on the warriors. The sun was behind them, but high enough that I wasn't blinded. A few carried rifles—ancient flintlocks that did not inspire fear. The others carried bows and short killing clubs, chunks of wood with protruding nails and decorated with feathers and blood-stained pieces of fur. Most of the warriors were older, encouraging in one way because hotheaded young bucks are usually the ones responsible for dead whites, but discouraging because seasoned warriors fight smarter.

"I understand the mechanism," Rebecca said.

"Good. If they attack, I'll empty the rifle first. We'll reload it later if we can. Otherwise, I'll be firing one revolver while you load the other. Shells are in the saddlebag. I intend to fire five shots and hand the revolver back with one shell remaining. You'll hand me the fresh pistol with six bullets in the chamber."

"One shell remaining? Why not fire six?"

"Because of why you should pray they kill you. If I'm hit bad, you'll have one bullet left for yourself."

A sharp intake of breath from her. Still, it was no time to candy words. "You don't want to be captured alive," I said. "Not when they'll kill you slow over the next week. Not with twenty of them wanting turns for their fun with you."

"No." She had disbelief in her voice.

"No?" I kept my chin almost on Charlie's rump and stared at the braves. "I've found men buried in the sand up to their chin. Blind from the sun because their eyelids had been cut off. Faces chewed away because the Injuns had led a trail of honey from a nearby antpile to their ears and nostrils."

Rebecca placed her hand on my arm. "I shall believe you," she said quietly. "Please don't make this horrible waiting any worse."

"You understand, then." There was plenty more I could tell her about Indian trouble, but my burdens were my own.

"I don't want to, but I can tell by your face that you mean it." She removed her hand from my arm as a warrior broke away from the group and rode slowly toward us.

"Interesting," I commented. "Stay behind the horses."

I stepped in front. So far, no rifles had been raised, no bows taken in hand. I figured I'd have enough time to duck behind the horses should any warrior make a move, and there was no harm now in appearing brave and fearless—two qualities of any fool in battle.

The warrior rode to the cottonwoods. He had to be conscious of my rifle. I'd guess he was gambling that if I meant to shoot, I'd have started. Now *he* could appear brave and fearless, which only proved that blustering stupidity is common to menfolk regardless of the color of their skin.

Just before reaching the cottonwood trees, he jabbed his spear downward and plucked Rebecca's coat from the ground where she had first dropped it at my insistence.

The warrior turned and rode equally slowly back to his companions. There, the oldest ones pointed at the coat and conferred for several minutes. Finally, the warrior left his companions and rode toward us again.

He continued through the cottonwoods and moved so close to us that I could see the wrinkles at the corners of his eyes and the single strands of gray hair among the black that fell to his shoulders.

He wore a feather medallion on the side of his head—white ermine skins dangled from it and fell almost to his chest. He'd painted his face and bare upper body with swirling designs of red. His horse, too, like the horses of all the warriors behind, was marked with sacred designs of war paint. There was a decorated buffalo robe slung across his saddle. A fire-hardened buffalo shield lay across his back. And great dignity in his steady gaze. I prepared myself for the slow and ungainly difficulties of negotiation through sign language.

"Ghost Rider," he said, slow and heavy. "We wish to speak."

I should have been surprised that he spoke English. But more surprises now were like extra rain in a heavy flood. They just rolled off me.

"No man here is called Ghost Rider," I said.

He motioned behind him. "That is what you are called. For our best trackers lost your trail every night. As if you were a spirit. You knew you were followed?"

I shrugged. I hadn't, of course, or I wouldn't have spent so much time in this draw. It had just been my usual precautions before making camp. But it wouldn't hurt to let them think I knew more than I did.

"Why do the Pawnee follow?" I asked. He showed no

surprise that I knew enough of Indian tribes to know they were Pawnee. I didn't ask his name. That was an insult to Indians. He'd tell me if he wanted.

"Why follow? For the same reason that the old ones called one who speaks the white men's tongue to join these warriors," he replied. "To speak to you without causing bloodshed."

He understood my questioning look.

"We have no wish for you to die. You punished the men who supplied our people with the devil's drink."

The men at the buffalo hunt. I thought that over. He still hadn't given me the reason for their pursuit. If it was gratitude, they didn't need warriors to express it.

I tried the same question from a different angle. "If you do not wish me to die, why so many warriors?"

"Ghost Rider," he said. "It is your companion we seek. The one who wore the coat."

That, of course, didn't surprise me either. Not after all the other trouble she had managed to attract.

"You wish to send greetings?"

"No." Not even a smile at my attempted humor. "She must travel with us."

It complicated things that they knew Rebecca was not a he. Had a scout seen her bathing?

"For what reason must she travel?" I tried to keep a poker face that matched his.

"The old ones seek her."

I shook my head. "My companion has hired me as a guide."

"Ghost Rider," the Indian said in the same measured tones, "the old ones have sent with us many furs as a gift to you. Yet they have also commanded us to return with your companion. Even if we must kill to do so."

While the terms were now clear—give up Rebecca or die—the why had escaped me.

"For what reason?" I asked again.

"If I turn my horse away from you," he said, "it means we attack."

"Many of yours shall die, too."

"The old ones have spoken. So shall it be." He stared at me for another minute. I said nothing. Finally, without expression, he nudged his pony away from me and returned to the war party.

They did not attack immediately. Not when it was certain that some of them would be killed. The Indian way was to wait until they could do the most damage with the least amount of risk.

From their vantage point, this was perfect. We were bottled in a deep hole in the side of the bank. All they needed was to make camp in the gully to cork us in solid.

I told Rebecca to settle in for a long wait.

CHAPTER 20

I'D NEVER SEEN NOR HEARD of an Indian battle quite like this one. The warriors almost ignored us. Only a couple hundred yards away and well within rifle range, they set up tepees and made fires and strolled and chatted as if they were squaws behind a buffalo hunt.

Their reason for staying near was obvious. Any farther away and we could easily slip past them out of the gully during the night. Instead, by camping so close, they effectively sealed us in, for if we tried to move our horses past them while they slept, their dogs would give clear alarm. And it was unthinkable that we move without our horses. Men on foot simply do not survive.

The Indians must have decided that I realized the stupidity of firing on their camp. I'd be lucky to kill more than one or two warriors before they found cover, and there was little percentage in me beginning a pitched gunfight.

On the other hand, I decided that they realized the stupidity of a frontal attack on me. With my repeating rifle and six-shot revolvers, I'd have an excellent chance at dropping a dozen of them before they covered half the distance between us and the camp. Attack from above was impossible, with the gully bank so steep and our cave so deep into the side of the bank.

What I couldn't figure, though, was why they hadn't taken any potshots from a distance. Were their guns empty of ammo? That happened often enough. Sometimes Indians fired nails or small stones from their muskets. Other times they'd dig out cartridge balls that had been shot at them. Regardless of their reason, I was happier to be watching than fighting.

After lending Rebecca a pair of pants from my saddlebag, I'd managed to drag a few logs close and pile dirt around them, two hours of silent dirty work that Rebecca had shared without complaint. By the time we finished, we had a crude waist-high barricade, with room for a fire behind. We tethered our horses to the side—if the Indians got close enough to steal them, they were close enough to kill me, and I figured at that point horse rustling would be the least of my problems. Our canteens were three-quarters full, and I'd be able to crawl to the creek during the night, so I didn't worry about water. We still had plenty of dried fruit and pemmican. It meant we could last a couple weeks if we managed to stay alert that long.

"We'll sleep in shifts," I told Rebecca at the end of our preparations. We had about an hour of sunlight left. Already orange and purple streaks of cloud lined the sky at the horizon, a sight I'd appreciate under any other circumstances. "I'm sure they'll attack at night."

She nodded. Clumps of dirt had stuck to the side of her sweating face. I dabbed water from my canteen onto the bunched end of my handkerchief and offered it to her. She smiled and sighed and sat back as she mopped her face clean.

"Well," I said. "Unless you play cards, time'll pass mighty slow."

"You're not afraid?"

"More'n you'd guess," I said. "But we got plenty reason for hope."

"They are camped in a horde. We are only two."

I shook my head. "Injuns are coyote smart." I snorted. "Not like whites. In a spot like this, since an army general stays behind and watches the fight, he figures out how many men he might lose. He's got twenty soldiers, decides five are going to die to take the two of us, and his math tells him that leaves fifteen soldiers for the next fight. A white soldier does his math, too. Five outta twenty are gonna die? He's got a three in four chance of surviving, and because the alternative is court martial, he lets the general send him ahead. Not Injuns. They fight together and like dying as little as you and I. Drives army men crazy that Injuns won't hang around to fight like was done by both armies in the Civil War. Unless Injuns figure there's a good chance of no one dying, they attack later. Or find an easier target. All we need to do is convince them there's a good chance a couple will die, and they'll leave us alone."

She looked at me for long moments, as if undecided what to say next. What came out surprised me.

"That scar," Rebecca said. "Is it part of how you know so much about life out here?"

I raised an eyebrow.

"We've traveled all these miles," she explained. "It's readily apparent you belong on the frontier. You know the habits of these Indians. I thought perhaps the scar . . ."

In reflex, I rubbed my cheek. Along a thin diagonal line, the scar led from just off the side of my nose down to my jawbone. Most days it still itched. All days it provided for an extra five minutes of shaving as I scraped around it.

"No," I told her, "it was a result of knowing too little."

I stared off at the Indian camp. I could see no one staring back.

"Will you tell me more?"

"Man hit me with the barrel of his revolver," I said flatly. "Front sight ripped open what you see now."

Then I realized that she, of course, could not know how painful my memories were, so I relaxed the flat anger that I felt.

"Mighta been worse," I told her with a rueful smile. "Couple seconds earlier, he had that gun barrel pressed into my nose and ready to pull the trigger."

It flashed through my mind, an image of Gray Eyes and the pleasure in his face to have me on my knees and facing death at his hand.

"How about we have you answer a few questions instead," I said immediately. I motioned at the Indian camp. "There's time, and I can't see the situation getting much worse."

I moved behind her and picked up the medicine bag. "Start with this," I said.

She took it from me, her face half flared in panic for the briefest of heartbeats. Then she, too, relaxed.

"My apologies," she said. "It's just that this satchel is all that links me to my mother."

I waited.

Rebecca loosed the leather drawstring of the medicine bag. She removed a small flat cloth-wrapped object. It took several minutes for her to untie the string around the cloth, for she worked very carefully. She peeled back the cloth to reveal two almost square slats of thin wood, one atop the other.

"Please be careful as you lift it apart," she said as she handed it to me.

I was careful. I discovered a photograph. Silvers, whites, and blacks in sharp outlines. It showed a small group of Indians in full Plains dress, with stern scowled faces. Yet the background was not horizon and sky. It was brick buildings, dulled in this photo by a lack of sunlight.

"At the far right," Rebecca said. "That was my mother."

The lines of the photograph had grown fuzzy with age, but not so much that I couldn't see that the woman in the buckskin dress on the right-hand side was young and beautiful and bore an uncanny resemblance to Rebecca. In front of her legs, two small Indian children stood and also faced the camera. Beside her, although there was a gap between her and the next, were those Indians of different ages, from a squat, gray-haired squaw to young bucks.

"That you?" I asked, referring to the children.

"No," Rebecca said. "As near as I can know, they belonged to another woman. I was only a baby, already in the orphanage."

I gave her back the photograph. She spent the next moments reverently wrapping the slats in cloth and retying the string around it.

"I'll tell you all I know," she said. "For what do I have left to lose?"

There was no answer to that, no matter how brightly I'd tried to paint our situation with my talk about the ways that Indians fought and how our death was not certain.

"My mother and the other Indians were captured by an English expedition to the Great American Desert in 1853," Rebecca said. "This land here was called that, wasn't it? Before the frontier was pushed this far?"

I nodded. It did not feel civilized at this moment—not with twenty braves holding us at bay—but in comparison to

'53, the territories now were models of settlement. Back then the mountain men were nearly the only ones who knew the country. Yes, it had been a vast wilderness.

"When I left London this spring," Rebecca said, "the English were still fascinated with American savages. In 1853, I imagine, it fascinated them much more, to hear rumors of red-skinned barbarians who hunted buffalo with arrows and spears. The expedition had one purpose, of course. To find a family of Injuns and take them back to England."

"Which explains the brick wall background of that photo."

"Yes," she said. "The Injuns were paraded around the country to the applause of great crowds. The newspaper reports I found even told of a live buffalo that traveled the train with them. At each stop, the Injuns set up tepees and admission was charged. The business partners who sponsored this made a fancy profit, for the Injuns were little more than slaves to them."

I could see her tenseness in the slight quivering of muscles along her jawline.

"We just fought a war over slavery," I said. "Times are changing."

She nodded slightly, but from the rigid way she now sat, I knew this was not easy for her to discuss. *Would I be telling her about Gray Eyes*, I wondered. *No, that was much worse.*

"I was born shortly after the expedition's arrival in London," she finally began again, "Apparently, it was"—an angry wrinkle furrowed her forehead—"'less than convenient for the showmen. Perhaps if they'd been equipped with a papoose, I too would have been paraded from train stop to train stop. Instead, they placed me in an orphanage. My mother died— all of the Indians died—within a year. Influenza."

Rebecca looked me full in the face. Her dark eyes gleamed with the beginning of tears. "I've wondered again and again how it felt for my mother to have her baby taken away. First stolen from her land, then parted from me. Did my mother feel anguish to have me taken away? Or relief?"

I met her grief without flinching. During the quietness, I thought about what she'd just told me.

"The satchel," I said after a minute of silence. "How did you get it?"

"From the sisters."

"You mentioned that. What I mean is where did the sisters get it? From your mother? Did she leave it behind at the orphanage when they took you away from her?"

Rebecca nodded.

"First understand that it's not a satchel," I said. "It's a medicine bag. Injuns hold the medicine bag to be sacred. At that Pawnee camp, I saw you scatter dried bones and feathers from that bag, feathers and bones the Injuns believed you could use to tell the future, call ancestors, ward off evil, cure ills."

Rebecca's eyes widened.

"I'm picturing a young woman about to lose her baby, knowing she'll never be able to give her daughter a thing," I continued, to share what I had decided in the earlier silence. "No love, no songs to lull you to sleep in her arms. I reckon in place of all that, she left behind for you the most important object in her life. The medicine bag."

"Thank you," Rebecca said softly. Her posture softened, and she held the medicine bag close to her chest.

I hardly heard her. What had I just said? *I saw you scatter dried bones and feathers from that bag.* And hadn't the old squaws seen it, too, just before beginning their unceasing wails?

"Let's have a closer look at the medicine bag. Maybe those old squaws recognized it because of the beading."

It was, I thought, a good guess. The beadwork on the

front and back was distinctive. It showed a bright Sioux pattern of thunderbirds and stars, beading that must have taken hours and hours of quillwork.

I squinted in puzzlement. Sioux beadwork. Why would old Pawnee squaws have an interest in something Sioux? I tried a different tact.

"Rebecca, what else is in the bag?"

She stiffened again.

"I won't take it from you," I said. "Just show me."

She reached in and pulled out a bear's claw amulet.

I whistled. "That's strong medicine," I said. "Most Injuns hold a grizzly is a man returned from the dead, from the way it looks after it's been skinned. Killing one is like counting coup."

She showed me a weasel skin, eagle feather, a short piece of an army cartridge belt, and a bracelet of tightly strung blue beads. She also didn't show me the one object that she had to fish around to retrieve the rest. I suspected it had to do with the gold. But I didn't push.

I motioned with my head at the Indian camp down the gully. "Didn't he tell us that the elders sent him along with the warriors?"

Rebecca agreed.

"Can you think of any reason at all the Pawnee elders would want you?"

"No. I've only just arrived here by train."

"Then all I can guess is that those squaws recognized your medicine bag or more likely something from it, and word got back to the elders. Whatever it was—if I'm guessing right—it's important enough that they don't want you dead."

And, if I was guessing right, that's why they hadn't yet begun to snipe bullets in our direction. Maybe they were afraid a stray shot might kill my companion.

Rebecca could recall nothing of her past to agree or disagree, and by her quietness, it appeared she wanted to lose herself in her own thoughts. So as the sun set, I studied on my theory for a while. Until another event cleanly took my mind from those studies.

Another dozen warriors rode into camp. That in itself was not so unusual. What did get my attention was the white man who rode with them. Will O'Neal.

CHAPTER 21

REBECCA HAD ANSWERED two of my questions: I now understood who she was, and that, as she'd confirmed, it had been my ill-timed attempt to rescue her from Harrison that had convinced her to place some trust in me, the passing stranger.

I had a host of other questions, of course. Who was behind the telegrams? Was it the same person from Denver who'd sent the telegram ordering Smickles to kill me, who had also given orders to Harrison and O'Neal? And why was O'Neal now in the camp just down the draw? These, however, were questions I didn't expect Rebecca to answer. Yet she *could* tell me what we were chasing. And how John Harrison had been involved.

Unfortunately, little daylight remained. I did not dare delay much past dark to move us, since rather than remain behind our barricade, I preferred to hide nearby where I could shoot any Indians who tried to ambush our campfire.

And once we moved, there could be no conversation to give away our presence. So, if we survived the night, I'd have to wait until morning for her next answers.

I explained to her why I was packing up the Winchester, pistols, and boxes of cartridges.

"When we find cover," I said, "sleep if you can. I'll be watching for Injuns the night through and will expect you to let me sleep during the day. But don't be surprised if you wake up to guns firing, for I have no intention of letting them take our horses. And once I start firing, we'll have to move around."

"We'll be away from our little fort," she said. "Won't they be able to—"

"If we stay in our fort, they'll be able to sneak close at night and make an effective charge. If we stay out of the fort, they won't be able to pin us down in the dark. We know anybody not *us* is *them*. So I'll have the luxury of shooting anything that moves. Once one or two get killed, they'll leave us alone."

She looked upward at the overhang of earth. "If we are able to move out of here in the dark," she said, "can we not scale the walls of this gully and escape?"

"Sure," I replied, "if you want to be dead before noon tomorrow."

"I don't understand."

"Our horses can't scale the walls," I told her. "On foot we might be able to make ten miles by dawn. These Injuns would track us down before the sun has burned away the dew."

She nodded understanding. I warned her again that nothing more could be said until daylight, not even a whisper, and she nodded again.

We crept away from our barricade. I led her to the spot I'd chosen during daylight, a small group of boulders that would give us cover, yet let me watch our fire and the light it gave me to aim. Once among the boulders, I knew we were invisible. The only risk would occur when I snuck back to push more logs to keep the fire alive as our decoy.

———————

Several hours passed, hours during which I worried and gnawed at all the questions, an activity that did little more than frustrate me, yet served to keep me awake.

I sat with my back against a boulder and counted the slow progress of time by the arc of the full moon as it traveled from the horizon upward. Few clouds blurred the brilliance of the stars, and as my eyes adjusted to the pale, almost blue moonlight, I found it easy to scan the trees and gully for movement. That helped me relax. We were reasonably close to the fire, and the earlier I could see and shoot at any approaching Indians, the better our chances.

Rebecca shifted in her sleep. She, too, was sitting up, and the movement caused her to fall against me. I did not push her way.

Lonely, thin howls of a coyote broke the silence, to be answered by yipping much farther away.

It reminded me of a she-coyote beyond the campfire, and I remembered my earlier vows not to trust the unseen Rebecca Montcalm. Now she was almost in my arms, and her nearness had an impact I could not ignore. Not when I could recall the half hitch in my breathing when I'd first studied her face. Not when I could recall that glimpse of the outline of her womanly profile when she'd begun to peel the long johns down to her shoulders.

Still, something disturbed me. I searched my mind for long minutes before I found it. Hadn't she begun to tell me her story by pointing at the Indian camp and admitting she had nothing to lose? Did that mean she would have hidden things about herself if she thought we would actually survive? And had I been right in deciding there was something in the medicine bag that she wanted hidden from me?

She pressed harder against me in her sleep, then, as if seeking warmth, rolled toward me and clutched her arms around my upper body.

I did not move. Her deep even breaths continued, and she settled against me, asleep almost in my lap.

I let my arms rest on top of her side, for I wanted to be able to shoot quickly should the shadows of any Indians appear.

Her breathing changed. She did not move. Rather, she became completely motionless. Awake? Aware of our closeness? I did not have to wonder long, because her hand stole softly up my chest and neck, and she lightly touched my lips with the tip of her forefinger.

I kept watching the trees for Indians.

She turned her head upward. I could feel her staring at my face.

I kept watching the trees for Indians.

Her breathing grew deep again, so deep and warm that I could feel her ribs expand and contract with each breath, but this breathing did not have the ordered rhythm of sleep.

I kept watching the trees for Indians.

She pulled herself up and lightly, slowly kissed the scar on my face. Her hair was satin, and I relaxed the grip on one of my Colts to lift my hand and run my fingers through its softness. She kissed me again, less lightly, less softly, as she moved her lips from my cheek to my own lips.

Had the Indians chosen that moment to steal forward, our capture would have been certain, for I finally bowed my head downward and for long moments returned her hunger.

I'd been kissed before. This was different. Innocent, yet charged with passion. This kiss was without calculation, timeless and untaught. She'd been in a convent her whole life until this spring, a lifetime in a world without men. I could not believe she was anything more or less than she appeared, and I forgot all thoughts about the she-coyote beyond the camp-fire.

She pulled tighter and closer as we kissed without sound, and from that kiss by itself I felt more completeness than there had ever been from women who'd given much more. It hadn't been since Clara that my heart responded like this to any act of love.

Yet, I could not help but skitter at a kiss that could seem to mean so much. And I realized why. What did I represent to her, so soon after the convent, to be the man who had saved her life and now protected her? Had the kiss meant less, I probably would have continued. But I could not risk the feelings she now brought, could not risk returning what she was giving, for I knew my pains too well. And the first man in her life should not be one to leave her.

I willed myself to push away from our kiss.

She pulled my head toward her, and again, I resolutely pushed away. I caught her startled glance in the moonlight. What she saw in my face, I cannot say. But she withdrew from me and found her original position and sat back against the rock.

I stared straight ahead and resumed my vigil. Not a single word had been exchanged, yet I knew already a trust had been offered and spurned.

I cursed myself. Only days earlier, I had declined a woman's invitation because it held no meaning, and now I had done so again because of too much meaning. Through the night watch's long hours my mind kept returning to the ache of my final night in jail, when that long look into the barrels of Smickles' shotgun had forced me to acknowledge there was something beyond life, something powerful and unknowable that whispered to a man's instincts when he permitted quietness around his soul. Rebecca's kiss had been so rich with promise that, for a moment, it seemed as though I had reached into that beyond to touch part of what might fill the ache I always carefully ignored. It made it that much worse now, the return of withered hollowness when I could still feel so clearly the small part of fullness that had just been offered.

I don't believe Rebecca slept either, and when occasionally her shoulder touched mine, she flinched. It was small consolation that dawn arrived and we returned to the small fort without incident.

The sight that greeted us with the rising sun was O'Neal, hanging by his wrists from a leather rope attached to the branch of a lone tree at the edge of their camp. His feet barely touched the ground.

If he did not support his weight by pushing upward with his toes—an agony impossible to sustain—he would be forced to hang slackly so that his arms almost pulled from their sockets, with the leather cord around his wrists cutting into his skin. To compound his agony, he was helpless against flies, mosquitoes, and thirst. And the day would not get cooler.

"Why?" Rebecca asked. Those were her first words to me, breaking a silence that had somehow made our cramped quarters behind the barricade seem like wide open range.

I had been asking myself the same.

"You're sure he's not familiar," I said. "Maybe his face is clearer now in the daylight."

She shook her head no, the same answer she'd given the previous evening when O'Neal had been on horseback.

"What I didn't tell you last night was that I did know

him." I watched O'Neal twist at the end of the leather rope as he vainly stabbed his toes downward. "Now it appears you don't have much to worry about. Leastways in regards to him."

"I don't understand," she said.

"First met him in Laramie," I replied. "In jail. Said he was a journalist from New York. By the eastern accent, I believe New York. For other reasons, I disbelieve journalist. Instead, I think he was chasing you, something I didn't want to mention last night because you had plenty other concerns."

"I do not need to be coddled."

By her standoffishness since our kiss, that was something needlessly said. I preferred to remain on the subject of O'Neal, so I continued.

"Being as he is from New York, and being as I understand you arrived in New York from London, I'd gamble that's where he picked up your trail."

I told her about the telegram O'Neal had received in Potter:

HARRISON ARRIVES TOMORROW STOP DELIVER THE GOODS STOP THEN FOLLOW STOP

To me, that suggested he'd stayed on her trail from New York and along the way telegraphed ahead his progress to the mystery man in Denver, the man who had in return sent Harrison to get her and sent O'Neal those curt instructions.

"With Harrison dead," I said, and pointed again at the man who hung from the tree branch, "O'Neal has stayed with you."

"From New York?"

"And from Laramie. He was asking me about you during the interview in jail. I'm guessing he followed you to the train when we left the sheriff's office, and that made it easy for him to disembark in Potter when we did."

I informed her that O'Neal must have been the one who arranged for the two drunk cowboys in Potter to shoot at her feet, probably hoping I'd get killed as I tried to stop them. That would clear the way for him to kidnap her or follow farther without worrying about me.

"I find that impossible," she said.

"The cowboys had no reason to lie. And they described a slicker who had just purchased new clothes. How many like him would be in Potter?"

She shook her head. "Impossible that anyone would know who I was in New York, let alone have reason to follow."

"No one in London knew you would be on a ship?"

"Not a soul. I . . . I had no friends close to me." She looked away when she said that.

And in the lonely terror of waiting in the dark to fend off an Indian attack, when she'd turned to me, I'd turned away. I bit my tongue in anger. Perhaps this was as good a time as any to try digging myself out of that hole.

"About last night—"

"Nothing happened last night," she said curtly, as if she had rehearsed that response. She pointed at O'Neal. "What are we going to do about that man's suffering?"

I rubbed my eyes. Ten years ago, riding herd I could live on no sleep for a couple of days. Now it left me kicked out and empty. Not to mention that the Indian camp was now showing plenty of activity, and that meant another day of finding a way to survive.

"We could shoot him," I suggested. I half meant it. "I doubt anyone will be by to rescue him, and he'd probably prefer to die fast."

"I find your humor to be lacking." She busied herself at the campfire—I noticed that this time she did put the grounds in the percolator of the coffeepot—and ignored me.

I kept my focus on O'Neal and the warrior camp behind him.

This situation was too strange.

Last night, O'Neal had ridden in with Indians. Now he was being tortured. Something in his situation had changed. But what?

Last night, we had not been attacked. It did not make sense, for the Indians could not have known that Rebecca and I were away from our fire, and if they had known our location, they certainly would have found a way to trap us. No, these Indians were too careful, too patient.

I backtracked in my thinking, put myself in O'Neal's position and realized something that did make sense. To follow us from Potter, a man from New York would probably hire scouts. Pawnee scouts. That explained why he had been so relaxed as he rode among them.

What, I asked myself, could I conclude from there? The first group of warriors wanted Rebecca badly, for reasons unknown to me. Now the second group rides in with a white man who also wants Rebecca badly, for different reasons unknown to me and unknown to the first group of Indians. If Rebecca was the prize she appeared to be, then I could understand why the Indians would try to force answers from O'Neal. Hence, the torture.

But why would O'Neal remain silent? What did Rebecca have that was so valuable?

I almost asked her but decided to ease into new conversation with my question about Harrison instead. It appeared we had all day. "If you never saw O'Neal in Potter, when did you first see Harrison?"

Rebecca moved away from the fire and stood closer where I could see her without taking my attention from the Indian camp.

"Potter," she said. "It was in Potter that I first decided I might make easier progress if I did not appear as a woman. I purchased clothes from a native." She wrinkled her nose. "It was a far cry from a clothier shop in London."

"Harrison took you at gunpoint, then?"

"No. I'd made the change. He approached me on the street in front of the hotel as I was leaving. Told me he knew who I was and that I'd find what I was looking for in Laramie."

"That didn't startle you?"

Her eyes flashed. "Of course it did. My first moments in disguise and not only did he know I was a woman, he knew I'd arrived from London. But I was here in the West and I had to start somewhere. He refused to tell me anything else. It was broad daylight. We would be traveling by train. I thought I was safe and a couple days' delay to satisfy my curiosity could not hurt. Then in Laramie . . ."

Had to start somewhere. What was it she sought? And because of it now was sought herself? It didn't seem the moment to interrupt her.

". . . then in Laramie, he changed. Grabbed me from the hotel, told me we'd be heading north by horseback, and that if I tried to stop him, no one would care because I looked like a worthless Injun. It was then you arrived."

I nodded.

"You were shot and rode away, and I followed because I didn't know what else to do. When you passed out, I tried getting you back on the horse, but you were too heavy. I didn't want to be found with you because I thought I would help you escape and, in turn, you'd help me with . . . with what I was looking for."

She let that hang there. I wanted badly to know what it was that had us both here somewhere south of the Black

Hills, surrounded by hostile warriors.

So I asked. I posed my question in as flat a voice as possible. "What is it in the Black Hills that has driven you here from London?"

CHAPTER 22

REBECCA GREW STILL.

I lifted my hat and waved some flies away from my face.

She walked away from me. Returned beside me at the barricade. Walked away and returned again.

"I should prefer not to tell you," she finally said.

"You should prefer not to tell me." Mix anger and disbelief and that's how my strangled voice sounded.

She nodded.

I could think of no suitable reply to vent my anger, so I moved behind her, put my arm on top of her shoulder, and pointed so that her eyes could travel the straight line from my finger to the Injun camp.

"I'm going to sleep," I said. If she wanted more reaction from me, she'd be sorely disappointed. "While I sleep, watch careful. Don't even blink, you're gonna watch so careful. Call at the first sign of anything that looks like the beginnings of an attack. Right about then I'll decide if . . ." I paused and mimicked her accent. ". . . if I should prefer not to fight."

"Samuel," she tried to protest.

I stepped aside, eased myself to the ground, and lay back, hat over my face. She tried one or two more times but only succeeded in giving me a malicious cheerfulness to be able to ignore her pleas. She gave up. In the silence, it surprised me that I fell asleep so quickly.

When I woke, the fire was white, dead ash. My back ached from the few hours on the ground. I was sweating from the rising heat, my mouth was filled with the taste of sour exhaustion, and I had to shake dust and ants from my jeans as I rose.

Rebecca was where I had left her. Her shoulders were square under the shirt that covered her like a loose tent, her borrowed bulky jeans tightened with a rope around her waist and tucked into her boots. She didn't turn at the noises of my stirring.

To see her ramrod straight with forced dignity, I felt a sudden remorse at having been so hard-nosed. Sometimes it'll happen that way, won't it, how when a person won't yield and gives the appearance of tough uncaring, you'll inflict punishment that doesn't seem to hurt them, only to realize later the damage you've done. How must Rebecca feel at this moment? She was an ocean and a month of frontier travel from the comforting civilization of her London, staring at hostiles who had gathered for the sole purpose of her capture, and her only apparent hope was the man who had spurned her and now treated her no better than a dog.

I coughed, searching for words to begin my apology. After all, looking at it from her viewpoint, she probably had good reason for not trusting me with what O'Neal and Harrison had tried to take from her.

"Rebecca," I said softly as I moved closer.

She turned away.

"Rebecca . . ."

I touched her shoulder. She ducked her head and kept her back to me.

I shot a quick glance at the Indian camp. O'Neal still twisted at the end of the cord. Indians still moved casually from fire to fire. One buck was dragging a dead pronghorn antelope off the back of his horse. Beyond that, all their other horses, hobbled, grazed near the small stream.

"Please don't look at me," Rebecca said, a hitch in her voice.

I realized with wonder that she was crying, silently and without movement, the kind of tears that hurt most to watch.

"If I were you," she continued, "I would have long since abandoned me. All I have caused you is grief and trouble. You've treated me like a lady in a situation where I've learned others would not. And—"

"Rebecca . . ."

"No. I must finish. And last night, I threw myself at you. I should not have dreamed you might feel the way I do. You're the man who can have any woman. Miss Ackerman. She wasn't pretty but isn't a half-breed. And the woman Marshal Evrett said visited you in the night. Why would you want me? I'm half . . ."

She drew a deep breath so that she could say it with dignity. "I'm half-Indian and an illegitimate child."

Tears now flowed freely, after all she had endured in silence over the last weeks. I closed my eyes at her pain. The tears and that admission said so much. Her mixed ancestry must always be foremost in her thoughts, especially since she'd grown up with the names "savage girl" and "circus girl" ringing in her ears. Did she not know the obvious, what would be foremost in my mind, her character and beauty?

I stepped closer and reached to lift her chin so that I could look directly in her eyes. "You're a beautiful woman," I said. "Only a fool would look at the color of your skin."

She wiped her eyes clear and shook her head. Her control had returned. "That is exactly what I'd expect you to say."

"But—"

"You were correct to push me away last night. We shall discuss that no more."

I saw she was close to tears again, so I stepped back. Later, I'd explain about Miss Ackerman and about Suzanne's visit, and maybe we'd both find amusement in the misunderstanding.

Rebecca lifted her medicine bag. Her voice had more strength now. "When you asked what brought me here, it was hurt pride that led me to refuse to answer. A spite you did not deserve."

She took another breath to steady herself and pulled a small object from her medicine bag, the object she had kept from me the day before. Like the photograph, it too was wrapped in cloth. She unwrapped it.

"A ring," she said. "I'm looking for the man who owned it."

She dropped it into my hand. Heavy and gold, it felt like a small rock. The wide band held a stone of deep red. Inscriptions around the stone and on the outside of the rest of the band showed tiny engraved words, words I could not read because they were, I guess, Latin. I did recognize one phrase. West Point Academy.

"He's in the military," I said without looking up from the ring, "without a doubt, an officer."

"Yes."

I studied it further. Held the ring at an angle that let sunlight play across the inside of the band. *Louis Wilcombe—'48.*

I gave it back to her, and she carefully rewrapped it.

I again scrutinized the Indian camp. Nothing seemed un-usual. The Indian buck with the pronghorn had already slit its belly and pulled free most of the animal's entrails. The sight comforted me. If they were bringing game into camp for an evening feed, I could assume a frontal attack was not immi-nent. On the other hand, it was strange that the Indians were willing to outwait us. How could it possibly have anything to do with the only explanation that had been offered to me, Rebecca's search for a Louis Wilcombe, a man who had grad-uated from West Point in 1848?

"It seems to me," I began, "every time you give me an answer, it leads to a host more questions. I'm thinking, if you're looking for a military man, why not start at one of the outposts? I'm thinking, how can your search be so important that it causes all this trouble? I'm thinking, how is it possible that anyone else knew about your search? And lastly . . ."

I softened my voice. "Lastly, Rebecca, are you going to be disappointed to discover that Louis Wilcombe is dead?"

"Dead?"

"The piece of cartridge belt in your medicine bag. Mean-ingless to us. To Injuns? Strong medicine. The Injuns hold that anything taken from a brave foe killed in battle is a pow-erful charm piece."

She lifted her chin. "Are you informing me that we may consider the same about the ring?"

I nodded.

"I pray not," she said. "I believe Louis Wilcombe to be my father."

CHAPTER 23

AT THAT POINT, she pulled her shirt loose from her pants, and I discovered another reason why she had been so reluctant to strip earlier—the crudely sewn cloth money belt around her waist. She reached beneath her shirt and pulled it loose without exposing any of her belly. As she twisted it in her hands to open a wide flap on the outside of the belt, I saw lines of dampness on the inner band.

She withdrew folded wax paper from that flap, unfolded it, and handed me an envelope. As I opened it, she tucked her shirt back into her pants.

The envelope was addressed to Rebecca Montcalm, in care of Holy Sisters Retreat, 36 Coventry Road, London. The return address was of the West Point Academy and proudly showed the West Point Academy seal and its date of establishment, 1802.

"You'll watch the Injun camp while I read?"

"Yes."

I concentrated on the firm, clear handwriting.

Dear Rebecca Montcalm:

In following military tradition, discretion, and prudence, the Academy makes it policy to offer few details of the lives of our graduates. We can only confirm that Louis Wilcombe did indeed graduate in '48, as you have suggested in earlier correspondence, and was stationed at Fort Laramie to perform duties as a soldier and translator for the Sioux tribes common to that area. Should you wish to know more of his military record, we suggest you contact the proper authorities in Washington to pursue further privileged information. Please be warned, however, that you will undoubtedly be required to make a case for the information, and should have an argument based on immediate family ties or any compelling issue that you feel is appropriate.

> *Sincerely,*
> *Stefan Winokur*
> *Administrative Secretary*
> *West Point Academy*

I refolded the letter.

"Seems to me that you didn't take Mr. Winokur's advice," I said. "We're a long ways from Washington. And I doubt these Injuns will have much to say on the subject of Louis Wilcombe."

"But I did take his advice." A half smile from her. "After I arrived in New York, I took the train to Washington," she said. "I spent a week there."

I tried to picture the capital, brick buildings slick smooth in the rain, the way I'd seen it in a photo. But I couldn't imagine what it might be like there. The stretch was too much from here, with savages camped down the gully, their campfires smudging the sky, and a lone white man in silent agony within a stone's throw of the nearest tepee.

"Washington," I echoed. "Was it you that ruffled feathers there? Or was it the name Louis Wilcombe?"

"How did you know?" she asked sharply.

I pointed at O'Neal. I didn't feel right to observe his agony and be helpless to stop it, but we had no choice. "That's got to be where he picked up your trail. And he wouldn't follow you this far without good reason."

She gathered her thoughts, then she told me what she knew about Louis Wilcombe.

He'd been assigned to learn Sioux and be a translator at Fort Laramie, Wyoming's first military outpost, built on the Oregon Trail at the junction of the North Platte and Laramie Rivers, and some hundred miles north and east of the later-established railroad town of Laramie. Soldiers' duties as "mounted rifles" at Fort Laramie consisted of helping the thousands of passing wagonbound travelers, settling their disputes, and remaining visible as a military deterrent to the increasingly hostile Sioux.

Wilcombe's last military assignment—in 1852—had been with troops sent to guard a wagon detail as it made a supply trip into Fort Laramie from Omaha, a steamship drop-off point on the Missouri River. The supply wagons kept to the Mormon Trail along the north bank of the Platte, a relatively civilized trip—as by then thousands of settlers traveled the same route. Among the twenty or so wagons and all the supplies was a secret shipment of rifles and paymaster's gold coin.

When the troops and wagons reached the Rawhide River, hundreds of miles of grueling travel from Omaha, and only ten miles downstream from Fort Laramie, word had reached the sergeant-in-charge that the Sioux had massed and were threatening to attack the ferry that brought settlers across the Platte River into the fort. The sergeant-in-charge remained with a skeleton force of ten men to guard the supply wagons and sent ahead the remaining troops. Louis Wilcombe was among the soldiers left behind.

The threatened attack on the ferry had only been that. A threat. The Sioux had another force of one hundred fifty that swept down on the supply trains and, according to the few survivors, decimated them within minutes. The Sioux took only the rifles and gold, as the bulk of the other supplies would have slowed the warriors in their successful escape from the Fort Laramie reinforcements.

Louis Wilcombe was not among the dead. Nor among the three survivors.

Rumors later circulated that he had been seen in Indian camps, and military officials concluded that he had made an earlier decision to go native, then conspired with the Sioux to set up the attack on the supply wagons.

The three survivors agreed with the assessment: John Harrison, Sergeant Steven Byrne, and one name Rebecca did not know, as he wasn't a military man. Rebecca hoped to eventually find them as well if she did not locate Louis Wilcombe.

"John Harrison!" I said, when she paused. "He—"

"I did not know the man that met me in Potter was John Harrison until after you killed him," she said, almost wearily. "At that point, however, I realized he must have heard of my arrival in Washington."

"Logical," I said. "It seems to me that the people in Washington were more than liberal with privileged information."

She smiled at my implied question. "I was able to present a compelling issue. I'll show you the same thing I showed the officer in Washington," she said. At that, she lifted another flap on the money bag she still held in her hands. She dug out a gold coin. "Part of the paymaster's gold."

Though it was difficult to believe that a London-born woman held coin that had been lost to the Sioux, I could not disagree with her. The coin was plainly stamped with U.S. military markings and must have also been convincing to the Washington officials.

"It's been nigh twenty years," I said. "How did—" I stopped myself and answered my own question. "The medicine bag."

"When the sisters gave me my inheritance, I discovered I was moderately wealthy. I did not know, then, the source of that wealth, but in Washington, after I showed one of my coins, they had a multitude of questions."

"Horse trading." I whistled in admiration. "Questions you weren't about to answer unless they supplied a few answers of their own."

She curtsied at the compliment, an elegant movement despite the bagged jeans and bulky shirt that covered her.

"They wanted all of the gold I had," she said. "But a dress and girdle can hide a lot, and I didn't let them know about this." She hefted her money belt. "So they contented themselves by confiscating the one coin I'd shown them as proof of my story."

I thought back to my gunfight with Harrison and mentioned the gold coin that Harrison had held out to me. "He got that from you?"

"Not by my choice," she said. "He forced me to open the medicine bag, and when he saw the coin . . . when he saw it, he wanted to know if there was more. I refused to tell him. That's when he threw me to the ground."

And when that Indian had intruded into my solitude. I half smiled at the thought.

A movement from the Indian camp caught my eye. The same warrior who had spoken to us yesterday was again approaching on horseback.

"Tell me," I said, "why are you convinced Louis Wilcombe is your father?" I wanted to keep the conversation going, to let her understand by my lack of panic that there was nothing to fear at the warrior's approach.

"Arithmetic," she said.

I squinted puzzlement.

"Samuel." She smiled fully, the first since I'd woken, and the smile lit her eyes, transforming her face from exotically mysterious to openly happy. I was prepared at that moment to believe only she and I existed in the world.

"Samuel, the sisters raised me, but even I know that babies spend nine months in the womb. I doubt that after capturing the Indians here the expedition took more than four months to return to London. I was born shortly after the expedition's arrival in England, so simple arithmetic tells me that my father was not part of the expedition, but someone with my mother nearly a half year earlier, a white man who had met my mother. The ring, I believe, was a gift from him to her."

I thought she was wrong. Had there only been the ring in the medicine bag, maybe not wrong. But there was also the piece of cartridge belt, which I could not view as a token of esteem or affection. I did not want to take away from her the hope of meeting her father, so I merely nodded in agreement with her arithmetic.

The Pawnee warrior reached us moments later.

He dismounted. The horse was a gray paint, not too scrawny considering how Indians usually pushed their horses, one I wouldn't have minded trading for under other circumstances. The warrior moved away from the haunch of his horse, and I saw why it was not yet scrawny. A cavalry brand. This horse had been stolen recently, not an uncommon occurrence.

"Ghost Rider, you can see I do not carry a weapon." He had the feather medallion placed in his hair, the shield across his back, and paint reapplied to the swirling designs on his chest and shoulders, but no weapon.

"No peace pipe, neither," I said.

He grinned broadly. "We have not yet declared war."

He stood several yards in front of me now, feet planted, and despite his age, he seemed as rooted as a mountain.

"Yesterday," I said, "you declared I would die."

"Were you visited last night?"

"Are any of your braves dead?"

He grinned again. "Ghost Rider, we could dance with words until the sun sets."

I motioned at his camp. "I suspect I'll be here until then."

"Release to us the woman," he said. "You will be long past the horizon before nightfall."

I shook my head.

"A night of waiting in fear did not convince you the stupidity of refusal?" the warrior asked.

He knew the answer to that already. I decided to try my theory on him. "You fear that any attack might kill her."

"Yes." He did not do me the disservice of pretending surprise at my deduction.

"What is it the old ones seek?" I asked. I found myself speaking with his cadence.

His eyes focused on a point past me. The breeze toyed with his decoration feathers; the sun cast his sharp-edged shadow onto the bent grass between us. I knew better than to break the silence. Above us, the scream of a wheeling hawk as it tried to startle small game into movement that might betray their position. Behind me, Rebecca, quiet as she sat cross-legged close to the back edge of the bank.

I again studied the Indian camp. O'Neal had stopped his twisting and struggles, as if he was too exhausted to care any longer about the terrible strain on his arms and shoulders and wrists. Other warriors stood in a small group, motionless as they stared across the distance between us.

"Evening Star," the warrior finally grunted. "She carries the medicine bag of one we remembered as Evening Star."

"Many summers have led to many winters since one named Evening Star carried the medicine bag," I said, guessing this was Rebecca's mother. "How can such a thing lead the old ones to send you here?"

"Since we lost Evening Star, many misfortunes have befallen our people. We have lost our land. Disease has struck. The buffalo have gone. To appease the evil spirits, we must have the medicine bag. This woman must die."

There were two things I did know about Indians. While often they made little sense to us, they did make sense to themselves. And no matter how little importance we attached to it, they would die for what they considered an issue of great importance. They would also kill for it.

"The woman is not Evening Star," I said. "She cannot help you."

"We have seen the medicine bag she carries. She hid herself as a man as she crossed our land," the warrior said. "We hold the coat she wore."

Now I shook my head. "It was not from you that she hid."

"That is for the old ones to decide."

More silence. The hawk gave a loud *skree,* then dove. It disappeared in tall grass, then rose with a ground squirrel in its claws. Death was never far from any of us.

"And what of the white man in your camp," I said. "Did he not hire a party of your braves as scouts?"

"It was his bad luck that he too sought Evening Star. More bad luck that he will not give us the answers we seek. I have come to warn you that you will suffer as he does unless you give us the woman."

"I must fight," I said.

"You must then die."

He turned his back on me, mounted his horse, and in the same way as the day before rode back to camp. Unlike the day before, I knew there was no chance he was bluffing. And unlike the day before, I believed I knew how we could escape.

CHAPTER 24

ON THE PLAINS, a man without a horse is a dead man.

That was such a known and understood certainty that those of us with experience—the Indians on one side and me on the other—naturally assumed that since it was impossible for my horses to pass by the camp unnoticed, it was impossible for Rebecca and me to escape. Therefore, when someone green with lack of experience—Rebecca—had earlier suggested to me that we climb the gully walls and walk away during the night, my ears had heard only the obviously ridiculous. Only a fool would walk.

Admiring the Indian's stolen gray paint, however, had opened my eyes to the first half of Rebecca's notion. It was not stupid to consider climbing the gully walls. Did we necessarily need *our* horses to ride away? Especially when theirs were already behind their camp, gathered in a small roped-off area of grass.

Indians took great satisfaction and reaped

great honor for bravery, daring, and skill in the theft of horses from other tribes. For them, it was safer to steal horses from whites than from other tribes, for whites had little sense of observation or tracking skills and knew it was easier to replace a horse than to find the Indian who took it.

Therefore, I was about to gamble on one aspect of human nature. In the same way that the hunters rarely look back on their trail to see if they are prey, I guessed Indian horse thieves would never expect a white to steal horses from them.

So, shortly after the warrior had returned to the Indian camp, I began to unravel my lariat. I stood at the barricade, guns beside me within easy reach. While I doubted their attack would happen till nightfall, I preferred to be ready.

"My mother's name was Evening Star," Rebecca said, almost with awe and wonder, her first words since he'd left. "The nuns never did know."

"Was she Sioux or Pawnee?" Louis had gone native among the Sioux, which should mean, if indeed he was Rebecca's father, that Evening Star was Sioux and Rebecca half-Sioux. Why then the Pawnee pursuit, unless Evening Star had been Pawnee?

"I . . . I . . . don't know. I thought all Indians . . ."

"All Injuns were the same? No, ma'am. Injuns have more politics than whites." The lariat was made of hemp, and four main strands had been woven together. I did not intend to further unravel each of those four strands. "Remember in Scottsbluff—that talk about General Custer ready to end the Injun trouble? How it's said he figures no Injun could match a white soldier in fighting? I figure he's just lucky that Injuns are worse at politics than whites. If Injun braves ever followed one chief like white soldiers follow one general, Custer would get a lickin' in a big hurry."

There was interest on her face. I realized this London girl was trying to learn plenty about who the other half of her was.

"Take the Sioux," I continued with a grunt as I pulled hard at the strands. "Whilst we call them that, none of them do, not with seven different tribes worth of Sioux. There's Oglala, Sichangu, Miniconjou, Hunkpap, Sihasap, Itazipcho, and Oohenonpa."

I grinned, because I knew I was showing off. But around this woman it was getting more and more difficult not to want to show off.

"Then you got Cheyenne and Pawnee," I said. "Now the Cheyenne, they're tight with the Sioux, because in '43, the Sioux took back a handful of sacred arrows that the Pawnee had first stolen from the Cheyenne, and the Sioux actually returned those arrows to the Cheyenne."

I'd worked a third of my lariat into the separate strands, and Rebecca had not yet commented on my strange behavior. Just as well. I wasn't about to tell her until dark. No sense in having her fret all day.

"After the Sioux, Pawnee, and Cheyenne," I said, "you go further in any direction. Find Soshonis, Blackfeet, Cree, Ponca, Ojibways . . ."

"Is your knowledge remarkable?" she asked. "I mean, are all cowboys like you? Wiping our trail at night as we travel. Reciting Indian history back to 1843. Able to talk in sign language."

"Where'd you . . . oh, in jail." I snorted. "At least now I understand why you didn't sign back. Just as well. You were a sorry sight as a buck."

"Well?" she demanded.

"Ma'am?"

"You don't restrain yourself in asking others questions. But I never hear you say anything about *your* past."

I felt the familiar knot of pain hit my stomach as unwanted memories rushed through the cracks of the walls that held them in place.

"Not much to say."

Silence.

I looked up from my rope work, and before she turned away, I caught on her face the same startled pain I'd seen in the moonlight after pushing away from her kisses.

Had my voice just been that curt?

"You've told me plenty," I said, more softly. "It's probably not right that I do my own holding back. It's just that I'm accustomed to leaving my past in the past."

She slowly turned back. "The scar?"

I bent my head and resumed my unbraiding. My fingers, however, seemed to work on their own.

"The scar," I said. I would talk, but not about that. "Yes, ma'am. Among other things, that's part of the past."

"Other things?"

"My parents died when I was young." I looked at her again. "My brother and I were headed with them for free land and paradise on the Pacific coast. My pa, he left the Oregon Trail 'cause he heard a rumor about a trail that cut a couple hundred miles off the journey, and he had so much pride he figured he could prove what others were too afraid to try. Pa was right. It did cut off plenty travel. And went through wide valleys with good water and grass. Folks later called it the Bozeman Trail. Only Pa never had a chance to find out he was right. Crow Injuns took his scalp somewhere near Yellowstone."

What I didn't tell Rebecca was that the Crow hadn't killed him before they took it.

———————

It had been drizzling then, three days since crossing the Bighorn River, where, more than a decade too late for my parents, Fort Smith would be built to guard travelers along the Bozeman. The backbone of the Bighorn Mountains, which for a couple weeks had been to our left as we traveled northwest with the curve, was now blue shadow well behind us, and the foothills of that same range were shrinking in size as we reached the valley of the Yellowstone.

Drizzle and mist shrouded and dulled the distant green of the pines lining the foothills, and behind the team of oxen, our wagon lurched at every bump, something Jed and I were experiencing for the first time. Until that day we'd been free to wander on foot with our slingshots to annoy all game within hailing distance of the slow-moving wagon.

This day, however, we both suffered from colds, and Ma kept us under blankets in the wagon for fear the drizzle might make our conditions worse. She had no inkling that the same drizzle would save our lives. Thrice.

It first saved our lives because we were hidden under the wagon canvas when the whooping and screaming of Crow braves broke the silence of the heavy cold air.

Ma pushed us down and crawled to the front of the wagon. We ignored her push and followed. The opening at the front of the wagon gave me a glimpse of hell on horseback, because the Indians were riding in full color and waving war axes and spears. An arrow pierced the canvas cover and snapped us out of our spell.

As Ma turned inside, she finally noticed us on all fours behind her. "Get back," she hissed and whopped Jed across shoulders. I'd never seen her face so fierce with rage. Only later did I realize it hadn't been rage at all, but the intensity of a mother bear protecting her cubs. Her passion scared us so badly it never entered our minds to disobey when she pushed us into the false bottom of the wagon and covered it with the blankets we had to push aside when we crawled out much after the horror of the attack.

Not one gunshot rang out above the war whoops of the Indians. This was '50, before brass cartridges. Pa had a flintlock, notorious for fouling in damp weather, and the powder probably never had a chance to spark. Or maybe an arrow hit him before he even brought the barrel up to take aim. Jed and I would never know, because through the cracks of the warped wood of the belly of the wagon we saw nothing but the bottom of the spokes of the wagon wheels and the grass immediately below us.

The war whoops didn't last long. We heard a roar of rage that we recognized as Pa's, the roar that made us giggle when we were out of range of his leather-hard hands, but scared us silly when he finally caught up to us for our real or imagined offenses. His roar was cut short with a thud that made me flinch as I huddled against Jed. Shortly after began the screams. At first it did sound like Ma. But too soon it didn't. And after that, the screams became something no person would ever guess belonged to a human.

Mercifully, sheer terror distracted us from the sounds of our mother, for the wagon suddenly bounced from the weight of Indians jumping inside. They crawled around and spoke quickly in deep voices, but saw nothing of interest, and when they had jumped out again, her screams were barely more than whimpers.

The drizzle saved us the second time because the usually faded gray wood of the wagon in sunlight had become dark brown with absorbed moisture. Without that slick sheen there, the urine from our released bladders would have left an obvious trail as it seeped from our clothes through the cracks of the wood bottom. And the warrior at the side of the wagon would have surely guessed our nearby presence as he knelt and filled our view with his bent shoulders and ragged braids during his attempts to stoke a small fire in the grass.

The drizzle saved us the third time because the warrior's fire refused to catch, and the Indians had to amuse themselves by pushing the wagon down a steep incline and then groan with collective disappointment because a clump of pines had slowed it too quickly.

We probably waited an hour before crawling out.

I was slower than Jed, but at one year older, he had always been the leader. When I staggered to the top of the incline, he was there waiting, and not until he actually punched me four times full in the face and knocked me backward twice did I finally quit my attempts to get past him and see what had happened to Ma and Pa.

Later, much later, while drunk in a saloon, he told me that Pa had crawled in circles. That he knew because Pa had left a confused trail of smeared blood and bent grass in his blind efforts to find Ma, for a man without a nose or eyes or scalp can only mewl as he gropes for the woman he has brought into the wilderness to death. Jed told me he'd found Pa crawled on top of her, two arrows protruding from his back, fingers tangled in her hair, and what was left of his face buried in the crook of her neck. Drunk as Jed was when he'd told me this through great heaving gulps of tears, he refused to say what had happened to Ma.

That day of their deaths was the first of more than a few that showed Jed's determination to protect me and my life. His life, I think, was stolen that day there as the ravens gathered in at the tops of the trees and waited for us to leave. Because while my thrashing nightmares ended at the campfires of the mountain men who eventually found us, Jed never lost his dislike and fear of sleep for the memories it would bring him, memories that I had been spared.

———

I pulled myself from those memories to feel Rebecca touching my arm.

"Your mother died, too, that day?"

"Yes," I said, calm. "She did."

"Your brother?" She asked gently, and it did not seem like prying.

"No," I said. "Not that day."

"Will you tell me about it . . ." I started to shake my head ". . . sometime?"

"Yes," I lied.

We fell into a silence. Mine probably brooding. I broke it by telling her how some mountain men had found our trail a week later and tracked us to where we were waiting in a tree to drop a rock on anything that passed below us, we were so hungry.

She smiled at that, so I continued and told her how the mountain men fobbed us onto a band of friendly Injuns at a small rendezvous the next spring. I explained that a rendezvous brought together trappers and Indians to a prearranged site, and that well into the '30s, until the early forts had been established, a major rendezvous might bring together dozens of trappers and hundreds of Indians in a week-long frenzy and festivity of trading. I said I had plenty of fondly exaggerated stories from the memories of old mountain men if that's what she wanted.

She told me instead to give her more of my life, so I obliged by describing my next few years with those friendly Indians, Shoshonis, who to the best of my knowledge as a tribe had never gone on the war path against whites, neither before we began to fill the frontier, nor now as we were displacing their buffalo.

I went on to let her know how Jed had dragged me across the territories to Denver and left me at a dance hall for a few years to grow up during my teen years. I didn't tell her about Jed's burning wildness though, nor about the bounty hunting, nor about Clara at that dance hall.

When I finished, and pleaded my sore, dry throat and the

need to finish my preparations as an excuse to stop, dusk was only a few hours away.

Rebecca asked me what I meant to do with the remnants of my lariat, and I judged it was late enough in the day to explain.

So I did.

I gathered she did not have full faith in my efforts, for as the sun began to set, she bowed her head and began to pray.

CHAPTER 25

IT HAD BEEN DARK for an hour, and I wanted to move on the Indians before they moved on us. I armed myself with a knife and two revolvers. I gave Rebecca the Winchester and the rigged lariat rope.

"Repeat it to me," I said to her. I'd learned from Jed and from bounty hunting how easily the best intentions break down in the heat of battle. "Because once we're apart, you'll find enough confusion without adding mistakes."

The glow of the firelight made her face appear, if it were possible, even softer. Her eyes were steady on me as she spoke, and again I found myself admiring her spunk.

"I climb to the top of the gully," she said. "Count to five thousand. I lower this rope a few feet into the fire. After five or six bullets have exploded, I move down the ridge and shoot at their campfires. Four times. Go back to the rope, lower it more, let another three or four bullets explode. I move the opposite direction on the ridge and again shoot four bullets at their campfires. Drop the rope into the fire. Shoot twice more. Then walk away onto the prairie with your saddlebag. When I hear horses and two quick shots, I fire an answering shot, straight up, to let you know where I am. If I don't hear horses or two shots, I keep walking."

"Good," I said, smiling. She had repeated my terse instructions not only word for word, but dropped the elegance of her English accent to mimic my drawl. "Good," I repeated. "But not good enough. Tell me one more time."

Coiled at her feet was the rigged lariat rope. I'd taken all the strands and tied one to the other to give me a thin rope four times longer than the original lariat. Then I'd knotted bullets into the rope and spaced those knots about a foot apart.

Ours was a simple plan, and it relied on getting the Indians to believe both of us were still near the barricade. To do that, I needed gunfire to come from two separate sources. When Rebecca slowly lowered that rope into the fire from above, the bullets would explode, causing, I hoped, the Indians to believe someone was shooting from inside the barricade. I'd told Rebecca that when she moved down the ridge to fire the Winchester, her muzzle flash obvious against the night sky would show that the second series of shots did come from somewhere else.

I hadn't told her, however, why she was to only fire two sets of shots before heading across the prairies. I feared that if she kept a steady barrage of sniping, any number of braves would close in on the muzzle flash. Instead, she'd be long gone before the first brave got close, and not even Indians can track someone at night. Besides that, I didn't need her covering fire for long. If I hadn't succeeded while the brief barrage of bullets behind me was firing at the Indians, extra distraction wasn't going to do my dead body any good.

She finished reciting the plan.

"Once more."

"Samuel, I'm afraid, but not so afraid you need to find ways to delay us."

She was uncanny. The first step was the most difficult part of any action that might result in your death. Once committed, total focus on survival took you from fear.

"Well spoken," I said. "The saddlebags are halfway up the gully where you'll pass them on your way."

She nodded. A silence built between us.

"I'll miss my horses," I added. Anything to rid us of this awkwardness. "They've been good to me."

She shook her head at my obvious idiocy.

"It was a stupid thing to say," I agreed moments later. "It is the truth, and Charlie has been good to me, but it's something I could just as easily have kept to myself if that's the last words you'll hear from me."

She shook her head again. "It won't be the last—"

"Look, I don't know what you learned from the sisters, but I'll tell you this. Distrust whatever a man says whenever he's in the pursuit of money or women. He won't necessarily be lying, but if he's going to lie, that's when, and he might not even know he's lying himself."

I reached across the barricade and untethered Charlie and the horses. They'd stay where they were until the bullets began to explode, and when they bolted, it would not only add to the confusion, but deprive the Indians of using them later. Thinking of that moment, I patted Charlie's neck, not without sadness. Moments later, I picked up the coiled lariat rope and helped Rebecca put her arm through it so that it hung over her right shoulder.

"But when a man's facing death he can't avoid," I finally continued, "chances are whatever he says is true. Understand?"

"Yes." It was a barely heard whisper.

"You kissed me last night. It felt so good I never wanted to let go. Me pushing you away had nothing to do with who you are, but with who I am and where I've been. Remember that."

She studied my face. "I will," she said a few heartbeats later.

I moved into the night before I might say anything else.

————

I accomplished almost all that I promised. Almost.

I'd snuck within pistol range of the Indian camp, thankful every step that this was midsummer and that soft grass, not dry leaves, bent beneath my feet.

Once there, on my belly and covered thoroughly by a bush alongside the last tree of the cottonwood stand, I waited and watched the camp. Some Indians moved among the orange light cast by the fires, but there was not much else to see.

I waited more. My eyes were accustomed to the starlight now, and I was able to see that the horses behind the camp were guarded by a single brave.

I waited more. A count to five thousand, done slowly, should take an hour and a half, but I'd figured Rebecca to be nervous and count quicker, thus giving me much less leeway to cross the three hundred yards of darkness and cottonwoods. I was wrong about Rebecca's nerves, for long as I had taken to get here, the minutes dragged on without the gunfire I needed to hide my actions.

I marked the seconds by the thudding of my heart against the cold ground and paid for my miscalculation of Rebecca's nerves as mosquitoes added to the misery of waiting. I dared not risk movement to slap any, and they descended in blankets, drawn by my body heat in the cool night air.

I pushed my nose into the ground in an attempt to squash one on the tip growing fat with my blood. *Why would God create anything so useless and miserable as a mosquito*, I wondered in irritation. Which, I realized shortly after, was a question with two major assumptions. God was Creator. And everything had purpose. Two assumptions it seemed folks took for granted, but never really considered. So why would I now? To pass time and take my mind off the mosquitoes? Or because I'd been impressed by Rebecca's quiet courage after her time of prayer? Even had I the further inclination to puzzle those questions in these less-than-ideal circumstances, I wasn't given the chance, not when three braves stepped away from camp, as silent as the shadows that had released them.

I realized how shortsighted I had been, and how much I'd hurt my chances by assuming Rebecca would count quickly. To reduce the amount of my movement, my line from the barricade through the cottonwoods had been the straightest and shortest. For the same reason, I'd eased myself into position at the last tree on that straight line. I had not considered, however, a long wait, nor that Indians might choose the same line to advance on our camp, a line that was bringing them directly to my prone body.

The once long seconds now shrank in a brief panic of indecision. I could shoot, but once my revolvers fired, I lost all advantage of surprise, and it would be me against the entire camp. Yet the longer I waited, the more difficult was my firing angle from the ground.

I finally decided I had no choice. I eased a revolver forward and trained it on the closest Indian. I picked out a point on the ground. If they stepped past it, I would have to shoot, or die.

They crouched as they walked. I marveled at their quietness.

Two more steps and they were dead. Then, not much later, probably me.

One more step.

"Heathen Injuns!" a voice croaked loudly behind them. *O'Neal.*

They spun, as surprised as I was at life from the motionless figure that hung slackly from the leather cords.

"Roast in hell!" O'Neal tried to yell, and succeeded in hoarsening the croak. "Hah! Hah! Hah!"

His voice rose in volume as he shouted meaningless, jumbled taunts.

Nods and hurried discussion among the three Indians. They moved on O'Neal, something I would have done, too, to stop his noise from spoiling their surprise. One raised his war club.

"Keaton, you owe me!" I heard. The club whirred downward and, with the thud of wood on ripe melon, bounced off O'Neal's head.

His body did not sag farther. It could not against the already taut leather that suspended his wrists. When the Indians moved away, his body instead swayed from side to side, the dying of a pendulum. And now, as the Indians began to melt forward into the trees, they entered from a different angle, missing me by at least twenty or thirty feet.

Keaton, you owe me. I could think of only one reason he might utter those words. He'd seen my approach, known my location, and judged the Indians would stumble across me.

Was he dead?

I couldn't know.

The first bullet banged loud echoes from the fire behind me. Another. And a third.

Indians at the fires swarmed into motion.

This was the moment. Yet I hesitated.

Was O'Neal dead?

If not, I did owe him. The question paralyzed me.

Crashing reverberations from the Winchester. Excited voices rose in the Indian camp as bullets whined a deadly buzz among the braves.

I pushed to my feet and ran, pulling my knife free from its sheath in the same motion. I had to jump to slash the leather above O'Neal's wrists, and I caught him as he fell, and, still running, humped him across my right shoulder.

Now, answering fire from the Indian camp. Deeper booms, the massive explosions from musket rifles.

I skirted the edge of the camp, driven by such urgency to run that O'Neal was no more than a sack of potatoes. I stumbled, recovered, and plowed onward, knowing that the lone brave guarding the horses could not possibly miss my clumsy approach. He didn't. He shouted above the roar of confusion and, I guessed in the darkness, pulled his bow, for seconds later I heard a deadly hiss and felt something pluck at my shoulder.

I stopped. Shooting on the run would only waste bullets. Another hiss. And a thud that shook me. In the heat of adrenaline, I felt nothing but the Colt in my hand as it bucked once. Twice.

The Indian screamed. Horses cried high in terror.

Shouts from behind me as other Indians realized what was happening. More rifle shots from high on the ridge. The outlines of a dozen figures running at me through the blackness.

I threw O'Neal over a horse. Jumped on behind him. Fired backward at the yelling horde.

I knew once we had a couple horses headed away from camp, the others would stampede with them. But I needed to be sure. Without horses, the Indians couldn't follow.

I hated to do it, but once the blood smell reached the rest of the horses, they would be crazy with fear, and nothing would keep them here. I shot the nearest horse, slammed my gun back into the holster and goaded my horse by slamming my heels into its ribs. It needed little urging at the dying screams of the nearby horse.

With no saddle, and O'Neal in front of me across the horse, I nearly slipped off the smooth back as we plunged along the bottom of the draw. I found myself clutching at O'Neal's suspenders with one hand and the horse's mane in the other. To fall now would get us kicked to death by the horses that pounded close behind.

We rounded the bend and thundered past the trail that Rebecca and I had used to pick our way downward in the gully two days earlier.

O'Neal had complicated things. I'd planned earlier to put that lone guard down quietly and to have time to tether a few horses together before stampeding the rest of the herd, leaving me in a control that would let me pick my way up the trail we'd just passed. Now all I could do was hope and hold on until the stampede ended.

My horse was tiring with the double load, and we began to slip farther backward in the herd. Dust rose and clogged my throat, and the night remained a plunging, whirling, roaring confusion.

Ahead and to the right came a snap loud enough to be heard above the pounding of hooves, the snap as of a tree down in the wind, a horrible snap of bone bursting to the driving force of the momentum of full gallop suddenly stopped by the leg that had dropped into an animal hole. That horse pitched forward, rolling sideways over his neck and shoulders. Two others ran over it and fell but twisted to their feet and galloped forward. The first one did not and shrieked in agony as we left it behind.

It underscored what I already knew. This blind gallop was insane.

And O'Neal began to slip off the horse.

I held as long as I could, gritted my teeth until the last of the other horses passed us, but ours refused to halt, no matter how hard I yanked back on its mane with my other hand. Any second this horse too could snap a leg and kill us in that same swiftness of shattering power.

O'Neal was now so far down that he flopped against the horse's ribs, panicking the horse more. I prayed the ground near the creek was soft and flung O'Neal as far off the horse as I could. Then with both hands in the horse's mane, I pulled myself forward so that I could wrap my arms around his neck.

His head reared and ducked in his mad efforts to stay with the herd. It took all my strength to hold the neck, and when I finally had my mouth close, I bit down on the horse's ear. I bit until my teeth sheared through the soft cartilage, and the salt taste of blood gagged me. Still, I did not let go. It was an old trick but had never failed.

The horse stopped.

With one hand, I twisted the horse's other ear and released my teeth. The horse remained still, his eyes flaring and rolling a moon-reflected white in the darkness. I held on to that ear as I swung down. I reached below his chin to find the Indian bridle that hung loose.

I spit out blood and gasped for air.

As soon as I stopped heaving, I would lead this horse to O'Neal. If I found a heartbeat, he'd go across the horse's back. There was now plenty distance between us and the Indian camp, the urgency was gone, and I could walk us farther down the gully until we reached the other horses, for they would eventually stop and rest as a herd. Once we found them, I'd take a couple more, then stampede the others again. That would only leave me a long lonely trot as I backtracked across the prairie for Rebecca, with the fear for her safety a taste in my mouth far worse than thickness of the horse's blood that clung to my tongue and teeth.

An hour later, my two shots were answered by a single shot, and I almost reached to the horse beside me to shake O'Neal's limp hand in congratulatory excitement.

CHAPTER *26*

NOT UNTIL DAWN did I remember that the night before I had mistakenly thought I'd been hit by an arrow. Because as the sun's early glow first streamed into rays of light that bounced diamonds off the scattered grasslands dew, Rebecca gasped.

"O'Neal!"

We each rode the lead horses at a walk. O'Neal trailed us, so I had to turn to follow her pointing finger. She hadn't gasped because he was struggling to sit in the saddle. He was unconscious—I doubted he would ever recover—and slumped in place, hands tied together around the horse's neck, and feet tied together by a rope that circled beneath the horse's belly. No, she'd gasped because dawn's first light revealed blood caked brown and the arrow shaft broken off high in O'Neal's left shoulder, the arrow that would have plunged through my belly if I hadn't been carrying him.

It made his already slim chances slimmer.

Had the Indians dipped the arrow in snake venom or a rotted carcass, nothing would save him. As it was, too much time had passed for me to pull the arrow loose, something I explained to Rebecca.

"You must make the attempt," she said, "no matter how difficult."

"The difficulty don't bother me," I replied, "it's the futility."

She glared at me, and her jaw assumed a stubborn set that was starting to become too familiar.

"The mountain men that raised me knew more about arrow wounds than any surgeon," I said. "We try to pull the arrow loose, all we get is shaft. The arrowhead stays inside."

I told her why. War arrows were shorter than hunting arrows, and barbed, one of the reasons that they could not be pulled loose. The other was that the sinew and glue that attached the blade to the shaft would have long since loosened in the warmth of O'Neal's blood. The mountain men figured a half hour at most was all you could afford to wait if you expected to pull an arrow out in one piece.

"We can't simply leave the arrow there," she said.

I took a deep breath.

"We can't," she insisted, misunderstanding my hesitation.

I stopped the horse and dismounted.

"He'll be dead by nightfall, no matter what we do." Even as I said it, I knew it was a weak protest. He'd saved me twice. Once in diverting the Indians, and once by taking this arrow. I was obliged to do all I could for him.

"You'll have to hold him in place," I said. As Rebecca got down from her horse, I was into my saddlebag, searching for my last remaining shirt. I tore it into strips. She joined me alongside O'Neal.

"Firm your shoulder against the horse's chest," I told her.

"Keep a good grip on the tether and don't let the horse get its head up."

She nodded.

"And look away."

I estimated the direction of the arrow's entry. O'Neal had been face downward over my shoulder when the arrow hit. It appeared to have entered the fleshy part between his shoulder bone and ribs and, I guessed, would exit the meat above his collarbone. I didn't figure those facts would console him much, but it meant nothing vital had been pierced.

I took another deep breath. I did not want to do this.

But I did. Pushed the arrow slowly and firmly, pushed so hard I was braced against the horse's stance. The arrow moved some. O'Neal groaned. I kept pushing and finally the arrowhead broke the skin on the other side. I pulled his shirt apart at the neck, found blood streaming from the arrowhead, and pulled it through.

With my clean hand, I matted a few strips of cloth against the new wound.

"Rebecca, keep this in place," I said.

She stepped back from the horse. I was happy to see she held a firm grip on the tether. Horses don't like the smell of human blood, either. When she had her other hand pressed on the cloth, I moved away at a half run.

"Is it always like that?" she asked when I returned some minutes later.

I rinsed my mouth with water from my canteen. She took my silence for a reluctance to answer, which it was.

"After Harrison, and after the whiskey traders, and now—" she said. "I didn't mean to pry. It's just that you seem to have so much control, and . . ."

I glared at her. "And I puke my guts out every time I cause blood to be shed?"

"You don't frighten me."

"You'd best learn fear soon." I preferred fear as a subject over my brother's death. I took a leather cord from the saddlebag, and while Rebecca held the bandage in place, I tied it down around O'Neal's shoulder. I spoke as I worked. "We're three, maybe four days travel from Scottsbluff, even if we dare backtrack past the Pawnees whose horses we run off. Going north as we are, you won't find a settlement between here and the Missouri, and if that weren't enough trouble, all night through you've been insisting on this crazy notion about riding into the Black Hills among the Sioux to find a father who may or may not be yours and may or may not be alive."

She stiffened. "How far to the Black Hills?"

I finished tying the last knot. "Two days." I could tell by the tone of her voice what she was thinking and wondered how far she would push.

"What direction?" she asked.

I pointed north and west. We had the White River to cross, then the Cheyenne. I hadn't been this way before, but around campfires and over beer in the saloons, talk was always traded, so that if a person listened with only half an ear, he still had a good idea of the lay of the land. It helped even more to study the survey maps at the railroad offices, which I did at every opportunity.

She pulled her shirttails loose and lifted out two gold coins from her money belt. "This should suffice for services as guide. I shall find my own way from here."

"Certainly, ma'am." I pocketed the coins. She had confirmed my guess, and I was amused now. "Just ask directions at the next street corner."

"Your arrogance is insufferable."

"As is your stubbornness, ma'am."

She marched to her horse. Amazing, I thought, how quickly pride replaced her concern for O'Neal.

I did know she would ride north without me, if it came to that. I also knew—for reasons ranging from curiosity to an unwillingness to let her commit suicide to stirrings of the heart that I wanted to ignore—that I would not let her ride alone. But I sure wasn't going to let her get a head start and put me in the foolish position of having to chase after her. While she struggled to climb onto her horse, I reached mine and swung atop with the ease of years of practice.

We rode almost all the day in silence.

————————

I'd been stopping to pluck coneflowers whenever I saw their pale purple flower heads in the tall grass, so that when we bedded down for the evening, I was finally able to tend more properly to O'Neal.

The coneflower—some call it black sampson—has a stout, bristly stem of two or three feet, but I was more interested in the plant's roots. Over the buffalo-chip fire, I boiled scrapings from the roots for half an hour, then drained the dark liquid into a tin cup. Rebecca poured some down the unconscious man's throat while I took the mash from the pot and formed it into a poultice. O'Neal's heart beat faintly, but other than that, he was dead to our world.

"Indian medicine or mountain-man medicine?"

"Injun. Shoshoni. Supposed to pull poison from the blood."

"Will it be effective?"

I shrugged. O'Neal's face had swollen almost black from the insect bites he'd endured at the end of the leather rope. He'd taken a terrible crunch across the head, stopped an arrow, and been thrown from a galloping horse. I was impressed he'd lasted this long. But I'd also seen men die from lesser injuries, and others survive worse. So there was nothing to do but shrug.

"If he lives," I added to that shrug, "he might be able to tell us who put him on our trail."

"Does it matter now?" Rebecca asked. "We're too far from any town to be found. And it is my father that I seek."

I squatted beside the fire and stared at the sky. Orange, reflected from dying sunlight below the horizon's clouds, had darkened to purples. In contrast, miles away, a thunderhead mushroomed a gray column that grew so quickly against the purple that I could see the movement as clouds bulged outward. I loved the sky, a picture that was as constant as it was changing.

"Does it matter?" I repeated. "To someone it does. You're holding gold coin that's probably only a small part of what got stole. Maybe that's what they want—why O'Neal was sent."

A coyote's howl reached us.

I tilted my head back and howled in return, to be answered again by the high-pitched yipping that cuts so clearly through prairie night. The response made me grin.

Rebecca shook her head at my levity.

"You don't understand, do you, why I want to find my father."

"I understand we have a good chance of being killed," I told her. "Sioux are the meanest fighters you'll find. And they been pushed plenty hard the last few years."

Not that I blamed them for their anger. There were those days I ached with joy at the freedom of crossing the valleys beneath all the sky. The buffalo gave the Sioux everything they needed to live in that freedom, and we were moving in with cattle and whiskey and wolf poison.

"You're an orphan," she persisted. "But at least you knew your parents. If I can find my own father . . ."

"Rebecca . . ." Looking at her wistfulness as she sat cross-legged across the fire, I wanted to stand and pull her close and hold her so that my chin rested in her soft hair, to tell her that there would be no more pain, no more need to fight the loneliness that had formed her dreams. So I didn't finish the further pessimism that I had intended to pass along. While I did not believe Louis Wilcombe had been her father, if she clung to the hope that a ring and a piece of cartridge belt made her part of his flesh and blood, and if she hoped even harder that he was still alive after all these years, I would not tell her otherwise.

It seemed our stubbornness and anger had dissolved with the peacefulness of the fire.

"Rebecca . . ." I searched to finish without the pessimism and found a question that had been with me all day. "You prayed last night. Why?"

She folded her hands together and regarded me with seriousness. The fire glowed in her eyes.

"Because I didn't want you killed."

I smiled. "Gathered that. What I meant was, why'd you believe it would help?"

"The sisters forced me every day to pray," she answered slowly. "It never felt like much more than a ritual, kneeling at the pews or whispering in the confession box. But at night, when I was alone, in the darkness, it felt as if . . ."

She faltered.

"Go on," I said softly. "I am truly curious."

". . . as if once I'd gotten away from all the distractions, my soul could finally listen, and as I prayed, I no longer felt alone."

Away from the distractions.

I was well past thirty, nearly old in these parts. My years had been spent among capable men, strong and tough and resourceful, men who had ridden thousands of miles in land unforgiving of the slightest mistake. Among these men, I fought and gambled, roped and branded cattle, drank and chased women my full share. Around us, death was never more than a single miscalculation away. Pull your gun too slow, or at the wrong time, death. Slip off your horse in a stampede, death. Catch a knife in a barroom brawl, death. Rattlesnakes, hostile Indians, prairie fires, blizzards, or just plain bad luck, all meant death. Daily, without flinching, we faced that death, yet in our quieter moments together, we pretended death did not exist. I could not recall a single conversation—short of the hymn singing and preachers' words that we endured to please womenfolk—where words had turned with any seriousness to the meaning of death or what might lie beyond, this against the plain evidence that death would find all of us, most likely with little warning.

And here Rebecca had spoken of the distractions that had kept her soul from listening. Distractions. The same word that had crossed my thoughts in the aftermath of facing death at Smickles' shotgun. What was it that would lead a woman whose life had shared none of mine to understand and feel in her childhood halfway across the world the same instinct that had touched me in my quietness?

"It's one or t'other," I said, more to myself than her.

"I beg your pardon?"

I raised my head and tried to sort my thoughts by speaking them. "It's nothing beyond death or it's something. Clear-cut logic. One or t'other. Nothing between."

I mused on that, pushed the end of a log farther into the fire with my toe. "If it's nothing beyond, I can't see that it matters much how a man lives or dies. He might as well grab what he can while the grabbing is good."

Two logs collapsed at the movement in the fire, and sparks shot a small tower into the dark.

But it did matter how a man lived. Why else would the memory of my brother cut so deeply? Why else love and sadness? Why else the clarity of despair in the one single moment

Smickles and his shotgun had forced me to finally understand that death would take me as surely as it had taken all the men that I had seen fall?

"If it's something beyond, that casts a new light, don't it?" I said, not seeking Rebecca's reply. "And a man best prepare as best as possible. Asking questions. Looking for what lies ahead."

Was it that simple? That, despite the compelling matters of living, much of a man's business was to decide matters of his death and matters of his soul? It struck me that should there be a God who followed our thoughts, He would have more compassion for the one who faced the question and decided against Him than for the fool who ignored the clear-cut logic that it must be one or t'other.

Was it that simple? If it was t'other and He did wait beyond—yet how could I decide upon what my eyes could not see—there would be new meaning in the stars above or the turning of the seasons or the touch of a woman, a new meaning—almost wonderment—to try to comprehend anything or anyone who might lie at the source of all of it.

I said none of this aloud to Rebecca. Nor did I tell her it was her presence in my life leading me to these thoughts.

When I eventually looked up from the fire and away from my thoughts, she was regarding me with a smile of such peaceful beauty that I again wanted to hold her warm against the night air.

Instead, I first built the fire before moving her and our bedrolls well into the darkness nearly a quarter mile away. Whatever might lie beyond the compelling matters of living and in the land of death, I was in no particular hurry to get there, and prudence on the edge of Sioux country would delay my arrival.

CHAPTER 27

DESPITE MY GRUMBLINGS and dire warnings over the next day and a half of easy riding through the tall grass of gently sloped hills, I did not believe the Sioux would cut us down without mercy or warning. Otherwise I would have taken us northeast and found safer valleys and hills to take Rebecca away from the Black Hills. I would have lied and pointed out other hills as the Black Hills, then expressed my sympathy and disappointment that we weren't able to find any Sioux.

No, I was allowing that Sioux curiosity would be stronger than bloodlust. At night, we slept away from the campfire, for darkness would give them little reason to question anything except our presence, and freshened curiosity on their part at dawn would do us little good if we were already dead. During daylight, however, it would be obvious that we were not soldiers or prospectors—both hazardous occupations in Sioux country. Sioux scouts, too, would easily see that Rebecca was not white. There was O'Neal, unconscious over the horse's neck. And most compelling of all, I hoped, were the Pawnee war markings not yet worn from the hides of our horses.

Still, I was not ready to gamble that Sioux curiosity would be provoked merely by a bedraggled caravan as strange as ours headed into the heart of their established territory. I rode with a stripped sapling as long as a flag pole, and indeed carried that pole upright as if I were leading us with a flag. Atop that pole, however, was no unfurled cloth. Instead, it held the Sioux medicine bag that Rebecca had been reluctant to let me pry from her hands.

Midway through the morning of the second day after our escape from the Pawnee, we were forced to halt because of buffalo. The herd filled a small valley and moved westward in a rumbling flow of dust and thunder. There was no way around this herd—buffalo stretched as far as we could see in both directions—and no way through. We waited and watched for several hours, unable to speak above the noise until just before the last of the stragglers had passed by. During that time, I alternated between wondering at the immensity of so much life and—as Rebecca was so enthralled she did not notice—studying Rebecca's face and her childlike joy to behold the herd in all its majesty.

After, we continued to ride slowly, letting our horses graze frequently and water as often as possible. Again and again I checked the rounded edges of the horizon for signs of men or horses, but even as I scanned, I knew that the Sioux would more probably appear without warning.

Several hours later, I drew our horses to a halt as we broached a rise in the grasslands.

Rebecca dismounted and stood in waist-deep grass and stared into the wind that pushed against our faces.

"The hills," she said without looking back at me. She

lifted her hands and spread her fingers, as if feeling the wind for the first time. "We are here."

I did not need to answer.

We stood on a ridge of grasslands. Ahead, the land stretched downward for many miles, unbroken by anything except for the occasional movement of pronghorn. Then the broad, vast slope rose upward, and clumps of firs began to dot the faraway smoothness of the grass. As the land swept higher, the deep green of the firs became more solid as the flat lines of the grassland horizon were replaced by an almost mountainous rim, at this distance dark with trees.

The Black Hills of Dakota. Sharp contrast to the prairie that surrounded them. Hundreds of square miles of timber, game, and crystal clear water.

I'd heard rumors for years that these domed mountains contained pockets of gold, heard story after story of Indians appearing at Fort Laramie, south to the other side of those mountains, with bags full of gold nuggets to be exchanged for guns, whiskey, blankets, and trinkets. Post commanders hated these rumors and feared their men would desert to search the hills.

Soldiers, however, valued their scalps more than gold. These hills were sacred ground to the Sioux and had been given to them in the treaty of '68, a treaty that had stopped their war raids in the territory south of the North Platte River, while returning to them everything north that included all the forts on the Bozeman Trail—which the Sioux had burned so immediately that departing soldiers could look back over their shoulders to see the rising smoke. For every rumor of gold that circled a mining camp or saloon, there were three sworn stories about the men who had entered these hills and not returned. Had there been a pickax flopping against the side of my horse, I, too, would be going no farther than this view.

Rebecca lowered her hands and turned slowly back to our horses.

"You don't have to take me any farther," she said.

I shook my head.

"Are you certain? There may be great trouble for you."

"If I die," I said. "You're forgiven. If I live, we'll see."

She smiled and moved back onto her horse. "How will we find the Sioux?" she asked. "I'd pictured one or two hills. A circle of tepees. That we could just ride up. But to see all of it now filling the entire horizon . . ."

"How will we find them? We won't." She began to frown, so I continued. "They'll find us."

———————

By early evening, we had reached the interior of the hills. We were following the river upstream, picking our way along the banks. The walls of the canyon on each side began to close as the river narrowed to less than a stone's throw in width. The walls began to block the sun, and more and more we had to move our horses into the water when the banks disappeared in the sheer rise of granite. Wafts of coolness rose from the water to our faces whenever the breeze trembled through the leaves of overhanging trees. It was a lazy river, making no sound. What I didn't like was the rest of the silence. No birds. No rustling.

My first warning of the Sioux came from the river itself. We were in the water again, and I saw wide gray plumes of silt drift toward us from upstream. The same sort of plumes that our own horses kicked downstream behind us.

I pointed at the plumes for Rebecca's benefit.

"It'd be real nice if the Sioux show the same respect for your medicine bag as did the Pawnee," I said. "Because I suspect they'll be on us real soon."

I was right. Except it was only one. And she appeared to

be older than the nearby ledge of worn boulders that served to dry a red blanket. She did not look up at our horses' splashing but continued to hum in singsong tones as she wrung another blanket with wrists that seemed as frail as chicken bones.

"Good afternoon," Rebecca called.

With a wave of my hand, I cut anything else Rebecca might have said. She glared at me with pursed lips.

I stepped off my horse and enjoyed briefly the rush of cool water that filled my boots. I handed the medicine bag pole to Rebecca, halter-led my horse to a nearby tree, and looped the reins around a branch. Then I dug some chewing tobacco from a small can in my saddlebag and waded upstream to the woman.

She showed no sign she knew I was there.

I set the tobacco on a nearby boulder, then squatted on my haunches at the edge of the shoreline and joined her in silence. I could only see the back of her head, hair gray in two braids. She wore a buckskin dress, greasy with matted fringes. Her shoulders hardly moved as her hands and elbows dipped and rose with the efficiency born of thousands of days of beading and awl work. She pulled another blanket out of the river, slapped it against a boulder a half dozen times, and wrung it as she had done the others. A small stack of blankets lay submerged just beneath the surface of the river, held down by stones.

Fleas and lice, I guessed. Indians didn't place much stock in soap—and who's to say that the smell of lye soap is any better than fire grease? But fleas and lice were a different matter. If I was right, she was drowning them.

The underside of my thighs began to ache before she swiped that chaw of tobacco from the rock and stuffed it into her mouth. She grunted with pleasure.

I said nothing. Only showed respect by waiting for her to speak first.

Finally, she did. But without turning, and it came out in Sioux. When I still said nothing, she pivoted and fixed her black eyes upon me. Her cheeks bunched into soft, wrinkled apples as she grinned. A green thread of tobacco juice from the side of her mouth marked one of the grooves of her old skin.

I signed a greeting.

Her eyes widened slightly before she too raised her hands and greeted me with sure, quick movements of her bent fingers. Had our conversation been verbal, it might have sounded like this:

"Have you come to trade?"

"No."

"The girl. She was worth many rifles."

"I did not trade for her."

"The horses. With war paint. What warrior would trade blankets for a horse?"

"I did not trade."

"Gold, then. For a bottle of whiskey, I will give you this." She fingered a small pouch of soft leather and pulled out a nugget the size of a bullet. "For more whiskey, I will lead you to its source."

"I have not come to trade. I carry no whiskey. Gold is not worth the price that many pay to obtain it."

A nod of agreement.

"The medicine bag." I pointed. "We seek its rightful owner."

She studied my face. I did not look away.

She stood and cupped her hands around her mouth and called several sharp words in Sioux, words that bounced off the canyon walls.

Seconds later, five braves rode out from an invisible crevice along the cliff walls.

None wore war paint, none carried ceremonial spears. This was not even a hunting party. Their knives were sheathed, rifles hanging on straps across their backs. They seemed more like braves recruited on a moment's notice from the nearest campfires.

Strangely, I found it more frightening that they appeared so casual. It was a strong message indeed that I was in their territory, and that they were in such command there was no need to show fierceness.

The brave on the lead horse barked several more words at the old woman. She lifted her skirt hem and crossed to the other side of the river.

All five braves stepped down from their horses. Unlike fort Indians, nothing marked association with whites. They wore no vests, no store-bought shirts, no black floppy hats. Instead, their smooth skin gleamed copper above their loincloths.

Two braves moved past me, neither veering to avoid me, nor deliberately crowding me. I refused to give in to the urge to turn my head to watch them. Should these Sioux want me dead, nothing I could do now would save my life. Even if I did manage to shoot all five, we were so far into the Black Hills that their brethren would have us tracked down and pegged across anthills before sundown. The skin between my shoulder blades itched, just to know they stood somewhere behind me.

The largest of the braves stepped in front of me. The last two moved up behind him.

"This is sacred ground," he signed. "Forbidden to those with pale skin."

My hunch was that my scalp would hang beside the others on his belt if I acted as a humble seeker of permission. Yet I dared not push too hard, either.

"I serve as a guide," I signed in return. "To one whose skin is not pale." Finally, I dared turn, using the need to point at Rebecca to see the positions of the braves behind me. One held the halter of Rebecca's horse. The other held O'Neal's horse.

"If she is of us, she needs no guide among the People."

"She comes from across the great water. She seeks to return the medicine bag to its rightful owner."

A flinching of the skin around his eyes betrayed interest. He pointed at O'Neal. "The other?"

"Taken from the Pawnee," I signed.

"With the horses?"

"With the horses."

Without removing his stare from my face, the brave spoke quickly to the others. He then pointed at her, pointed at me, jabbed his chest to sign, "She is your woman?"

I shrugged.

More guttural Sioux.

Moments later, I heard Rebecca cry out. I spun. The brave had dropped the reins and was pulling her from her horse.

Was this a test?

The old woman surely had been. There had been too many plumes of silt washing downstream to be merely from her, too few wet blankets on the ledge, and her questions too pointed. My guess was that we'd been seen much earlier, and that indeed curiosity had prompted them to set her in our path. Surrounded by Sioux braves, one would have little incentive to admit to seeking gold or trading whiskey. Treatment of a harmless old woman, on the other hand, would show an intruder's true intentions.

Rebecca cried out again as the brave grabbed her legs, threw her over his shoulders, and marched through the shallow water toward us. She could only pound helplessly at his back.

It was his leer of pleasure that removed any of my careful calculations on the best way to handle this.

Perhaps the brave had expected no reaction. Not here, not with the power of my life or death in the hands of the four other braves. In two strides, I reached him as he stepped onto the sand bank, and as his leer faded to puzzlement, I kicked him in the groin.

His upper body plunged forward as he clutched himself. Rebecca tumbled off his back. I brought my knee up and slammed it into his chin and at the same time brought both my hands down on the back of his neck.

Clean fury filled me, but he had no fight, and I dimly heard myself roaring disappointment above his crumpled body. I turned, and before any of the other braves reacted, I yanked at the buckle of my holster and let it drop to the ground.

"Come on," I said as I beckoned them forward. "No knives. No guns."

I don't know if I was bluffing. I do know that when black rage takes a man over, he will pit himself against a mountain. Foolish as it was, I was ready to die fighting.

I did not receive the chance.

"Samuel!"

I took a step forward.

"Samuel!"

I understood through my fog of anger that it was Rebecca. The lead brave's eyes shifted from me to her.

"Samuel!"

Rebecca had undone the top buttons of her shirt and was peeling it back to reveal the tops of her shoulders and her lower neck.

She was pointing at the bear's claw necklace.

"Tell them it belongs to Red Cloud," she said. "Tell them now."

Red Cloud? Chief of chiefs among the Sioux? I gaped at her.

"Yes," she pleaded. "Stop all of this. Tell them I am his granddaughter."

CHAPTER 28

SEVEN DIED WHILE WE waited in the Sioux camp for Red Cloud.

How many before, I could not say.

The four braves had reacted with stone faces to my own incredulous description of Rebecca as Red Cloud's granddaughter. The bear's claw necklace probably spoke more loudly than my gestures, for the largest brave had grunted more commands to the others, and Rebecca and I were allowed to return to our horses and follow. They had ignored the one on the ground, and I gathered by their contemptuous laughter that they felt he earned his punishment by failing to pay attention to a potential foe.

They had led us upward along a trail—I noted that they had left the old woman to find her own way without a horse—that wound through the hills for several miles. Long before reaching the tepees of camp, Rebecca and I saw the already dead.

They were on the high hills, silhouettes of sorrow set atop burial scaffolds. If we rode closer, I knew, we would see that each dark shadow consisted of a scaffold of four forked posts, high enough that wild animals could not reach the bodies. A cross frame of sturdy branches supported each bundle of tanned skin, hide wrapped around a body prepared for burial. I had only seen a Shoshoni funeral, so it was from hearsay provided by the mountain men that I knew a Sioux brave would have badges of his war record, eagle feathers, placed in his hair, and beside his body in that bundle would be placed those things he most cherished: his weapons, his war paint, his flute. I knew, too, that his best friend would, at the grave-site, kill the dead warrior's favorite horse so that they could travel together in the Land of Many Lodges. When a woman died, her face was painted and her awl case and sewing kit placed beside her in the death bundle.

That the edge of the high hills was dotted with burial scaf-folds told me many other people had already died, too, for such ceremony was only provided for those with honor. I could guess that for each scaffold, two or three or more of little consequence were buried in shallow graves near the crest of the hill.

Once in camp, I understood the cause of such sorrow. Smallpox.

I had a friend in boyhood who had died from it. Chills and high fever. A rash that filled with pus and swelled him so that I barely recognized his agonized features. Had he not died, it would have left him blind.

Throughout the next few days, Rebecca and I discovered how badly this camp was hit. During our wait, the Sioux made no effort to confine neither Rebecca nor me. Had we not risked our lives to seek Red Cloud? Why then would we leave? And if we did, where could we run to escape their trackers? O'Neal, of course, remained day and night on a bed of spruce boughs, tended occasionally by the old woman who we had first met on the river.

With that limited freedom, Rebecca and I spent most of our daylight hours among their sick. It was a rare tepee, unaffected either by the disease or by sorrow in its deadly aftermath.

Those afflicted suffered beneath buffalo robes, chilled and shaking one moment, and in the next, feverishly begging for water or throwing aside the robes to seek the cooler outside air.

Those in sorrow walked the camp circle, weeping and wailing and singing of their grief. Some of the women had, in expression of their agony, severed their little fingers at the first joint.

Rebecca and I did what we could. We tried to convince many of the Sioux to stay away from their stricken loved ones, that it only increased the chances of their own death to remain close-by. Our advice was ignored.

The savage irony was that we could walk from infected tepee to infected tepee to deliver water without fear of contracting smallpox. We had both in our childhood been dosed with vaccine made from cowpox serum.

Again and again, Rebecca complained bitterly that the strongest and mightiest of these Sioux were struck low by something so preventable. Again and again, Rebecca spoke of what she might do to help these people.

I only listened with half an ear. Whatever thoughts I had away from the suffering of these people was on what Rebecca insisted on keeping hidden from me.

I had asked Rebecca about her blood claim to Red Cloud only once, while we first rode into camp. She'd apologized for keeping it secret but had declared with much insistence that she could not tell me more. I decided right there it would be futile to inquire again. And I had my pride. For me, asking again would have been like begging. I'd thrown the dice by deciding to stay with her into the Black Hills, and they'd rolled so far I had no choice but to stay in the game.

After the seventh died, a boy barely out of the moss-filled swaddles of cloth that served as diapers, I found Rebecca in tears.

We were at the edge of the camp, surrounded by the hills and alone.

"How they must hate the white," she whispered. "My pain for this child is more than I knew could exist, and I am not the mother. How much more so if the child were mine?"

That was a question without an answer.

"The buffalo," she said. "I see how these people live. Every part of the buffalo is of use to them. And we took ten minutes to ride through a herd killed only for tongue and hide."

I put my arm around her shoulders and let her lean her head against the crook of my neck.

"Two different worlds," I said. "One can't understand the other. Sioux think it almost blasphemous that someone would claim a piece of land. White take ownership with a piece of paper, then barter that deed."

"Samuel, someone must speak for these people."

She began to cry again, silently, with tears that fell onto the young child in her lap. I was selfish enough to be glad that for once I was not responsible for those tears.

Until I realized I was part of the tribe that laid claim to land with paper deeds.

We were both quiet, then, each for different reasons, and that is how Red Cloud found us. Rebecca seated with the dead boy across her lap, me kneeling and staring at the ground, with my arms around her.

CHAPTER 29

H<small>E STOOD WITH THE SUN</small> behind him. Deliberately done, I suspected. Against the glare, I saw only the dark outlines of his head and the single eagle feather that rose above it.

I stood.

Rebecca did not. Lost in grief, she remained seated with the dead boy's body cradled in her lap, her head bowed low, hair fallen softly across the boy's still face. She stroked the boy's cheek with one hand and reached upward with the other to keep her fingers intertwined among mine as I stood beside her.

Without letting go of her hand, I shifted slightly to take the sun out of my eyes.

Red Cloud was fiercely wiry, a man easily older, smaller, and lighter than I, but with a fire in his eyes and long-set anger in the tight muscles of his face. His braids, bound with wraps of red cloth, reached well below his shoulders. He wore a once black but now dusty formal dinner jacket with wide lapels. Beneath it, a dark soldier's shirt with a rounded collar tightly buttoned at the neck. On anyone else, the combination would have seemed laughable. With Red Cloud's smoldering dignity, it belonged.

He spoke, at length, in Sioux.

I began to raise my free hand to sign that I did not speak his language.

"Why should you not be dead, Red Cloud says." The voice came from behind me.

I did not turn to see the translator, did not take my eyes from Red Cloud's. At mention of his name, Rebecca stirred.

"You are a white man in the land given us by the Great Spirit and by treaty," the voice continued. "The white man lies and steals. The white man wants all. My lodges were once many and because of the white man now are few. I have killed many of the soldiers to keep this land. Why should you not be dead?"

Red Cloud watched my face.

"Red Cloud is known far and wide as a warrior," I said. "One who fights without mercy. Yet he is also known as a man of honor. Is there honor in killing the man who guides one who seeks Red Cloud as the father of her mother?"

The man behind me spoke rapid Sioux.

Red Cloud grunted. My reply would not have surprised him. High, narrow trails of black smudge at the tops of several faraway hills over the last few days had been good indication that our presence had been communicated across the hills. Once arrived here—unless Red Cloud was a fool—he would have spoken to the braves who first stopped us. And Red Cloud was no fool, not the Sioux chief who had badgered travelers and forts along the Bozeman so effectively that he and his negotiations had become the most compelling reason that the Black Hills had been granted to his people in '68.

Red Cloud did not glance at Rebecca. Interest shown was

weakness shown. I was also willing to bet six months' wages that he had satisfied his curiosity earlier by watching her unseen.

A few words from Red Cloud.

After a pause, the voice behind me spoke. "Any person may make claims of kinship to Red Cloud."

"Few, however, are those who carry his blood," I said.

"Please help me, Samuel," Rebecca whispered. "Take the boy."

I did. He felt no heavier than the blanket around him, and it took no effort to hold him to my chest as she moved to her feet and faced Red Cloud.

"My mother gave me this medicine bag," Rebecca said and pulled it from her shoulder. "I have come to ask you if indeed she was your daughter."

Slow, measured Sioux words reached Red Cloud from behind me as the translator gave him Rebecca's words. Red Cloud replied to the translator, who stepped into view and took from Rebecca the medicine bag. The translator was a young brave, heavily muscled, and naked above his loincloth.

Red Cloud spoke in brief bursts, hardly allowing the translator to finish before starting the next flow of Sioux.

"Indeed, it has been since the year of Heavy Snow that I have seen this medicine bag. Woman Who Sings to Wolves took it from me and caused me some shame and much grief, for she was lovely to see and I loved her as a favorite daughter. Yet you cannot be of my blood, for she had not been given to a man and did not bear me grandchildren. She ran from us to the hills, and she was never heard from again."

I thought this through. The Sioux called Rebecca's mother Woman Who Sings to Wolves. The Pawnee called Rebecca's mother Evening Star. I could think of no reason for this, unless the Pawnee had stolen Woman Who Sings to Wolves.

"This necklace?" Rebecca asked. She removed it and, ignoring the translator, handed it directly to Red Cloud, who rolled it in his fingers as he examined it.

"This too once belonged to me," the translator said after Red Cloud spoke slowly in grave tones. "A gift I had passed on to Woman Who Sings to Wolves."

"She was my mother!" Rebecca cried.

Red Cloud waited to hear what she had said with such heat, then shook his head and told us again it could not be possible. He asked us who we had killed to steal both the necklace and medicine bag, and how we had known it belonged to him. I was ready to point out that knowing it had once belonged to him was a strong argument in our favor, when I remembered something else.

"Rebecca," I said. "Show him the photograph."

I spoke to the translator. "Open the bag. Take from it the flat parcel wrapped in cloth. Untie the strings and ask Red Cloud if he sees Woman Who Sings to Wolves."

We waited. Somewhere among the pines, a horse neighed and was answered by another. Muted voices reached us, too, as did the smoke from fires among the tepees. In the moments we waited, several jays bounced from branch to branch of a nearby tree, screaming at each other and flashing blue in the sunlight. And beyond all of this, burial scaffolds at the top of the hill reminded me of the light burden in my arms.

Why, with such reminders of death, did I not fear now? Red Cloud had led his warriors against Fetterman in '66, joining hundreds of other Sioux and Cheyenne who massacred one hundred sixty soldiers, almost within sight of Fort Phil Kearny. His embittered hatred at the loss of his land was legendary, his cruelty unparalleled, even among a tribe renowned across the Plains for savagery. Red Cloud need only nod his head and I would face a tortured death that would take days.

Red Cloud bent his head to study the photograph, and

after long seconds, he raised it again. I thought I could hear sadness in his voice.

"Take the dead child to his mother and return to us here," Red Cloud told us. I hid a grin of admiration. The old fox knew English and had hidden it from us. It was a great trick. "Among the living, there are many questions to be answered."

CHAPTER 30

WE SAT CROSS-LEGGED at the edge of a wide meadow. It had taken almost an hour to give Red Cloud the story that Rebecca had told me. The expedition of 1853. Her upbringing in an orphanage—a concept that had been difficult to explain and at which Red Cloud had asked many details about the barbaric practices of a people who abandoned their children to strangers. The medicine bag she had been given upon her birthday. Her trip across the ocean to this territory.

I then gave a brief narration of our journey but did not stint on any details of the theft of Pawnee horses. If the Sioux were anything like the Shoshoni who had raised me, I did not hurt myself by such immodesty. Unlike among the white, it is considered great form to recount and embellish any acts of bravery, and I hoped to make my stay easier among the Sioux by sparing no chance to let them know how I had bested their traditional enemies.

When Rebecca had finished her story, I mine, and Red Cloud his questions, we shared a silence, not unfriendly.

"You are truly the daughter of my daughter," Red Cloud finally said to Rebecca. "I knew that before you showed me the medicine bag, for you appear so much as her that my heart aches with sadness at the memories you bring."

He pondered that, then said. "Life is filled with strangeness."

I nodded, thinking of the chain of events that had brought all of us together.

"On the paper that holds the image of people," he said, "Woman Who Sings to Wolves stood among Pawnee. How can that be?"

I pulled my hat from my head, ran my fingers through my hair, and scratched the back of my head as I searched for a reply. I hadn't looked closely enough at the photograph earlier, and I was impressed by Red Cloud's powers of observation.

"I'd guess only Rebecca's mother would have the answer to that mystery," I began, "and she is—"

Red Cloud lifted a hand to silence me.

"Let my granddaughter speak," he said. "I believe she has hidden much."

Rebecca glanced at me. I read guilt on her face. Slowly, she nodded. "I am truly sorry, Samuel. When you discover what I kept from you, you will understand that I could not trust anyone, not even you."

"Go ahead and bare your soul to someone trustworthy like Red Cloud," I told her. "He ain't killed and tortured much more'n a couple hundred men over the last few years."

Red Cloud slapped his belly and chuckled. Having my sour humor duly appreciated did not ease my anger. I'd begun to place a trust in this woman, even been shot for her, and now . . .

Rebecca placed her hand on mine. "Samuel, I'm not blind. You've kept more than a couple of secrets from me, too."

I had no reply to that.

She turned to Red Cloud. "Why is it that you believe I have the answer?"

He replied with a question of his own. "Why is it that you believe I am the father of your mother when you spent your childhood among the white man far across the ocean?"

Again, I was impressed by the old fox's ability to think. It was easy to understand how he had bested the treaty negotiators in '68.

Rebecca reached for her medicine bag. She pulled out the piece of cartridge belt. "This belonged to a man named Louis Wilcombe. I fondly hope he is still alive among the Sioux."

"Louis Wilcombe!" The translator had spoken, not Red Cloud. The older Indian rebuked him sharply.

"Continue," Red Cloud commanded.

"This piece of belt holds a letter that had been folded and resewn between the canvas strips. I found it one day, read it, and hid it again," Rebecca said. "My mother left your camp to deliver this letter to soldiers at Omaha."

Omaha? That was clear to the eastern edge of Nebraska. There were easily a half dozen other outposts far closer, not the least of which was Fort Laramie.

Red Cloud remained impassive at her statement—while a swirl of questions raised dust in my mind.

Rebecca spoke softly to me. "When I told you that I had shown a piece of gold to the army officials in Washington, Samuel, I did not tell you that I'd also hinted to them about the letter."

"You could have let them investigate."

"As you will hear, I had reason to believe it might result in Louis Wilcombe's death, if he wasn't dead already. I wanted to come here and find him myself."

"I appreciate your previous forthrightness."

She shook her head at my sarcasm. "Did I have reason to believe I could trust you? Or anyone?"

"Read the letter," I said dryly.

"I shall," she said. "From memory. I do not want to take apart the canvas."

Rebecca closed her eyes and in a steady voice recited in slow and measured words. " 'June 3, 1853. To the commanding officer at Fort Omaha. I can only pray that this letter reaches you. Notwithstanding grave injury which prevents me from travel, I also fear for my life at the hands of our own soldiers. Thus, this messenger. Please treat her with the respect due to the daughter of a great warrior, Red Cloud of the Oglala Sioux. I write from his camp because of a raid upon the supply train bound for Fort Laramie from your command in Omaha. I have no doubt that in the last year news of the raid has both reached your ears and also been blamed squarely upon the Sioux. I believe I am the only white witness to say otherwise, and for this reason, I fear death at the hands of the three soldiers responsible for the carnage of the raid. My report is as follows . . .' "

The translator broke in and spoke hurriedly in Sioux. Red Cloud absorbed his words, then nodded.

Rebecca began again. " 'Our supply wagons had reached the Rawhide River when shortly after noon on the fifth of May a rider appeared with a message for Sergeant Steven Byrne that the Sioux were massing for attack on Fort Laramie and reinforcements were crucial. Sergeant Byrne sent most of the soldiers ahead. No sooner had the dust of their departing horses settled when Sergeant Byrne pulled his rifle and calmly shot the soldier beside me. Four others, including the rider who had delivered the message, also began to shoot at the rest of us. My life was saved only because I sat on the buckboard of a supply wagon, and my team of horses bolted, causing the bullet from Sergeant Byrne's rifle to pierce only my shoulder. I am quite sure all the soldiers were slaughtered, but, as I was urging my horses to flee, I cannot confirm this. Shortly thereafter Sioux warriors did appear and engaged Sergeant Byrne in battle, an action that prevented them from pursuing me.' "

Rebecca paused once more for the translator to catch up.

Now Red Cloud nodded for her to continue.

" 'In the months since, as a guest among the Sioux and an able translator, which enables me to rely on their reports, I have been able to determine the intent of Sergeant Byrne and the aftermath of what happened. The sergeant and his four soldiers sought the gold and rifles hidden in the wagon I drove from them. Two of his men were slain by the Sioux. I have heard also that Sergeant Byrne and the two other survivors began to take scalps from the dead soldiers around them, which I conclude was done to place blame upon the Sioux. I believe it was John Harrison, the surviving soldier, who with Byrne turned on their fellow men. The other survivor, the messenger, I could not identify, but I do not believe he is a military man. Should this letter reach you, I urge you to begin an immediate investigation. Until then, I shall remain among the Sioux, for I believe that Byrne and Harrison will murder me on sight and justify their actions by accusing me of betraying the troops to the Sioux who now keep me among their camps. Yours sincerely, Lieutenant Louis Wilcombe.' "

Rebecca opened her eyes again. I should have been mesmerized by the letter she had just recounted to us. Woman Who Sings to Wolves was trying to help Louis Wilcombe by getting the letter to an unbiased military man who might open the investigation.

And I was mesmerized by the letter to a degree, but moreso I was struck by how much it thrilled my heart to observe her, despite the momentous news of that letter. I felt my anger at her secretiveness fade.

She turned to me. "Samuel . . ."

I shook my head. "Were I you, I would have played my cards equally close to my chest."

The letter explained much. Hearing John Harrison mentioned again had been like a lightning bolt to my nerves, for now I understood the connection. And Wilcombe had guessed rightly that the survivors would wrongfully put the blame of the Rawhide River Massacre on the Sioux, as that is how Washington had told the story to Rebecca.

The letter also explained her need to keep her knowledge from me until she was safe among the Sioux. It was a letter that held a two-decade secret of gold, rifles, and murder, exposing John Harrison, Sergeant Steven Byrne, and the third unnamed man as traitors, thieves, and murderers. Only a fool would trust a stranger with that knowledge, and, new to this land, all men in the territories were strangers to her. The letter explained her unwavering determination to reach the Sioux. And it explained why O'Neal had been following her since Washington: someone there did not want murder exposed, even twenty years later. And there was, of course, the gold and rifles.

Or was there?

I looked at Red Cloud. "You let Louis Wilcombe live in your camp?"

"He bartered for his life" came the reply.

I tried to imagine his headlong flight from the butchery at Rawhide River. Indians and soldiers behind, unknown trails ahead. And the bulky clattering of a loaded supply wagon. A slow supply wagon. Had not the Sioux descended, the soldiers would have easily caught him. So, too, the Sioux later at their leisure. Wilcombe would never have had an opportunity to ditch the gold or rifles.

"What did he have to barter?" I asked. "He could not have hid the gold or rifles. You immediately took both from him."

Red Cloud grinned, exposing broken teeth.

"I remember that day well," Red Cloud said. "We traveled in a small war party and heard shooting. It was with great delight that we saw white soldiers killing each other. To be generous, we did not delay in offering assistance in such a tiresome task. The one soldier who fled also gave us great delight, for he fell unconscious and was unable to protect his wagon. Yet greater delight awaited us inside the wagon, for we found gold and rifles."

I grinned at a thought. "Gold that later appeared at Fort Laramie?"

Red Cloud chuckled. "We thought it wise to turn the coins into lumps of gold to hide from the military that it was their gold." He frowned. "Yet it was unwise. It has brought soldiers again into the hills. The general with long yellow hair. They believe this gold comes from the hills. It has brought other whites into our sacred land."

I nodded. Custer's foray.

Rebecca interrupted our conversation. "You say Louis Wilcombe was unconscious, and that you had found the gold and rifles. Why did you not kill him?"

Red Cloud brought his dark, glittering eyes around to stare at her and answered slowly. "As I raised my killing club, Louis Wilcombe opened his eyes and spoke to us in Sioux. Louis Wilcombe told us he could help. Then fell back. I stayed the killing club until he awoke again. I asked him to explain. He said he would teach us to speak the white man's language. I asked him why we should learn. He replied by asking if I trusted any of the white translators." Red Cloud smiled, bringing the shadow of his wrinkles dark into his face. "I saw his wisdom. Many times since has it helped me to listen to white men who believed I could not understand their words."

The young brave lifted his head from its respectful bow. Red Cloud noticed the movement.

"You may speak of Louis Wilcombe now," Red Cloud said.

"Louis Wilcombe, my father," the brave said, "taught me, too, the words of the white."

Rebecca sat forward, as startled as I was. "Our father! He is alive."

"Two winters ago, fever took him from us."

She sat back, but I could see her watching the young brave, and I could almost hear the thoughts she held. This was a half brother.

"Yes," Red Cloud told her. "Louis Wilcombe remained among us. He told me often that he had no faith his story would be believed at the fort. His word against three others. And who would doubt that the Sioux"—a wolfish grin appeared—"were not the ones responsible for dead soldiers?"

As a sun going behind clouds, so was the disappearance of that grin. "Yet had I known that before he took a wife and fathered his son here, that earlier he had shared the blanket with Woman Who Sings to Wolves . . ."

Red Cloud straightened his legs and with little effort stood from the grass. "I have spoken much," he said. "we shall talk of decisions later."

Decisions?

Red Cloud read my face moments after I had struggled more heavily to my own feet. "No. You will not be held among us. You have my gratitude for guiding my granddaughter to her people. Word shall go out among the tribes that the man with the long scar on his face is not to be harmed. And unless it is in battle that you meet our warriors, that word shall be followed until the mountains move."

He turned with dignity to hold his arms out to Rebecca. She stepped forward and clasped his forearms.

"I believe it is her decision that shall be discussed at the fires of camp," he said.

"Rebecca?" I asked. But already my heart sensed her answer, an answer my mind should have known much, much earlier. This was the woman who had lived and dreamed for the day she could claim and be claimed. This was the woman I had pushed away during the black, lonely hours when she had offered all. I waited with dread for her next words to send me to the edge of the abyss that held darkness in front of me.

"I did not seek rifles or gold, but family," she said. Her face was grave. "I wish to remain among the Sioux."

CHAPTER *31*

THREE OF US RODE to Fort Laramie. Two would return to the Black Hills—Rebecca and Moves Dancing, her half brother, the Sioux who had learned English from their father, Louis Wilcombe. They intended to purchase supplies, in particular medical supplies and smallpox vaccine for Rebecca to administer, as Fort Laramie had the only stores within two-weeks travel of the Sioux camps.

I knew, too, that Rebecca—satisfied by Red Cloud's confirmation of Louis Wilcombe's version of the Rawhide River slaughter—now wanted to prod the military into beginning an inquiry that would clear her father's name.

My own destination after Fort Laramie was less sure. I did have to return to the town of Laramie, some hundred miles south and west of the fort, to discharge my obligation to Marshal Evrett. What might come after was something I had no urge to consider.

Before all of this had begun with an irksome Indian thrust into my path, I had earned a truce with myself, a truce based on seeking the most comfortable level of survival.

Rightly or wrongly, in the aftermath of Smickles' shotgun, I had hoped I might find a way back to the peace it took to endure the hours of solitude that came with moving through the territories alone. I was prepared to examine my soul's destiny in that solitude and live with what I learned.

Now I no longer had the confidence I could accomplish that, not with the squeeze on my heart from Rebecca's decision to stay with the Sioux. I did not want to be alone anymore.

To ease the burden on my heart as we moved, hour by slow hour, out of the Black Hills into the parched, rolling grasslands of the basins, I forced myself to ponder the unanswerable. Who had directed O'Neal—finally conscious but delirious with fever among the Sioux—to follow Rebecca? Who had directed Harrison? One of the other survivors of the Rawhide River Massacre? Why get O'Neal to then follow Harrison? What was it that had driven the Pawnee to such lengths to capture Rebecca?

Yet even with those questions to distract me, often I caught myself close to the edge of the abyss of darkness that threatened when I thought of saying good-bye to Rebecca at Fort Laramie. During those moments, as each plodding horse step brought us closer to parting, I told myself again and again to tear down the walls I had built between us, to let her understand how badly I wanted to have that chance once more where she might put her body into my arms and her soul into my trust.

But I could not.

Because to do so with any honor would require that she understood all of me, and there are some walls that a man builds with good reason. I knew too much of me would remain a stranger to her, unless the day might arrive when I could finally close my eyes and not find the image of those gray eyes boring into mine as Henry Reed waited for me to beg for mercy from the pistol pressed against my nose.

I could not forgive myself for that day.

So I rode in the silence, without telling Rebecca of how I longed for her.

Days later, we crested the hills north of Fort Laramie for our first view again of the Bighorn Mountains as they swept their hazy blue majesty in a ridge north to south as far as the eye could see, crests visible against the equally blue sky only because of the snow that lined the peaks, a refreshing contrast to the browns and dusty greens of the folded land in front.

I noted the stillness on Rebecca's face as she drank in that view.

"Looks some different from horseback than from train, don't it?"

She smiled, as if I had read her thoughts. I had not guarded my heart against her unexpected smile, and whatever crossed my face must have suggested some of the pain it brought, for she attempted to place a hand on my arm.

"Twenty, maybe thirty miles as the crow flies, ma'am," I said. "We'll be at the fort before noon tomorrow. Then I reckon you'll be glad to be rid of me."

At the cold tone of my voice, she withdrew her hand from my arm.

————

Some folks held that the collection of buildings on the flatlands at the confluence of the Laramie and North Platte Rivers was a rose in the wilderness. Others called it a miserable apology for a fort. My own guess was that a body's opinion depended on where he'd been and where he was headed. Coming out of the great wilderness of the Rockies and back to this semblance of civilization, it was a rose indeed. But fresh from memories of Omaha or Kansas City or points farther east, this grouping of tents and wood shacks would hardly appear to be the important way station it was for a cavalcade of trappers, traders, missionaries, immigrants, Pony Express Riders, and, of course, soldiers.

On our approach at midmorning, we rode along the flat, bottom river land, crossed the deep grooves left by settlers' wagons, skirted various groups of sullen or drunk Indians, and moved into the irregular stream of foot and horse traffic that crossed the bridge that had replaced the Laramie River ferry.

"This can't be the fort," Rebecca said once we'd crossed the bridge. "It has no walls."

I pointed at a haze of dust rising from the center of the fort buildings—cavalrymen turning their horses in full gallop with pinwheel precision on the large parade grounds.

"Doesn't need walls," I said. "Injuns can't get within a mile unseen, and there's enough men, horses, and cannon that even Red Cloud wouldn't attack."

We continued to ride, and as if to confirm my opinion, she scanned both directions to take in the stables off far ahead to our right, the rows of barracks that formed a loose square around the parade grounds up and to our left, and the scattered buildings that lined the road that cut left from the bridge and wound around the barracks and parade grounds like a huge horseshoe. Fort Laramie was almost a town now, with the bustling activity of off-duty soldiers, officers' wives, and settlers in rough-hewn clothing.

Moves Dancing did not bother to gaze at his surroundings. He'd been here, of course, more than once with his grandfather, and faced the need to carry himself with the dignity befitting someone of his rank within the Sioux.

I pointed again, this time at a building straight ahead, at

the other side of the horseshoe formed by the road. "Cut across behind the barracks," I told Rebecca. "Alongside that building with the flag, you'll find the post trader's store. I'll be along shortly."

She did not ask my destination, and I would have been hard pressed to explain my whim, for a small stone church at the opposite end of the parade grounds had caught my eye, and the thought of cool, quiet darkness inside drew me like a deer to water.

Moves Dancing and Rebecca continued ahead, and I dismounted shortly after in front of that church. I pulled my hat from my head, clutched it in my right hand, and walked in slowly, probably with the same hesitation that a deer approaches a water hole at dusk. It was as cool and quiet inside as I had expected.

My boots clicked softly on the stone floor. I did not stop until I had reached the front of the church. Sunlight cut across the wood altar. The candles atop it had not been changed, and the stumps were heavy with cooled drippings of wax.

I leaned my left hand against the roughness of the pew beside me. A twinge of pain ran up my arm to remind me of the gunshot wound so recently healed. So much had happened since my shoot-out with Harrison. Not only events, but a shifting of my heart that now filled me with a sad loneliness I did not like.

Was that why I was here in this church? Because that sad loneliness was a wedge driving me to acknowledge I could not be my own island? Regardless of the reason, I did not know what to do next alongside the pew. To me, in our settled hometown before the Oregon Trail excursion, churches had first been a place where old ladies presented Bible stories as fairy tales, describing angels who plucked people from the ground like benevolent eagles, and who also spoke about a throne standing on the very same clouds that, at the age of eight, I plainly knew could not even bear the pressure of a light wind without breaking into pieces, let alone carry a palace and throne. Later, churches to me had been a place to learn about hellfire and brimstone, shouted at me by scrawny preachers with the spit of passion on their beards, preachers who didn't half measure up to the hardworking grit of the men and women who squirmed on the benches under their dire thunder. Or churches were the tents of the revivalists who ranted about saving souls, worked their crowds into chanting mobs eager to fill collection bags, and released their own passion, more often than not, with the swooning women who followed them into the darkness beyond the campers. Where was God in all of this?

Silence covered me in a blanket of peace, and I found myself staring at the cross high up on the wall behind the altar.

Where, indeed, was God? And how could a body find the truth behind all the noise of those who carried the trumpets and banners of religion as a way to proclaim their own righteousness?

Then I saw in my mind the picture of Rebecca with her head bowed in prayer the evening we had made our plan to escape the Pawnee and her head bowed all those mornings I had returned to camp with dew so heavy on the grass it soaked the sound of my approaching footsteps. I remembered her pain to witness the pain of others as she tended to the stricken Sioux, and I remembered her grief to hold the dying Sioux boy she had never once spoken to before his death. A grief of love. Love that spoke much louder than trumpets and banners.

I thought of the other loves I had witnessed in my life. The sacrifices of my mother along the wagon trail. How my dying father had cared about nothing in his agony except cradling a woman already dead. The fierce determination of Jed to protect me. My own pain at Jed's death. The instinct for the wholeness I'd felt so briefly as Rebecca kissed me.

And, strong as were the total loves of my own witness, I was only a small flame out of all the lives that had ever flickered a brief defiance at death. How much more the sum of the love that had burned and glowed in each life of the countless generations of men and women who had spanned the centuries and horizons of this world?

How could I attempt to believe, then, that we were only meat and bones doomed to become dust when, frail as we were, something as invisible and unexplainable as love mocked the very notion of a body without soul, and when something as enduring and unchanging as love was the glue that held all of us together across all of those centuries. What if all that love came from one source and reflected one source? What if a body found that source behind all the noise of religion, would there then be God and the beyond and something to take away the sting of death without meaning?

The silence of the church seemed to grow inside of me, and—was it something I imagined—I felt a peace as surely as if I had been touched, and when it departed slowly, I was wiser and sadder and stronger than in the moments before I had closed my eyes and bowed my head.

I wondered if it was too much to ask for a sign that it hadn't been my imagination.

"Lord," I said aloud, "begging your forgiveness, but you don't make it real easy to be found. I hope you know I'll keep my eyes wide open, but I'd appreciate a little help from your end."

I twisted my hat in my hands, almost uncomfortable. It had been that long since I'd prayed.

"I guess that's it. Amen."

As I shut the church door behind me, it did feel like a load had been taken from me. Reluctant to break my peace by speaking aloud to Rebecca or Moves Dancing, I decided not to ride and instead walked my horse down the road to the post trader's store.

That's how long my quiet mood lasted.

Because just as I reached the store, a short man stepped from the shadows between two buildings. A man with a buckskin jacket open to show two pistols tucked in his waistband, handles toward each other. A man who walked as if rolling on oiled wheels. A man with empty eyes as cold and gray as lead bullets. A man whose face had appeared in every nightmare I'd had since the day I'd watched my brother die. A man with a scatter-gun leveled at my belly. Henry Reed, sheriff of the entire Wyoming Territory.

He grinned at the shock on my face. "Drop the reins of that horse, boy. Then raise your hands real slow, 'cause I'm looking for any excuse to let the sun shine a big chunk of daylight through the center of your gut."

I did as directed.

If this was a sign from above, God had a powerful sense of humor.

CHAPTER 32

WITH HIM STANDING in front of me, it all came back in a jumbled rush that I could no longer avoid, the happenings around my brother's death, which I'd misrepresented to Marshal Evrett during our final conversation in the town jail of Laramie.

Yes, as I'd mentioned to Evrett, we'd been ambushed in Pueblo, and yes, I'd been wrongly accused of the bank robbery.

Yes, a woman bystander did die during the shoot-out near the stables outside our hotel. And yes, she—and Jed—had both fallen in ambush to the bounty hunter, Henry Reed, the man now standing in front of me.

I had not, however, informed Marshal Evrett of the woman's name—Leanna Whittington—or that she was more than a bystander, or why, because of her, Jed had neglected his customary caution and gone without me to take our prisoner, Nick Caxton, to our horses at the stable that fateful dawn.

Jed and I had met Leanna Whittington in a dance hall a month earlier. He'd watched in admiration from across the floor as she slapped the face of a cowboy who'd whispered one word too many during a quiet dance. Jed had actually pushed aside the man in his hurry to introduce himself, his eyebrows arched above the devil's smile that few women could resist and none could ignore. Jed and Leanna each burned with a seething wildness that set them apart from the mere mortals who they lit with their comet orbits, a wildness each recognized immediately in the other—and which drew them together that night as surely as two moths struggling to reach the same candle flame.

At that time, we were trailing Nick Caxton for the bounty money, asking after him from town to town. To quit pursuit was unthinkable to Jed. But before the evening had ended, it was equally unthinkable that he move on without Leanna Whittington. She joined us the next morning as we rode into the Colorado mountains. I don't think it took much persuasion on Jed's part.

As the third person on our ride through the territories, I had no jealousy at their obvious passion—in arguments and in love—for each other. Clara filled my heart, and even without that, I decided I felt no attraction for Leanna. The danger of her wildness intoxicated Jed but led me only to the same mild fascination I'd once felt to be standing outside a cage that held a panther. Unlike Jed, I told myself, I had no urge to enter the cage.

In Pueblo, shortly after we had successfully ambushed Nick Caxton in the saloon where his pockets were flush with bank notes and he with whiskey, Jed and Leanna had a toe-to-toe shouting match, and she stomped off into the night, leaving Jed and me to alternate vigils over the bound prisoner.

It was nearly dawn, during Jed's turn at guard duty in the other room, that a soft knock awoke me from the dreams of the woman that I loved. I sat up on the narrow bed. I did not have to reach far to lay grip on my gun, not fully clothed, boots on, and lying on top of the bedcovers.

I swung my feet off the bed and lit the oil lamp before I moved forward. I stood with my gun waist high in my right hand and turned the door knob with my left to keep my right shoulder and arm hidden to the person in the hallway. If I needed, I could shoot through the wood as I opened the door.

It was Leanna, armed only with two bottles of wine. I relaxed.

"Jed's down the hall in the other room," I told her. "Guarding Caxton."

She did not, as I expected, turn away. Instead, she smiled and pushed in.

"After our fight, Jed and I are not quite speaking yet." Her eyes, a brown that reflected no light, were open wide and frank. "I'm looking for brotherly advice."

She closed the door behind her.

Whatever breathing space there was in that cramped room seemed to disappear in the force of her presence. Jed could do it, too, say nothing and draw in awareness and attention as surely as if he had his guns out and ready to fire.

"I'm not sure advice will help when it comes to Jed," I replied. "He's got a mind no one can bend."

"He listens to you," she said. "He pretends like he's leading, but he doesn't do anything unless you give him the nod. It's like you're stronger and you gentle him."

I considered that but could not see it as true, and said as much.

She smiled. Her auburn hair was mussed, as if she had been running her hands through its thickness again and again.

I was conscious of the freckles that dotted her cream skin, too conscious of her presence and warmth.

She set one wine bottle down on the floor and with her strong, white teeth pulled the cork loose from the other. She tilted the bottle back and drank deeply. Trickles of wine escaped the corners of her mouth and flowed onto her neck like thin streams of blood.

This was one of the things that Jed craved about her. Her womanhood was inescapable—it hit you like a blast of heat—but she dressed in jeans, shirt, and vest like a man and had no compunction about keeping the manners of a man, one of these manners to pass a bottle without striking a dainty pose by insisting on glasses.

I shook my head.

She smiled again, drew another mouthful, and without warning moved herself to me, pulled the back of my head downward to press her lips against mine, and squirted the warm liquid into my mouth.

My swallow was a gasp of surprise. I stepped back and glared but could no longer deny to myself her effect on me.

"Jed's already told me he wants me gone," she said. "Nothing I do matters."

I wiped my mouth with the back of my hand. "Then why ask for advice?"

"Not advice," she said, "more like words to let me understand him."

She offered me the bottle. I shook my head again. In a few hours, Jed and I would be riding across open land with a bounty prisoner. Having bounty stolen by other hunters was not uncommon. I wanted a clear head.

"Afraid?" Her taunt was low and throaty.

At nineteen years of age, I was afraid of nothing. And had a need to prove it. I took the bottle from her hand. Each gulp warmed me like the lust in my blood.

"Tell me," she said as she moved closer. "Have you always traveled with Jed?"

I sat, heavily. She remained standing, where she could look down on me with the edge of the mocking smile that curved her lips upward.

"Ask Jed." But my brave front was useless, for the croak in my words had betrayed me.

The smile curved more, as if she had tasted something delicious. Drops of the red wine glistened on her lips.

"There's a price on his head, too," she said. "Did you know that?"

I'd read tales about a snake in the exotic Far East, one that fixed you with a stare and held you in that stare while you helplessly waited for it to strike. That is how I felt.

"No," I said. "It can't be."

She lowered the bottle down to my lips and laughed softly as she poured into my mouth. I gulped as fast as possible, but still it spilled onto my neck, which only caused her to laugh again.

"No? Then let me ask you again. Have you always traveled with him?"

I had not. He'd left me at that dance hall in Denver and for three years returned only in the summers.

"California," she whispered. "He killed a man in California."

"No." The wine was hitting me now. "No," I repeated, as if saying it louder would give it the conviction it lacked.

She lowered her head and stared into my eyes, her lips only inches from mine and her breathing so close that it felt as though I took her air into my lungs.

I believe I would have had the strength to push her away from me. Yes, I did want to kiss her, and I hated myself for it. But Jed was everything to me, and even if he no longer wanted her, I could not bring myself to become the traitor.

But I did not have the chance to push her away.

As she buried her face into my neck and ran her lips against my skin, I could see past her to the door, where Jed now stood and surveyed the room.

We locked eyes.

Panic, fear, shame, all paralyzed me into silence.

He shut the door on me.

I tried pushing Leanna away. She did not know what had happened behind her and only held me tighter.

The door opened.

"I'll be taking Caxton in alone," Jed told me from the hallway. His face showed no emotion. "I'll send your share of the money ahead to Denver. Wait for it there."

"Jed!"

"Don't follow," he finished with the same cold neutrality. "From here on, we ride separate trails."

That was it. The door closed on me.

Leanna pressed harder against me. I leveraged the heel of my hand against her forehead and pushed her back. I stood and let her tumble to the floor. I had to reach Jed.

But the room swirled. I'd drunk too much wine, too quickly.

Minutes later, I stumbled onto the street in front of the hotel and sucked in lungfuls of the cool air. Jed was already ahead of me, and first light was already gray.

Halfway to the stable, I realized that Leanna was following.

It did not matter. I had to reach Jed to explain.

That's when I heard the unmistakable echo of a gunshot. Then several more.

I broke into a weaving, shambling run. At the corner of the building I stopped. Despite my thick head, it was all clear, like a stage in front of me. Two horses standing along the side of the street, Nick Caxton, hands bound, cowering behind them both. Jed was ducked behind a water trough, flat on the ground. Water poured from bullet holes in the trough. There was a mushroom of blood at Jed's shoulder. Someone had shot him from ambush.

"Jed!" I called to let him know I was there to back him.

Jed spun in without rising at the sound of my voice and raised his gun.

He recognized me in time and lowered his arm. The crash of exploding gunpowder came instead from across the street, and a bullet crunched wood above my head, spraying my face with splinters. I ducked back.

Jed was still in my range of vision. He buried his chin in his shoulders as he turned his head to say something to me.

The light of early dawn was not yet strong, and in the stone's throw between us, I could only see the shadow of his face. He raised his gun again and pointed it at me.

I waited for the bullet, almost welcomed it, for the sickness inside me told me that I deserved it.

He waved me aside. I did not understand. Because I did not move, he had to rise to get a bead on the figure approaching behind me. He squeezed off a shot that sounded like two. Barely a moment later, I comprehended that it *was* two shots that had been fired.

The first bullet was Jed's, which caught Leanna just under the chin. She dropped, dead. Her gun had been out as she ran forward to help our gunfight, and in the dim light, he must not have recognized her as someone helping us.

The other shot came from the rifle across the street, and it smashed Jed in the right half of his chest.

I dove forward to reach him, and behind the safety of the water trough and in the mud forming in the water that gushed onto the dust, I held him.

"Jed, I didn't—"

"It hurts," he said.

Did he mean the bullets or what I had done? I can only torment myself with that question, for Jed coughed blood and died in my arms.

I looked up through a veil of tears to see the man with the gray eyes.

He kicked my gun—I'd dropped it beside me to hold Jed—away from me, stepped a few paces back to get position on the helpless Caxton, aimed briefly, and fired the shot that took him in the heart. The man with the gray eyes trained his gun back on me, walked backward as he moved to Caxton, pulled a Bowie knife loose from the sheath on his belt, bent, and swiftly cut loose the rope around the dead man's hands.

Gray Eyes pocketed the pieces of rope, stepped forward to me again and pressed the barrel against my nose and stared those cold gray eyes into mine.

"Beg, boy," he said, "beg for your life."

I pressed my lips together and prayed he would pull the trigger.

"Come on, boy, beg." He slashed the barrel against my face, raking my cheek with the gunsight.

"Hey!" A shout came from down the street. People were gathering to see the cause of all the commotion.

Gray Eyes smiled.

"You think I'm holstering this gun 'cause we got witnesses?" His voice was as cold as the smile. "Not a chance, boy. It's already been arranged, that you and your brother get the blame for robbing the bank in La Junta. With this rope in my pocket, it appears as if you and Caxton were set to leave town together. 'Nother words, you dead now saves a hanging later."

He smiled again. "No, boy, I ain't gonna pull the trigger. It'll give me more pleasure having you remember it was you that got your brother killed."

He kicked me in the chest and sent me flat backward in the mud. His next kick was like a railroad tie across my head, and when I woke, I was in jail, charged with murder and bank robbery and hoping they'd hang me soon.

CHAPTER 33

"YOU GONNA DENY you're Samuel Keaton?" Henry Reed flicked his eyes up and down, measuring me, his voice taking me back from my memory.

I said nothing.

"Not many with a scar like yours," he continued. "You'd be a fool to do so."

Still, I said nothing. My guts churned with hatred and fear. If there was any man in this world who could paralyze me, it was this one, the man who'd pistol-whipped me as I cringed in the time of my worst shame.

He studied me for several more seconds before speaking again. "By the powers vested in me by the territory of Wyoming," Henry Reed intoned, "I arrest you for the cold-blooded murder of Deputy John Harrison and for unlawful escape of custody."

He then grinned and cocked the scattergun. "Now that we got the paper work finished, you interested in resisting arrest?"

I made no move.

"That's a disappointment," he said.

He motioned with the scatter-gun. "What we're gonna do, boy, is have you turn around slow. Real slow. These soldiers behind me have as much hate for a man what killed a lawman as I do."

Three soldiers, peach fuzz and fear across their white faces, stepped out from the corner of the post trader's store behind Henry Reed, each armed with extended pistols trained on my head, as if they really did expect me to resist arrest. I wondered what tales Henry Reed had told of me.

I glanced at the door to the post trader's store.

Henry Reed caught that glance.

"Don't worry none about them Injuns you rode in with. They's in handcuffs, too."

The soldiers advanced. Two kept their pistols high. The third fumbled with handcuffs. When I turned—very, very slowly—the third soldier stood as far from me as possible as he cuffed my hands together, then tossed the key to Henry Reed.

"Get him on his horse," Reed commanded. That done, he spoke again. "Obliged, men. Give my thanks to Corporal Braude for volunteering your help. I should have my prisoners in Cheyenne by the end of the week."

The soldiers—they were barely more than boys—saluted Reed before departing.

He took the reins of my horse and began to lead me past the post trader's store.

"Well, boy, it appears I should have put you out of your misery back in Pueblo."

I found my voice. "You have no call to arrest the other two."

He stopped and turned to watch my face. "Judge'll see it different, being how they sheltered an escaped murderer." He shrugged. "Whatever happens to them lands on your shoulders, boy. Just like how you got your brother kilt."

I tasted blood on my tongue and realized then I'd bitten it through my clenched jaws.

We reached the far corner of the post trader's store, and Henry Reed stopped again. He tied the reins of my horse to a hitching post.

"You can always drop from your horse and run, but I'll just shoot you down."

He walked away without looking back. I struggled with my handcuffs but knew I would remain atop the horse.

A half minute later, Reed returned, riding his horse. A rope tied to his saddle led back to the halters of two other horses. In deference to her womanhood, the soldiers had handcuffed Rebecca's hands in front of her stomach. Moves Dancing, like me, had been handcuffed behind his back. It was not a joyful reunion.

———

Several hours out of Fort Laramie, Henry Reed turned our horses off the stagecoach road and walked us along a dried creek bed, westward to the shadows of the Bighorns. My skin—dry and dusty—now prickled cold as fresh fear sweat broke through. It was too early to set up camp. Thus, I couldn't see any good reasons for this diversion.

Until this, I'd managed to convince myself that Reed had taken us from Fort Laramie for the reasons he'd given the soldiers. My arrest for shooting John Harrison, and Rebecca and Moves Dancing for riding with me. I'd convinced myself that Deputy Smickles had gladly given my description to Reed, or that Evrett had done it in the course of his duty as a red-faced marshal tied by the escaping prisoner.

This detour, however, did not bode any good. All of this had begun with John Harrison's death. Harrison was also the man who'd seen through Rebecca's disguise in the town of Potter, exactly as if he'd been watching and expecting her. Harrison was the one who, behind that saloon, had tried to shake Rebecca down for the gold. Harrison was one of the three survivors of the Rawhide River Massacre. And John Harrison was the half brother to this man who rode shotgun on us. Much as I wanted to believe in coincidence, I was forced to admit to myself that Reed's determination to take all of us away from Fort Laramie into these remote hills was not part of the duty of a hardworking sheriff.

Our horses plodded through the sand of the creek bed. At this time of day, little moved. Not even the hawks swept the sky. All that interrupted the silence was the shifting of sand from hooves and the scratchy hum of insects.

An hour later, Henry Reed stopped.

He walked up to my horse and pushed me off the saddle. I crashed, shoulder first, into the dry brush that lined the creek bed. Before I could straighten into a sitting position, he'd done the same to Rebecca and Moves Dancing. Like sacks of potatoes, we formed a random line where we lay on the ground: me, Rebecca between, Moves Dancing.

Henry Reed tied the reins of all the horses to the branch of a nearby tree, turned and regarded our positions, hummed satisfaction, and pulled out a revolver.

"That's good," he said, "the three of you spread out like that. I want y'all to roll over."

We stared.

"Belly over," he said, almost pleasant. "Face first. That ways you won't be tempted to try something hasty and stupid while I enjoy a leisurely search of your belongings."

We didn't move. He smiled. Then shot Moves Dancing in the fleshly part of his lower leg. Moves Dancing popped out a grunt of air, as if he been punched in the gut.

We turned over, but not before I saw how easily the sand soaked blood.

It put considerable strain on my shoulders to keep my head above the ground with my hands cuffed behind my back. The position was so awkward, I could barely watch Henry Reed, let alone think about any action.

He began to search all of our belongings, ripping things apart, throwing items to the ground. He was thorough and slow.

He took so long, I finally had to let my head fall onto the ground. Stray ants explored my face, but I would not give Henry Reed the pleasure of knowing how it crazed me—not now when I still had the strength for foolish pride. So I did not attempt to blow them off my face or to shake them loose.

I turned my head the other way, hoping the weight of my cheek would squash the ants and found myself staring directly into Rebecca's eyes, as she, too, had laid her head on the ground.

"I'm truly sorry," I said to her.

"Shut up," Reed said in conversational tones.

I remembered the bullet in Moves Dancing's leg. I shut.

Maybe another five minutes passed, five minutes of feeling, or imagining that I felt, hordes of chiggers and sand fleas crawl into the cracks of my clothing.

"All right now," Reed said. "Roll back over and sit up."

We did. Moves Dancing had his teeth gritted and was doing his best not to look downward at his leg.

"We have ourselves a predicament," Henry Reed said. "See, I'm convinced you have something I desire. Only, I can't seem to find it."

CHAPTER 34

SEVERAL SECONDS OF SILENCE.

Reed squatted in front of Rebecca and touched his forefinger to her throat. He ran the finger up to her chin and lifted it so that she had to look him directly in the eyes.

"The letter, woman," he said. "The letter that stirred up a beehive in Washington. Where's it hid?"

Her eyes squinted hatred. He ran his finger back down to her throat, then began to part the collar of her shirt. She raised her cuffed hands to fight, and he slapped them down.

"Maybe she's saying nothing because she has no idea what you want," I said.

Reed stood.

"You were mighty quick to speak out." A leer put on his face the first expression I'd seen across it. "Maybe you don't like the way I'm handling your squaw."

My fear evaporated as cold fury stopped the churning of my guts. "Maybe I'm figuring the only way a woman would let you touch her," I said, "is if she can't move to get out of your way."

He smiled, then kicked me in the chest.

It almost felt good, to have the pain crash through me as a physical release for my hatred and anger. And Reed's attention was off Rebecca.

He rolled me back up to a sitting position.

"Keaton," he said. "*You* tell me what you found in the hills."

I smiled in return.

He reached out and in a blurring motion slapped Rebecca so hard she fell back.

"Keaton," he repeated. "*You* tell me what you found in the hills."

"Sure." The knives of pain in my ribs were a focus to keep my mind sharp in the storm of my fury. "As long as we're both talking about Louis Wilcombe."

"That was the wrong name to say, boy. You were dead anyway, but proving you know too much justifies the price of the bullet that I'll put through your head."

His answer confirmed my half-formed thoughts. This had to be about Rawhide River. Otherwise, all of this was just coincidence. And if this was about Rawhide River, chances were he was involved for only one reason.

"You're the messenger," I said. "You rode to Rawhide River and let the soldiers believe that the Sioux were about to attack Fort Laramie. And when they left, you helped shoot on Wilcombe and the remaining men. You want the missing army gold. And the letter Louis Wilcombe wrote that condemns you completely."

He dug into his pocket for chewing tobacco.

I liked that. Dead to be as I was, I'd managed to spook him into fumbling for time to think.

Three had survived the Rawhide Massacre. The three had

never been suspected for their roles in it. John Harrison was now dead. Sergeant Byrne was somewhere in the military. And Henry Reed was in front of us now. None of them had been safe from the moment Rebecca arrived in Washington with her letter.

He chewed some. Spat. Spoke. "I am that third man. You're intent on digging your grave as deep as possible."

I thought about the letter Rebecca had recited from memory to Red Cloud, and I came up with the names I wanted. "Sergeant Byrne. He didn't dare waltz in to Fort Laramie and try to arrest us. Someone might remember him. But you weren't a soldier. No one would remember you from the Rawhide Massacre. Where is Byrne? Did he change his name? Run from the military?"

Reed spit again. Brown juice hung in small drops from his mustache.

"Where's the gold, Keaton?"

"You sent the telegram to Smickles, didn't you? The one telling him to find the letter, then kill me. Why?"

"He'd wired me in Rawlins about you and the Injun. Where's the gold, Keaton?"

"If it sounds like I know lots," I said. "I do. Fact is, a letter with all this is already on the way to Washington. Set us loose, and they'll go easy on you."

"You bluff worse than a drunk nun," he said. "Where's the gold?"

I grinned. "The Injuns spent it."

He kicked me again. This time, he didn't assist me back into my sitting position. Only watched as I struggled upward to sit again.

"The gold." His voice was flat.

"Tell me first about O'Neal. Why'd you have him follow Harrison? Didn't you trust your own half brother once he got a hold of Rebecca?"

"Maybe I kicked you too hard," he said. "Something got knocked loose in your head. I'm asking you about gold."

"O'Neal," I repeated. "The man who followed Harrison back to Laramie from the town of Potter."

I don't know why I was so stubborn, playing for time. Did it matter if I died in three minutes or ten?

"You are touched, boy." After a thoughtful stare at me, Reed turned to Rebecca. "The letter. The gold. Where?"

She glared defiance.

Reed sighed theatrically. He left us to untie the reins of one of the horses and brought that horse close to me. He went to the saddlebag of his horse and returned with two lariats. He winked at Rebecca, then squatted in front of me and tied the end of one of the lariats around my left ankle.

He stood again and admired his handiwork. "It's like this," he said to Rebecca. "Give me what I want, and the man dies easy."

He squatted to tie the second lariat around my right ankle. When finished, he stood and tested the knots by yanking. I slid several inches in the loose sand.

"Don't give me what I want, and he dies hard." Reed scratched his chin. "What I can't figure is whether I should tie him to one horse and let him get dragged to death. Or loosen another horse, tie one leg to each, and send them in opposite directions."

Rebecca did not hesitate. "The letter is sewn into the cartridge belt that you'll find in my medicine bag."

Reed smiled. "Let me confirm that, ma'am." He whipped his Bowie knife loose, searched for the cartridge belt, and cut it apart. He whistled tunelessly as he read the letter.

"Obliged, ma'am." He reached into a pocket for a match, flicked its head against his thumbnail, and lit the letter before dropping it on the sand. He watched it burn to black curling leaves, then kicked apart the ashes. "As you can guess, this takes a big load off. Hate to have a promising law career cut short by something so incriminating."

He faced me. "Keaton. Or should I call you Adams? No matter. I still haven't forgot Pueblo. What that means is that it'd stick in my craw to let you die easy. What I've decided is to tie you to one horse and fire the shot that'll get you dragged to death. Reason is, I've caused a man to get tore apart by two horses before, and messy as it appears, the dying happens too quick."

Rebecca began to cry out.

Reed stopped her with an uplifted hand. "I know I promised different, ma'am. Trust me. In a half hour, you won't care." His leer bloomed. "'Cause I got plans for you, too."

The horse was three steps back from where Reed stood. I knew that's all I had left. The three steps to the horse, and as long as it took for him to secure the rope ends to the saddle and fire his revolver a few inches away from the horse's ear to send it running with me dragging behind.

There was no way I would not die. The horse would bolt and panic as it felt the drag of my weight—leading to more panic and a gallop that would only end when the horse was exhausted. If my skull wasn't crushed quickly by running into a big rock, I'd feel myself skinned raw because it would take miles for the horse to run itself out.

Three steps left until Reed reached the horse.

Henry Reed grinned at me and took the first step.

Two steps left.

"Rebecca," I said. "I want you to know that I truly love you with every part of my heart and soul."

Reed paused.

One step. "Ain't that touching," he snorted.

He reached the horse and patted its rump. He held the lariat in his left hand and paused once more to look at Rebecca. "I want you to know that this here man who professes love for you is also wanted for a Colorado bank robbery and murder. That's why I called him Adams.''

Reed laughed a short burst and turned his back on us to begin tying the rope to the horn of the saddle.

I closed my eyes against the injustice. Rebecca would re-member me only for Reed's words. Yet in that moment, as I closed my eyes and waited for death, I found something else besides anger at the injustice. A peace of acceptance. Very close to the peace that had reached me inside the church. I would die, but not without the love that I'd allowed to grow for Rebecca, and there was meaning in that, even if it wasn't returned, meaning enough to replace the hollowness I'd faced looking into Smickles' shotgun. In that moment, with death so close, there came utter clarity as the rags of the illusions of the importance of my earthly life fell away in the face of eter-nity. I found the faith to understand how the love we shared reflected the love of One much greater, and my only sadness was that I could no longer explore this life with that faith. All of this hit me in a flash of understanding, and as I waited with my eyes closed for Reed to complete the knot and fire the revolver to send the horse on its way with me behind, I pre-pared myself not for death itself, but for the short pain that would take me through the curtain of death to what waited beyond.

Then, in the darkness of my closed eyes, the shot rang.

Hooves pounded.

I grimaced in anticipation of the surge that would come as the power of the horse snapped tight the slack of the lariat.

Nothing.

I opened my eyes.

The horse was galloping down the draw, dust drifting downward behind it. And Henry Reed was writhing belly first on the ground, the lariat fallen beside him, and his revolver flung far ahead.

Disbelief froze me until Moves Dancing shouted. I could not understand the words, for he'd shouted in Sioux, but the noise caused me to look over, and I saw that Rebecca held a smoking derringer in her hands. Rebecca. The last person I or Henry Reed would expect to carry one, let alone use to kill a man.

Moves Dancing shouted again, and my mind was able to sort the words because he'd dropped the Sioux. "Get him before he gets the gun! I can't move. You get him!"

I pushed myself to kneel on one knee.

Henry Reed started to roll over.

I got to my second knee, then onto my feet.

He was on his back now, struggling to sit, and reaching for the remaining gun in his belt.

I lurched forward, but my hands were helpless, cuffed behind my back, and I had no way to strike him.

His hand was now on the butt of his pistol.

I did the only thing possible. I dropped forward, using the full weight of my body to drive my knees into his chest. The force slammed him backward.

He clawed feebly at me as I stood again. Now I knew how I would kill him. I'd push as high as I could and drop, using my knees as a battering ram to crush his ribs, his chest, his neck, to rise and drop again and again in savage joy.

His hands twitched.

"Reach for your gun!" I roared and readied myself to spear him with my knees. His eyes opened. Fluttered shut. "Reach!"

His head lolled sideways, and I could find nothing to sustain the black storm of anger that was driving me. I did not fall upon him.

I stared downward and gulped. He was nothing more now than a slight man in clothes filled with the blood that leaked from the blast of the derringer. Whether he was dead or not mattered little; I could not bring myself to venting my fear and hatred and anger upon him.

I lifted my foot and placed it, almost gently, on his windpipe. "Rebecca," I said, and was surprised at my hoarseness. "Crawl forward. Take the gun from his belt and throw it aside."

She hesitated. I wondered if it was a reaction to killing him or fear of him. Or fear of me.

"You must," I said, almost a pleading whisper. I could feel my revulsion at violent death build inside me. And, as always happened around violent death, I could only see Jed dying in my arms. "Hurry. Please. Then search him for the keys to our handcuffs."

She did not need to fear Henry Reed. He truly was dead. Nor did she need to fear me. I was spent of emotion, drained to the point of weakness, and had to stumble down the creek bed to find a private place to endure the heaves of my emptying stomach.

———

Five minutes later, the three of us were free from our handcuffs.

"What now?" Rebecca asked.

I drew in a lungful of air. "We ride as far as we can," I said. "With the letter burned, we have no proof he meant to kill us, no way to justify what has happened. And when he doesn't show up in Cheyenne, there will be no one to blame but us."

"How long do we ride?" Moves Dancing asked.

"For the rest of our lives."

CHAPTER 35

As we headed up the dry creek bed into the shadows of the Bighorns, we all rode in silence. The events were too raw in our minds, I guess, and I knew for my part of the silence that I had no urge to discover what Rebecca now thought about me, a man she undoubtedly believed was a bank robber and murderer, a notion reinforced by my near loss of sanity in the heat of wanting to kill the man who'd shot my brother.

I was silent, too, because something niggled my mind and would not quit. It took until the sun was just about behind the peaks of the mountains before I realized what was bothering me.

I stopped my horse so that Rebecca and Moves Dancing caught up and halted alongside me.

"Where did Henry Reed arrest you?" I asked Rebecca.

"In the post trader's store." She could not meet my eyes as we spoke.

"Just like that? He walked in and announced it?"

"I don't understand."

"It may mean something, it may not," I said. "Think carefully. Did he arrest you immediately, or did he strike up conversation first?"

She looked at me directly for the first time since leaving Henry Reed in his shallow grave in the creek bed. "We spoke first—he asked me if we'd just arrived—then he left. A few minutes later, he returned with the soldiers."

I gnawed on that thought. Moves Dancing and Rebecca watched me without comment.

"He walked up to you and started a conversation. Just like that? In English?"

She closed her eyes in recollection before nodding.

"It fits," I said. "Maybe there's a reason we should turn back."

"Back where?" Moves Dancing asked.

"Back to Fort Laramie. We'll bring in the body and tell the corporal what happened."

"You said without the letter that we didn't have a chance to—"

"It'll be a gamble," I agreed to Rebecca's protest. "If it doesn't work, all three of us hang."

I explained what I had in mind and why it would be worth the gamble. What I didn't explain was that the best I could hope for was to earn a pardon as Samuel Keaton. I'd still have to face the law as Robert Adams on that long-ago bank robbery and murder in Colorado. But that was my business, not theirs.

Moves Dancing thought it through as the shadows lengthened.

"It should be done," he finally said to Rebecca. With reluctance, Moves Dancing turned his horse in the direction we'd come. "It is no wonder that the Sioux fare so badly against the whites," he continued. "The workings of your minds are as hidden as the movement of the wind."

For the first time in what seemed like months, I grinned. Rebecca caught my spirit, and it gave her the nerve to move her horse closer to mine.

Moves Dancing kept riding, and when he was out of ear-shot, she spoke.

"Samuel," she said gently. "We have traveled far together. Shared much time. And often when we are quiet and you think I am not watching, I have seen in your eyes that you keep a terrible secret."

I could not help myself. My back stiffened.

"What that terrible man said about you cannot be all true," she whispered, "for I have also seen enough of you to know you are a good man. Yet, I wonder what of it is true."

She waited for my response, but I gave no guidance.

"Samuel, the last words that you thought you might speak told me of your love. Can you not tell me what it is that re-mains as a wall between us? For I love you, too, but feel as if you drive me away, and it hurts to keep myself open to you. I find myself putting up my own walls."

It was close. I nearly began to speak. But when I opened my mouth, my throat became dry. How could I tell her I'd killed my brother because of the woman I betrayed him with?

She shook her head at my stubbornness and pushed away from me. She nudged her horse into a trot.

I caught up to her, searched for anything else to talk about. "May I thank you for my life?"

She stopped again. When she looked in my eyes this time, I saw only cold remoteness.

"No," she said. "You may not. Carry it for the rest of your life that you owe me. Carry it that you owe me for saving your life three times. Carry it, stew on it, and add that to whatever other burdens you are determined to wrap around yourself as a blanket of self-pitying nobility. And leave me alone so that I can become one more sad secret in your eyes as you run away."

I said the only thing I could think of. "Three times. The buffalo hunters, yes. Now, yes. But the third time?"

"You are a fool, Samuel Keaton. In more ways than one." Her words were chilled as she held up her derringer. "I saved you on the day we met. Who do you think shot John Harrison with this as you fanned bullets in all directions around him?"

CHAPTER *36*

TWO DAYS PASSED after Henry Reed died.

Two days passed until I found myself in a cramped hotel room smelling of stale sweat and dried beer.

It felt too much like that night long, long ago, when Leanna Whittington stepped into my hotel room and changed my life for the worse. Moonlight shining cold and hard through torn drapes. Me lying on a narrow hard bed. Fully clothed. Boots on. And a soft knock on the door to interrupt thoughts of a woman who I missed so badly it was an ache.

This night, however, was the better part of two decades away from Pueblo, and far north of the town where Jed died. This night, the woman who filled my thoughts was not Clara, but Rebecca. This night, the hotel was alongside the rail tracks in Cheyenne, the main stopping point south of Fort Laramie, east of the town of Laramie.

And on this night, I opened the door not

to Leanna Whittington, but to Marshal Evrett.

His lean face creased into a grin as he removed his hat and extended his hand. "Smart, to wait here and send me a telegram to meet you here. Had you come to Laramie, it'd be a mite compromising to meet my escaped prisoner in the same town he escaped from."

I shook his hand and motioned for him to step inside.

I'd left a bottle of whiskey and two glasses beside my gun and the oil lamp on the apple-crate nightstand near the head of the bed. Evrett poured an inch into each tumbler without waiting for me to ask and handed one to me. I sat on the edge of my bed. He pulled a chair up near to the nightstand, leaned it back, and propped his boots up near the bottle.

I smiled.

He smiled.

I smiled.

He groaned. "This again? Dragging words from you is worse than pulling teeth. Man's got to do a lot of guesswork when all he reads on the telegram is when and where to show up."

I smiled.

He sighed. "Start with the Injun. You stayed on his trail, right?"

"Her trail."

He sat forward so quickly his chair legs thumped the floor. "Injun was a she?"

"From England. Looking for her pa. A soldier by the name of Louis Wilcombe."

Evrett massaged the balding skin of his head with both hands. "How about you give me a blow by blow and quit getting me to ask questions that make me the fool."

"Fair enough." I told him everything. Leaving the train at Potter. The showdown with the Pawnee. The rescue of O'Neal—and that someone had sent him to follow Rebecca.

The fact that O'Neal had remained unconscious. Red Cloud and Rebecca. My arrest at Fort Laramie. How Henry Reed fit in. That the letter of proof had been burned.

Evrett poured himself another whiskey. "Army gold, huh. No matter. I don't mind keeping my half of the chest you brought into this hotel."

"You know about that?"

" 'Course. First thing I asked at the front desk was if you'd brought luggage. And your half of that gold oughta make it easy for you to live fancy in Mexico."

"Mexico?"

He shook his head. "I'm sorry, Keaton. I just can't see how I can help you duck the noose on Reed's death. What with that letter gone, Mexico's probably your best bet."

I grinned. "It *is* convenient that the Denver Pacific can run me right down to the Rio Grande, and how that track'll take me clear to El Paso. Not that I purchased my ticket already for the morning train."

He grinned back. "I knew that, too. Already checked at the train station. Just like at the front desk of this here hotel. Amazing what people will tell you once you flash a badge."

He leaned back in his chair and held his glass up to examine the amber contents against the dim yellow light of the oil lamp. "Keaton, you'd make a fine deputy. It's a real shame you can't stay."

He pushed my gun away from the edge of the nightstand to make room for the glass he set down. He reached to his holster and pulled out his Colt and idly spun the chamber. "Fact is, Keaton, it's a real shame you're about to resist arrest for shooting Henry Reed."

I made a move forward for the gun he had pushed out of my reach. He froze me in place by lifting the Colt.

"Like even now," he said. "Didn't take you long at all to realize all the meaning of that statement."

"You're taking all the gold," I said.

"Yup. You're on the run for killing Harrison, escaping jail, and shooting Henry Reed. And no one else knows about the gold. I just can't see how you're in a position to negotiate."

"'Specially since you're holding the gun."

"Don't sound bitter," he said. "You got dealt into a cheating game from the beginning."

"Care to explain?" I said. "It's a small thing to return for the pot you're taking."

"Why not? Move once, though, and I'll shoot you dead."

I nodded agreement. Saloon music filtered up from the dancing below. They were maybe ten feet away, straight below, all those cowboys carrying on with cards and whiskey and women, and none had any inkling of this one-sided show-down to death.

"Keaton, I do like you. Any other situation, we'd probably ride range together. And because I like you, I'll even give you a bonus for the gold you brought in."

I waited.

"Remember a night in Pueblo?" His teeth gleamed white. "Tut, tut. You promised no movement."

I forced myself to relax.

"Henry Reed arrived in Laramie the day you escaped. Arrived on the same train you left on. He found no humor in that. But when I showed him the Wanted poster with a sketch of Robert Adams, it cheered him up some. That's when I found out you two were already acquainted."

He leaned forward, elbows on his knees, and braced the unwavering gun with both hands. There was a couple steps distance between us. I had no chance if I made a play for my gun. We both knew it.

"Reed told me he often wondered when he'd run into you again. Said it would only be a matter of time. Said it would give him special pleasure to get you hanged after you missed the noose the first time."

I truly did not understand.

Evrett answered my puzzlement.

"This is too rich," he said. "The pity is that I won't ever be able to share this story with anyone."

"Pueblo," I said.

The gleam of white teeth. "It pleases me to see that there is something that brings a rise out of you."

"Pueblo."

"You don't know, do you? That's what's so rich." He watched my face. "Keaton, you and your brother killed Reed's woman. He hated you so bad he about spit nails when I showed him that poster. Swore up and down it wasn't enough that he framed you for the bank robbery and murder, 'specially since you escaped jail."

"We . . . killed . . . Reed's . . . woman." I'm not sure another sentence could have staggered me more.

He nodded. "They had this game. She'd move in on a bounty hunter. From what I hear, she was a good-looking wildcat. Nobody could say no. The way they worked it, Reed would stay close. And after the bounty hunter had done the dangerous work, she'd handle the bounty hunter for Reed. Used drugged wine, he said, had this play where she'd tilt the bottle back and pretend she was drinking, then she'd pass the bottle. Made it real easy for the two of them to claim the bounty for themselves."

"We killed Reed's woman," I repeated.

"Thought you might like to know that before you go. Reed told me how your brother stood to get a bead on the woman before she could shoot you from behind. How if he'd hit your brother a split second sooner, she'd still be alive and they'd still be together."

I felt myself sag. Leanna's toe-to-toe shouting argument with Jed had been no accident. Reed had been somewhere nearby, and Leanna had needed an excuse to make arrangements with Reed. I understood, too, why she had worked so hard to get me to drink the wine, and why I'd been so foggy after only a few gulps. And . . .

I groaned.

Jed hadn't shot her by mistake. He saw the gun out as she ran up behind me. He knew I'd be killed. Even after I'd betrayed him, he'd made the decision to stand to shoot around me in order to save my life. He died as he'd lived, looking out for me, the brother who didn't even have the decency to push away his woman.

I looked up at the sound of Evrett's voice. He was holding out a glass of whiskey and repeated the words that had blurred on me.

"I said I'll set this on the floor," he said. "You ease forward and take it. I won't deny a man his last cigarette or drink, and you look like you could use it."

I shook my head. "Whiskey's no cure for anything. And ain't anything a cure for what I got."

"Suit yourself."

I dry swallowed several times. "Tell me, Evrett. How come Reed told you all this? Admitted to framing me and killing a man in cold blood?"

"Wondered when you'd get to that. Reed and I knew each other a ways back. Fact is, I had just as good a reason to get that letter as he did."

I lifted my head to stare at Evrett. "The third survivor. Reed was the messenger, John Harrison was one soldier. And you were Sergeant Byrne."

"Almost ashamed to tell you, yes. 'Course, I had mutton-chop whiskers myself and a full head of hair. You ain't the only lobo that shaved and took a different name. Just as an aside, of course, that's what gave me the idea to look up those Wanted posters. Watching you so careful to shave reminded me of why I had a smooth face, and it got me to thinking."

Evrett slammed back a shot of whiskey from the glass he'd offered me. "Keaton, here's the rest of what you earned by getting me the gold. The whyfors of how you got dealt that cheating hand as soon as I knew you were a wanted man."

"Why'd that make a difference?" I asked.

"You'd been on the run for more'n fifteen years. Proved you weren't stupid. And I liked the recall factor."

"Meaning anytime you had the notion, you could bring me in, get rid of me, and have the justification to do it legal like."

He shrugged. "Don't take it personal. I needed someone to keep an eye on the woman come in from Washington."

"You had O'Neal," I said. "He followed us both."

"Told you you were sharp. Yes, O'Neal was in my employ, ever since a friend in Washington alerted me to Rebecca and her letter. When I brought O'Neal into your jail cell, I was hoping you'd answer for him some of the questions I couldn't ask. That's why I introduced him as a journalist. But O'Neal couldn't help with the woman, of course."

He took a sip of whiskey. "I'd heard about the Injun visiting you in jail. Knew about the disguise, of course. Got that from Harrison who got it from O'Neal."

Then, too, that was how Harrison had found Rebecca so easily once she'd donned the shabby clothes of a down-on-his-heels buck. O'Neal. Harrison must have decided there was no sense in forcing her out of that disguise. It'd be a lot easier bullying an Indian buck in public than a woman dressed as a British visitor, even if she did have Indian features.

"Wasn't hard to put it together," Evrett was saying. "She needs to turn to someone for help, why not the one person to risk his life for her? And maybe she was feeling guilty for getting you in there in the first place."

Evrett tapped his forehead with his index finger, pointing

at his brains. "So I figured it was the perfect setup. You'd bloodhound for her and me at the same time. And she'd never know you'd report back to the man looking for her gold."

"All right," I said, even though I thought I could guess the answer. "How did you know about her search in the first place?"

"Sergeant Byrne still lives." He grinned. "Still lives and collects what pension the army sends. I'd changed my name to be extra safe, against the long shot that Louis Wilcombe might someday come out of the hills. Only the person in Denver who picks up Sergeant Byrne's mail and telegrams ain't me. That's the same person that sends out the telegrams I need. From Denver, so they can't be traced to a small town like Laramie, where everybody'd know my business."

I nodded. The mysterious third person in Denver was just a puppet.

"That doesn't explain how you knew Rebecca was on her way to the Black Hills."

"What with your time so short, I can understand your impatience," he answered. He patted the barrel of his gun as if to emphasize its deadliness, then continued. "About two months ago a friend in Washington—an old army buddy who stayed on—wired Denver to say that a woman had come calling for information about Louis Wilcombe, and not only that, but she had gold and spoke of a letter and would return the next day to prove it. I wired back to have her followed—"

"O'Neal," I said.

"O'Neal. A Pinkerton man. And with him working so hard, it didn't seem dumb to have him stay nearby to follow Harrison." He shook his head. "Turned out to be real smart. No sooner did Harrison get an eyeful of that gold, when— I'm thinking—he tried to beat the information out of her so that he could get it himself. That's when you made your timely arrival, smack into a situation you had no idea was already twenty years old."

"I've had better luck," I agreed.

"It got worse," Evrett said.

I raised an eyebrow.

"Henry Reed was there when your telegram came in from Potter. I had to let him in on the game."

"And . . ."

"It appears he was less certain than me about what might happen if an investigation started. He thought it'd be too easy for someone to place him at Rawhide River, and he was still going under the name he'd always had. He couldn't afford to let you or Rebecca live. After your escape, he figured Fort Laramie was the logical place for you and the woman to show up with the letter. He made sure he was waiting at the fort, armed with a good excuse to take you out of there if you arrived."

"Doesn't appear that you had the best of intentions for me, either."

He shrugged again. "The letter's gone, and all the gold's here. Without Harrison or Reed to divide it like we agreed all those years ago. It's an opportunity too good to resist. And—"

A sneeze interrupted him.

I froze in fear.

Evrett's face tightened into a mask of evil. "That sneeze came from under the bed."

A second sneeze confirmed his guess. "Keaton," he said. "What's gonna happen if no one comes out after the count of three is that I'm gonna shoot you in the heart, then fire five more bullets under the bed."

"No," I said, then directed my voice downward. "Caleb, push your gun out onto the floor. And come out slow. Don't play the hero. Evrett's got the drop on both of us."

Sergeant Caleb Hutchens, carrying out special service to Colonel Braude of Fort Laramie, squeezed into sight from under the bed.

Evrett motioned for him to move to the far side of the room. "Sit and keep your hands on your head. One twitch and you're dead."

Evrett surveyed both of us. Slowly, a smile returned to his face.

"Interesting," he said. "And not much of a complication. Won't take long for me to arrange it so it appears that you two had a fallin' out and shot each other."

CHAPTER 37

"It won't work," I said. "He's been sent down here with me. Special orders from Colonel Braude at Fort Laramie. Kill us both and folks'll know it was a setup."

Evrett thought it through, then chuckled. "Keaton, you coyote. With that letter gone, you needed a witness to whatever I might tell you. And you got me chattier than a flock of magpies. Weren't for that sneeze . . ."

"Sir, I need to rub my nose real bad." Caleb Hutchens, blond hair smeared with the dirt that had accumulated for years beneath the bed, trembled in his fear as he called across the room. "You find it permissible that I reach with one hand?"

"Sure," Evrett said. "But try anything else, and I shoot Keaton. Can you live knowing you caused another man's death?"

I wondered if Evrett had been deliberately ironic with that question.

"Thank you, sir." Caleb rubbed until his

eyes watered, and finished, moved his hand back atop his head.

"How'd you know it was me?" Evrett demanded abruptly in my direction. "Reed wouldn't tell you. He hated you so bad he wouldn't give you the satisfaction."

I told him how I knew. And in no particular rush. Every extra minute now meant an extra minute when something might happen to save us. A drunk wandering into our room. Clerk from the hotel desk with a question. Any straw for a drowning man.

My wonderings had begun during our ride away from Reed's body, as I considered his presence in Fort Laramie. Understanding that he was the messenger at the Rawhide River Massacre helped, for that explained his need to take all three of us away from Fort Laramie.

But why had he been there in the first place? Not coincidence. While the territories are underpopulated, the spaces between towns are too great. I hadn't been able to accept that Reed could be so fortunate as to be in the one place at the right time to find us, not with the thousands of square miles of territories around Fort Laramie. I'd decided, instead, that he was there because Fort Laramie was the logical place to wait for someone coming from the Black Hills.

I'd puzzled through how Reed might originally have known of my Black Hills destination. Marshal Evrett was the first answer that came to mind but so hard to believe that I'd first told myself that Reed could also have known of my Black Hills destination from several sources—telegraph office, Smickles, anyone who had read the telegram, or, as had happened, because through official business Evrett had no choice but to report the telegram.

Yet all of those possibilities would have led Reed to believe that I was traveling alone. So I'd been forced to ask myself why he had arrested the two Indians that he undoubtedly saw

ride with me into Fort Laramie. Under ordinary circumstances it was a tall stretch to believe the reason was the one
he gave, that they'd been consorting with an escaped prisoner.
Not when they were Indians. Not when it'd be too easy a
defense for them that I'd just joined up with them as they
traveled. Not when the last thing Henry Reed would want
were two more complications as he took me from the fort.

When I'd come to that point in my musings, I'd queried
Rebecca about the circumstances of her arrest in the post
trader's store. Had Reed arrested her after accidentally over-
hearing her speak, I could have found a way to believe Evrett
was not responsible, that it was just our misfortune that Reed
had made the connection between my presence and that of
the only Indian in the whole territories who would have been
remotely likely to speak the King's English. But because Reed
had made a point of getting Rebecca to speak before initiating
the arrest, it seemed to show that he was indeed looking to
confirm her accent, something he would only do if he was also
looking for her. Only one person besides O'Neal could have
told Reed that I was traveling with Rebecca—Marshal Evrett,
the man who had sent me on my way with her.

Furthermore, I could not convince myself it had been
O'Neal who was the third surveyor, instead of Evrett—not
after Reed's lack of reaction to the mention of O'Neal. If he
hadn't known of O'Neal's involvement, it meant a third person did. Again, I'd asked myself if it was Evrett.

And I'd thought of the telegram, the one I'd found on
the floor after Smickles had almost beat me to death.

FIND LETTER STOP LEARN ALL YOU CAN STOP
SHOOT ESCAPING PRISONER STOP

Reed had admitted he'd sent it to Smickles. There was no
reason for Reed to be so anxious to have Smickles find Rebecca's letter from Louis Wilcombe, when Reed was about to

arrive shortly and could search me himself. Unless Reed believed that someone else might find the letter first, and to find it first, that someone else would have to be closer to me than was Reed. Evrett was the name that came up again.

That was exactly how I'd presented it to Colonel Braude, commander at Fort Laramie. He'd found it thin, very thin indeed, especially with Henry Reed's lifeless body to be such powerful incentive for me to make up any outrageous story. That's when we'd decided to place Rebecca and Moves Dancing in the fort stockade as hostages to my return and that I would try to prove my story by trying to get a confession from Evrett, with Caleb Hutchens as the hidden witness.

It would have worked. Except for the fact that Hutchens had sneezed.

"All of this," I finished my explanation to Evrett, "is a long way of saying that since Sergeant Hutchens was sent down here with me, no one at Fort Laramie will believe I shot him."

Evrett thought more. Loud arguing, muted by the floor below and the music around it, reached into our silence. Then the sound of chairs crashing, men cursing. The music did not let up.

"Keaton, you've been right about a considerable amount," he said after a long pause, as if this were high-stakes poker and he were deciding whether I had a fifth spade to match four showing. "The presence of this here soldier attests to that. But you're wrong—dead wrong—when you say that folks at Fort Laramie will call it a setup when you and Hutchens finish shooting each other."

Evrett shook his head, convincing himself as he spoke. Unfortunately, I knew he'd guessed right. All I held was a busted flush.

"What you're forgetting, Keaton, is this sergeant's job was to hear enough to get proof. With him dead, *his* proof is gone, just as surely as the proof disappeared when Reed burnt the letter. Which is a short way of saying that the best the army folks could do is suspect me, and suspicions alone never hanged no one."

He grinned triumph at me. "Fact is, with no proof to say otherwise, it'll probably look like you concocted all this with full intent to shoot this young man at the first opportunity, just to get away, uncaring what happened to the two people left behind in the fort stockade."

"Who you going to shoot first?" I asked after a pause.

He sighed. "You were so good, too. No begging, no whining. Admirable the way you had composed yourself until breaking nerve now."

"Shoot Hutchens first," I said, "and you got a problem. 'Cause folks will come running, and you'll have to shoot me quick, before I have the chance to tell you the problem with this gold. On the other hand, shoot me first, and you'll have the same problem."

His gun had been aimed at a point between Caleb and me. Now Evrett swiveled the gun until it was pointed at my heart.

I held my silence.

"Amuse me then," he said. "With you dead, what's my problem?"

"That chest don't contain gold."

A small muscle around his left eye twitched.

I pushed. "While the presence of this here soldier does testify that the army needs proof of your involvement at Rawhide River in '52, you're forgetting it also testifies to one other thing. I expected you to double-cross me."

He squinted now.

"And if I expected you to double-cross me," I said as slowly as I could above the hammering of my heart, "I'd be a fool to bring in the gold."

"You're bluffing," he said after deliberation. "What if I open the chest first thing I come into the room and find no gold? Then how do you get me talking for the sergeant to hear enough?"

This was as high as I'd ever placed stakes in any poker. I kept my voice even. "If you opened it first thing, the natural reaction is that you pull a gun on me and you ask me why I filled it with rocks. Then I tell you I figured you for the third survivor of the Rawhide River Massacre, and from there we begin the conversation that gets you hanged."

He studied me more.

"I die," I said, "the secret of the gold goes with me."

The silence was loud enough I could hear Caleb Hutchen's breathing through his mouth to get around that plugged-up nose.

"I'm willing," I said as I played the only ace I had, "to trade the gold for my life."

"We both know that chest is just under the bed," he told me. "Hook it with your foot and push it to me."

I hooked it from the edge of the bed and did as directed.

He pointed the gun at me. "Get back to Hutchens. Sit cross-legged and get your hands on your head. If this chest holds rocks, we have more discussion. If not, this iron will do the only talking here."

Everett fumbled with the lock with his left hand, his right hand steady with the gun pointed at us, and flicked his eyes back from me down to the lock, taking sharp attention that— despite my awkward position—I didn't make a last-ditch scramble to cross the space between us. He snapped his teeth together in frustration. "Keaton, the key."

I reached into my shirt pocket.

"Throw it soft. Make sure it lands near my feet."

He did not take his eyes off mine as I tossed it. This man was as careful as any. Without dropping his head, he reached around for it with his left hand and kept his eyes on us as he inserted the key into the lock.

It clicked and opened.

Still by feel only, he watched me without wavering his eyes and pulled the lock loose. Only as he lifted the lid did he glance downward.

I doubt he saw what hit him.

To me—and I was expecting it, for I'd muffled their rattles with wrapped cloth only hours before—the snakes were only blurs of savagery as they shot forward. One caught him in the left forearm. And the other in the tendons of his neck. I'd taken care to trap rattlesnakes as thick as clubs—and the shaking of the chest and confinement had them riled. They hit the gap of light offered by the opening of the chest and struck Evrett with such force that Evrett fell backward in his chair. It will always remain a photograph of horror in my mind, the snakes with jaws open so wide it appeared they were clamped onto his skin. And as Evrett rolled and shook in his spasms of terror, it only succeeded in driving their fangs in deeper.

I had not planned for the snakes to kill him. Only distract him enough that I could reach into my boot for Rebecca's derringer. Snake's venom generally only causes a powerful sickness; he'd have been ready for trial within a day or two. But the snake clamped onto his neck must have pumped itself dry of venom into the vein to his heart. Before the derringer was in my hand, Evrett shook in death tremors.

I rose slowly and went to the bed for the stick with the forked end hidden beneath the covers. As soon as the snakes worked themselves loose from Evrett's flesh, I'd pin them behind the neck to capture them just as I'd done earlier in the day in the dry hills just north of Cheyenne.

It saddened me that a man might die like this for the rocks that indeed rested within that chest. But when you come right down to it, gold's the same as rocks, only a little shinier.

EPILOGUE

"WILL O'NEAL REACHED Fort Laramie while you were waiting for the marshal," Rebecca told me. "Two of Red Cloud's men gave him escort to the fort. But he is no longer here. O'Neal then took the stagecoach to Cheyenne for an eastbound train."

"I heard," I said. "But not much more than that, beyond that he told the colonel enough to match the report given by Caleb Hutchens and establish us as clearly innocent."

Rebecca and I sat high up in the hills on a broad and flat rocky ledge that overlooked the North Platte River. It had been her suggestion, this meandering ride into the breezes that swept across the open land. And she'd said little as we let our horses wander. As if we both needed time and the winds to scrub ourselves clean of the noise and bustle of Fort Laramie.

"O'Neal made a point to visit me in the stockade," Rebecca said. "He had many questions of course, as would I had I woken in a Sioux tepee."

"Before he departed, I'd have liked to be able to thank him for saving my life."

Rebecca turned her head to look me squarely in the eyes. The wind plucked at her hair, lifting it and setting it again on the shoulders of the pale buckskin of her dress. I wanted to drown in the depths of her dark eyes.

She stared at me moments longer. Without warning, her eyes began to tear, and she did not remove her gaze, nor wipe her cheeks as the tears rolled downward. Why is it that a man can fix fence, rope cattle, and survive a blizzard, yet feel as helpless as a straw in a river to face a woman's tears?

I found myself twisting my hat.

"Sam Keaton." It was almost a whisper. "My heart is filled with love for you."

"I can understand your sorrow."

She ignored my poor attempt at humor. "That man, O'Neal. You couldn't leave him behind to die with the Pawnee. You tended his wounds, kept him alive. Yet you want to thank him for your life. As if you've forgotten all you did for him."

I tried to protest that I'd only done what I owed him and wasn't happy, either, about those duties.

She continued, as did her tears. "That day we rode into the buffalo hunters. You didn't pause to think how it might get you killed, just did what you could. Then never spoke about it again."

"Wasn't right, them taking advantage of someone who couldn't fight back. Anybody would try to fix what wasn't right."

She didn't hear me. "The ways you protected me when all I was to you was that irksome Injun, as I heard you mutter time and again under your breath. You are truly a kind and decent man, and I've discovered how valuable that is."

She smiled through her tears, a smile of bravery. "But it isn't just kindness and decency that turn a woman's heart. No, Sam Keaton, the first time I saw that crooked grin of yours, I got fluttery inside."

She reached for my hand. "What I'm trying to say is that since I looked up from the ground and heard you trying to protect me from John Harrison in that quiet voice of yours, I have learned much about myself. And love."

She looked away from me, even as she intertwined her fingers among mine.

What's a man to reply to something like that? Especially a man whose heart aches with love in return. I concentrated on the lines of the far hills across the North Platte and told myself I was blinking this way because the breeze blew directly crossways into my eyes.

"I learned about Evening Star from O'Neal," she said, still faced away from me. "He passed on what he'd learned from his time in the Pawnee camp."

I waited.

"It's a Pawnee religious ceremony," she said. "According to their legend, the Morning Star is their protector against the Evening Star, which drives the sun into darkness. Every fourth year, Pawnee warriors capture a woman of beauty from an enemy camp. On the appointed day, she is tied to a scaffold, painted half-red to appear as the Morning Star, half-black to appear as the Evening Star. Then she is pierced with arrows. Her death blood flows as a blessing."

Rebecca lapsed into silence.

"Woman Who Sings to Wolves was captured by the Pawnee as she tried to deliver the letter to Omaha."

She nodded. "Before she could be sacrificed, the English expedition happened upon that Pawnee camp. In taking those Pawnee and Woman Who Sings to Wolves, they saved her life, at least until she lost it in England. To them she was known as Evening Star."

I considered how easily one random event changed forever the thin chains of what happened next, how one small stone kicked loose might begin an avalanche. Rebecca here from England because an Indian camp happened to be in the way of the march of an expedition. Me here because I had walked down an alley in Laramie at the particular moment that would embroil me in her life. I realized the way a man's life unfolded and depended so much on all the chains that had been linked before his birth. God did have a hand and a purpose in our destinies, for this journey had brought me closer to Him.

I took a deep breath, thinking, too, of Rebecca. "This journey has brought you amazing knowledge."

"It is not finished, this journey."

"No?"

She didn't pause, as if this were the question she most wanted to ask. "Can you tell me, Samuel, what happened in Colorado?"

It was involuntary, the pulling away of my hand from hers. But she did not let go. Only grasped tighter and placed her other hand over mine.

"You have been cleared of the old charges, too," she reminded me. "Caleb Hutchens, I'm told, took great pains to emphasize he also heard Marshal Evrett explain how Henry Reed had made it appear you and your brother had robbed the bank and murdered the people in it."

I thought long and hard. This was it, I knew. My chance to set it straight between the two of us, my chance to step back from the abyss of darkness that came with the thoughts of leaving this woman.

So I told it. The first time I'd repeated it aloud since I'd told Clara when she appeared in Pueblo two weeks after Jed's death to bust me loose, something she accomplished with a standard dance-hall trick of drugging the guard's beer on that moonless night. This time, however, my retelling was not the anguished confession and hope for absolution it had been the only other time I'd spoken the story aloud.

The other occasion was much more difficult. It had been to Clara as she visited me in jail so long ago. My agony of confession was worsened to watch the pain on her face as she listened to me tell her that in that brief moment with Leanna, I'd betrayed both her love and my brother. That night all those years ago, Clara was able to give me my freedom from jail and my life, for she had slipped me a revolver. But it had not brought me forgiveness, for Clara had bid me good-bye with frozen dignity and turned her back on me as she left me to later ride into the darkness alone.

In this moment, my second telling of that night, was I asking Rebecca for absolution? I don't think so. I told it as straightforwardly as I could, my eyes on the fixed point of a gap in the rounded hills far across the valley. It was not for Rebecca to give me absolution, just as it was not for Clara. Yet even now, knowing Leanna's determination to accomplish what she had in my brother's death, I was not prepared to place the blame on her.

Who was there to give absolution? That was one of the things I would be seeking. Squarely as the blame must be placed on my shoulders, I believed I might be able to go gentler on who I'd been that night at age nineteen, a boy in a man's body and out of his depth in a stormy sea he didn't even realize swirled around him.

My voice cracked, however, when it came to breaching the realization I'd had in the Cheyenne hotel room, that Jed had stood to die as he saved me from the woman with the gun in her hand, even in the face of my betrayal to him.

By that time, I was standing as I paced the ledge, something that surprised me when I stopped speaking, for I didn't remember getting to my feet.

"That's it, then," I said. "The entire story."

"Do you love her? Clara?"

"I don't let myself think about her."

More silence.

"Samuel, do you remember how you told me to look at my medicine bag differently? That you suggested it was the greatest gift my mother could leave me?"

"Yes."

"Ask yourself, why would your brother be so convinced that Leanna was ready to shoot you. After all, you assumed all these years that she had the gun out to back you up. Why wouldn't Jed?"

I had no answer.

"Jed shot her immediately, without thinking. Were I you, I'd believe that somehow, between your hotel room and reaching the ambush at the stable, he'd realized their argument the night before was deliberate, and that she'd betrayed him long before she forced herself upon you."

Rebecca stood and moved to me. She put her arms around my neck and placed her head against my chest. My chin, at last, rested on the softness of her hair as I held her in my arms.

"Samuel, when you look at it that way," she said so quietly I could barely hear it above the whisper of the breeze in my ears, "Jed died knowing that Leanna had set you up. And I don't believe a man can give his life for another man unless he's first forgiven him."

I closed my eyes and felt my heart thudding against hers. "That eases it much," I said, more to myself than to her.

She pushed back. Without breaking entirely free, she searched my eyes. "Will it be over, you think? Your determination to hide yourself from me?"

I grinned. "If not, we've got a good start on it."

"I don't need to hear much more than that," she said. "You'll ride back to Fort Laramie with me?"

"You noticed my saddlebags."

"Packed. Like they were every morning as we traveled. It wasn't hard to figure you were ready to move on."

In reply, I kissed her, and it was there once more, the completeness, the promise of what might fill the ache of hollowness. The kiss ended, as tender as it had begun, and she again rested her head against my chest.

And in those long minutes of silence as we shared a single heartbeat, as I held her and stared into the distance, I had a vision of the roads ahead. I gradually began to understand what I would have to say next.

"Rebecca." She tried to step back, but I held her tight. I could not bear to look into her face as I spoke.

"Rebecca. I listened to you as we rode back from Red Cloud to Fort Laramie, listened to you tell me why you wanted to remain among the Sioux, how you believed you could help. Vaccines. A fight against buffalo hunters. How your background could help them in legal battles against treaty breakers. That you'd found family."

"Yes?"

"Can you quit that?"

"I don't understand."

"I do." I held her tighter. "And wish I didn't. We have three roads. On the first, you join me in my world, the world of white men determined to conquer these territories. Yet you left England and braved this wilderness to find family. On that road, then, I believe you'll always wonder, maybe even begin to hate yourself or me for the reason you turned your back on a people who need you. It will sour our love, and in the end, you will have lost me and your people."

By her stillness, I think Rebecca began to understand. I continued. "The second road, I travel with you and live among the Sioux. Even if the Sioux could accept me, I already know that their life is not mine and I will always be the stranger."

I swallowed back deep sadness. "Rebecca, whatever love we share, I don't believe we can follow either road together, not now."

"I . . . I cannot accept that."

"There is the third road. Return to the people you have claimed and who have claimed you. Live among the Sioux until you are beyond wondering how you might help them or them you. Then, let us decide."

She moved to the edge of the rock and stood there, motionless, as she stared across the valley. When she turned back, I could see by the resolve in the lines of her chin that she too had seen the three roads before us and knew there was only one to follow.

"I will return to the Sioux," she said. "For you are right. I would always wonder. But I cannot say good-bye. Will you spend some time with me now and delay our parting? A day? Two days? A month?"

I trembled. Every nerve in my body told me to step forward and sweep her into my arms and satisfy that which raged between us. "Delay our parting, each knowing during each minute together the pain we will face to say good-bye?"

I held my arms open. "You make the decision."

She stared at me again. Tears reached her eyes again, and when she stepped forward now, it was quickly, to hold my face and kiss me hard and quick.

"Give me until spring, Samuel." She smiled through her tears. "Return to me. I know you can find me."

I swallowed. The great sadness in my throat was a lump of pain, and the sky and horizon blurred. "Yes, ma'am."

I swung onto my horse.

"Samuel," she called. "You know where I'll be. But what

about you. Where will you go?"

I did my best to give her a crooked grin.

"Laramie," I said with a tip of my hat. "Won't surprise me at all to discover they need a marshal there."